GWEN BRISTOW {
TWO AND TWO {

C000088018

GWEN Bristow was born in Marion, South Carolina in 1903, and Bruce Manning in Jersey City, New Jersey in 1902. In 1924, following Bristow's graduation from Judson College, her parents moved to New Orleans. In the late 1920s, Gwen Bristow and Bruce Manning, both Louisiana journalists at that point, met and married.

Their first joint novel, *The Invisible Host*, was a success, and enjoyed stage and film adaptations. Three further mysteries by the writing duo were to follow.

The couple moved to Hollywood in the early thirties, and there Bristow established herself as a prolific and bestselling writer of historical fiction, while Manning became a respected screenwriter, producer and director.

They continued to live in California until their respective deaths: Manning's in 1965, Bristow's in 1980.

GWEN BRISTOW

AND

BRUCE MANNING

TWO AND TWO MAKE
TWENTY-TWO

With an introduction by
Curtis Evans

DEAN STREET PRESS

Published by Dean Street Press 2021

Copyright © 1932 by Gwen Bristow and Bruce Manning. Renewed
1959. By arrangement with the Proprietor. All rights reserved.

Introduction © 2021 Curtis Evans

All Rights Reserved

The right of Gwen Bristow and Bruce Manning to be identified as the
Authors of the Work has been asserted by their estate in accordance
with the Copyright, Designs and Patents Act 1988.

First published in 1932 by The Mystery League

Cover by DSP

ISBN 978 1 915014 54 2

www.deanstreetpress.co.uk

To

OUR FRIENDS

IN THE

PASS

WHO SHOWED US WHERE

PARADISE ISLAND

SHOULD HAVE

BEEN

INTRODUCTION

OVER several years in the early 1930s the spousal writing team of Gwen Bristow (1903-1980) and Bruce Manning (1900-1965) published four crime novels: *The Invisible Host,* (which possibly inspired Agatha Christie's classic mystery *And Then There Were None*), *The Gutenberg Murders, Two and Two Make Twenty-Two* and *The Mardi Gras Murders.* The couple later went on to enjoy highly successful careers in entertainment, she writing historical fiction, including her bestselling Plantation Trilogy, he writing screenplays in Hollywood, including most of the scripts for the hugely popular films of youthful star Deanna Durbin. Before turning to writing crime fiction and these other rewarding pursuits, however, Bristow and Manning had experienced at first hand, during their time as Roaring Twenties newspaper reporters working the mean moonlight and magnolia streets of New Orleans, Louisiana, more than their share of real life crime, including a great deal of bloody murder. Bristow, a diminutive but daring brunette originally from South Carolina, particularly distinguished herself as what George W. Healy, Jr., a colleague of hers at the *New Orleans Times-Picayune*, the Bayou State's leading newspaper, termed "our star sob sister." Although "sob sister" was a somewhat condescending term for women journalists covering human interest stories (the most interesting of which invariably concerned murder), another of Bristow's colleague's recalled of her, with what he no doubt meant as the highest of praise: "She was the kind of woman reporter you'd send to do the type of story you'd send a man on. She was perfectly capable of doing it."

Bristow proved just how capable she was of doing nasty jobs in 1927, a banner year for bizarre and grisly killings in Louisiana, even by the old French colony's own impressive Baroque Gothic standard. First there came in July the murder of Morgan City utility company engineer James LeBoeuf. Murder in this case was only outed when the engineer's bloated body, which had been submerged with three hundred pounds of railroad irons in the depths of Lake Palourde, was exposed by receding water in the aftermath of the Great Mississippi River Flood. James's unfaithful wife Ada, the mother of the couple's four young children, was arrested and brought to trial for his shocking murder, along with an older, socially distinguished local doctor named Thomas Dreher, with whom Ada had been having an affair. The trial, which dragged on for two years, became an immediate sensation in the state and even made national newspaper headlines, with Ada LeBouef finally becoming the first white woman in the state's history to be judicially executed. The state hanged Dr. Dreher as well, on the same day as Ada.

Along with her colleague, drama critic Kenneth Thomas Knoblock (who later authored three crime novels himself, including one which drew directly on the infamous Moity murders; see below), Bristow handled coverage of the LeBoeuf-Dreher trial for the *Times-Picayune*. She "manfully" detailed every aspect of the affair for her readers, despite admitting in an anguished letter to her mother, written after the guilty verdicts had been handed down, that her job exacted an enormous emotional toll on her. The two year LeBoeuf-Dreher trial was "the most horrible experience I ever had," she confided. "When I rushed into the Western Union office behind the courtroom to flash my story, my hand was shaking so I could hardly write. I slept only three hours that night. . . ."

Bristow proved considerably more hard-boiled when, about four months after the James LeBoeuf murder, she and her colleague George Healy found themselves on the scene of a ghastly double trunk slaying in the French Quarter. Early on the morning of October 27, black "scrub woman" Nettie Compass, who lived in the back of the small stucco French creole style two and a half story building at 715 Ursulines Street with her husband Rocky and daughter Beatrice, trudged upstairs to clean at the second-story apartment of housepainter Henry Moity and his wife Theresa, a couple who lived unharmoniously in cramped and dingy quarters with their three small children and Theresa's sister Leonide, who recently had left her own husband, Henry's brother Joseph, and two children. Discovering a pool of blood seeping out from under the door to the Moity's apartment and down the stairs, Nettie promptly fled for her life, screaming for help in classic crime novel fashion.

Nettie's cries attracted two insurance salesmen who ran a business next door. After a brief inspection of the premises one of the men, Frank Silva, doubtlessly did what any other true blue American would have done. He alerted the press, which soon arrived on the scene in the form of the *Times-Picayune*'s intrepid George Healy. Silva, Healy and several local neighbors effected entry into the Moity apartment, where they found more blood on the floor and a large, partially open trunk in the couple's bedroom. Upon lifting the lid of the trunk, Healy discovered a dismembered woman's body, its severed limbs and head piled over the torso. Healy then doubtlessly did what any other true blue American reporter would have done. He alerted his city desk, asking for a lady reporter to be sent to the scene as soon as possible to help chronicle this blockbuster story. He also suggested that the city desk might want to get in touch with the police and the parish coroner.

Star sob sister Gwen Bristow arrived on the scene at the same time as the coroner, George F. Rowling, but she was in no way intimidated or inhibited by this man's official presence, bounding into the apartment at his side and immediately sighting several repellent objects on the bed in the Moitys' bedroom. "Look," she ghoulishly announced as she held these loathsome items up for the others in the room to descry, "ladyfingers." Four human fingers they were, severed from a woman's hand. Placing the "ladyfingers" back on the bed, Bristow then charged into the second bedroom, where Leonine had slept, and thereupon discovered a second trunk with another woman's body. The disjointed bodies being identified as those of the Moity wives, New Orleans Police Superintendent Thomas Healy, a "ruddy, pot-bellied Irishman" (who was no relation to George, though the two men had an amicable relationship), sent out an all-station bulletin calling for the arrest of the dead women's husbands.

Joseph Moity soon turned himself in the authorities, opining all the while that his brother Henry, driven to madness by Theresa's wanton ways with other men and resenting Leonide's influence over her sister, had committed the murder and fled; this indeed proved to be the case. There followed another bulletin from Superintendent Healey to the seven ships which had sailed from New Orleans on the day of the murders, warning their crews to keep a lookout for a desperate man with "dark, bushy hair," "very dark brown eyes" and a tattoo mark on his arm, depicting a flower with a woman's face and a nude female body.

The telltale tattoo did the trick and Henry, who had been working under an assumed name as a deck hand on a fishing lugger on Bayou Lafourche, soon was identified and turned over to the police. Once confronted with the ghastly killings, Henry attempted to pin the blame on a big, red-haired, psychotic Norwegian sailor he had dreamed up, but soon he broke down and confessed to the awful crimes. He admitted that after hearing rumors his unhappy wife was planning to run off with Joseph Caruso, the Moitys' landlord and the owner of a store on the ground floor of the building, he became possessed with thoughts of killing her and her meddlesome sister. Catching sight of Nettie Compass on the evening before the murders, he had whispered to the cleaner not to be frightened if she and her family heard the Moity children crying in the early morning hours. A few hours later, Henry after a heavy bout of drinking stabbed Theresa and Leonide to death, then expertly disjointed their bodies and deposited the pieces in the trunks. (His former employment as a butcher proved most helpful in this regard.) After cleansing himself of his bloody work in the bathroom he gathered the children and deposited them at a relative's and made his futile attempt at escape.

At the conclusion of his trial the next year Henry was sentenced to life imprisonment for the murders. Deemed a model prisoner by authorities, he was eventually placed under minimal supervision and as a result casually strolled to freedom by catching a cab in 1944. Although he was recaptured two years later, Henry received a pardon from Louisiana's governor in 1948, on the ground that he had committed the murders during a fit of temporary insanity (i.e., that bout of heavy drinking). It is interesting, and perhaps instructive, to compare the difference in the punishments which the state meted out to Ada LeBeouf for peripheral involvement in the murder of her husband and to Henry Moity for the bestial slaying and dismemberment of his wife and her sister. Henry went on eight years later to shoot his then girlfriend in the state of California. For this attempted murder (his bullet had pierced the woman's lung, but she managed to survive), he was sentenced to a term in prison at Folsom State Prison, where he passed away the next year.

George Healy and Gwen Bristow covered the Moity murder trial from start to finish, Healy writing the straight news report and Bristow the imaginative "color" (i.e., the sob sister stuff). However, near the end of the trial the two reporters, having gotten rather bored with the whole sordid mess, secretly switched bylines. George ruefully admitted that his color was not up to Bristow's impeccable standard and that it "was my last attempt to write like a woman." While he did not divulge how successfully Bristow had written "like a man" on this occasion, certainly she proved able to put her experiences covering murder trials to good use when she wrote four crime novels in collaboration with another male, her husband Bruce Manning, a fellow New Orleans newspaper reporter with black hair, dancing eyes and an infectious grin, whom she met and married while covering the LeBoeuf-Dreher trial.

* * * * * * *

Critics of Bristow and Manning's most successful crime novel, *The Invisible Host*, have carped over the wickedly baroque novel's artificial setting and general lack of realism, criticisms which to me seem entirely beside the point. The Golden Age of detective fiction for a time gloried in its very artificiality. However, the trio of Bristow and Manning crime novels which followed *The Invisible Host* are, if less outrageously inspired than *Host*, also more credible as well as quite enjoyable in their own right, demonstrating that the crime writing couple had not exhausted their murderous imaginations with a single book.

Although not published consecutively, *The Gutenberg Murders* (1931) and *The Mardi Gras Murders* (1932)—both of which novels, like *The Invisible Host*, are set in New Orleans— comprise a two book series and share a number of characters, both major and minor. The major series characters in the novel, all of whom are memorably presented, are Dan Farrell, district attorney of Orleans Parish ("not society but . . . nice people"), ace crime reporter Wade of the *Morning Creole* (decidedly homely but the possessor of a "sardonic grin that conveyed a perpetual assumption of the superiority behind the grin and the stupidity in front of it"), Captain Dennis Murphy of the New Orleans Homicide Squad ("broad, ruddy and Irish") and the *Creole*'s star photographer Wiggins (a "very small, very brown young man with a screwed-up face, hopping like a firecracker"). These colorful characters, along with assorted police and press men (sadly no sob sisters ever put in appearances) link and enliven the two novels, providing as well an air of big city verisimilitude to a genre that was then still dominated by the country house setting, both in the United Kingdom and the United States.

Although its milieu is more realistic than that of *The Invisible Host*, *The Gutenberg Murders* nevertheless offers readers an ingenious, highly classical puzzle, with D.A. Farrell, the police and the press all working together to discover the malefactor behind a rash of gruesome, fiery slayings of individuals associated with the Sheldon Memorial Library, which had already been reeling from the scandalous theft of its recent prized acquisition of nine leaves from the Gutenberg Bible. (Farrell improbably deputizes Wade, although in real life Bristow herself would seem to have had rather a cozy relationship with the police in the Big Easy.)

For murderous inspiration Bristow and Manning unexpectedly drew on the ancient Greek playwright Euripides. (Indeed the novel might have been called *The Euripides Murders*.) Another source of inspiration very likely came to the authors from England's recent Blazing Car Murder, a notorious killing which took place shortly after the passing of Guy Fawkes Night in the early morning of November 6, 1930. After a slain body was discovered in a burning automobile, another man, Alfred Rouse, was arrested and brought to trial for the crime on January 26 1931, and convicted and sentenced to death five days later. Upon the failure of his appeal, Rouse was executed on March 10. Bristow and Manning published *The Gutenberg Murders* four months later in July, likely after having been composed the novel during the winter of 1930-31, so assuredly would have been familiar with the case.

The second and final entry in what might be termed the Wade and Wiggins mystery series, *The Mardi Gras Murders*, was published in November 1932, about sixteen months after *The Gutenberg Murders* and eight months after the non-series *Two and Two Make Twenty-Two*. Farrell, Murphy, Wade and Wiggins all reappear, with Murphy's and Wiggins' roles enlarged from the first novel relative to Farrell's and Wade's. Indeed, Wiggins, whose first name we now learn is Tony, plays the leading role in solving the crime, as Wade had done in *Gutenberg*. The story concerns another rash of bizarre murders in New Orleans, this one taking place over Collop Monday, Shrove Tuesday and Ash Wednesday and plaguing members of the secretive and sinister Mardi Gras parade society Dis, dedicated to the Greek god of Inferno. Once again Bristow and Manning served up an intricately plotted mystery with fiendish murders (including a "locked room" killing on a parade float) and plenteous local color, although it must be admitted that *Mardi Gras Murders*, completed after the publication of Dashiell Hammett's hugely popular novels *The Maltese Falcon* and *The Glass Key*, has a more hard-boiled consistency to it than *Gutenberg*.

In particular Police Captain Murphy, with his repeated belli-cose threats of inflicting the "third degree" upon persons of interest in the case and his bigoted treatment of Cynthia Fonte-nay's black butler Jasper (an important witness in the case), likely will be viewed far less indulgently by modern readers than he is by Farrell, Wade and Wiggins. Yet should we really fault authors like Bristow and Manning for portraying things as they were in those days? (And of course many would question just how much things have changed today.) As New Orleans crime reporters themselves, Bristow and Manning knew of what they wrote, unlike most crime writers of the day (Dashiell Hammett certainly excepted), although they often shared the cynicism of their profession, a quality which they portray in their depic-tions of Wade and Wiggins, who often get so caught up in the story they are covering that they forget about the finer human feelings. Bristow and Manning refer to "the newspaperman's paradoxical quality of combining a genuine sympathy for people who got into trouble with a naïve eagerness to put their trou-bles in the paper," which is perhaps a bit too indulgent a way of characterizing it.

Wade and Wiggins are similarly indulgent in their view of Murphy's practice of "stowing away recalcitrant suspects" in the "dripping, rat-ridden, unlighted depths" of the Ninth Precinct station house under the authority of Ordinance 1436, on the assumption that a night or two spent there would loosen stiff tongues. "[E]ven the toughest of gangsters had been known to confess with teary appeals for mercy after two days in sparse fare among the rats," write Bristow and Manning, without any obvi-ous sense of disapproval. As the pair of former reporters would well have known, in real life Henry Moity had made his confession at the Ninth Precinct station house a few years earlier in 1927 and at his trial his legal team argued that he had confessed essentially, as George Healy out it, "to get away from the rats" in that "disintegrating, ill-kept, rodent-infested dungeon."

Two and Two Make Twenty-Two, the crime novel which appeared between *Gutenberg* and *Mardi Gras,* is more of a throwback to the pleasing artificiality of *The Invisible Host,* at least in terms of its enclosed setting on an island off the Mississippi Gulf Coast, which is obviously drawn from the time which Bristow and Manning themselves spent in the area in 1930-31. As a powerful storm bears down on the high-toned pleasure resort of Paradise Island, the small number of hotel personnel and guests remaining there has to cope not only with a squall but drug running and a most determined murderer. Regular police being absent from the scene, the case is solved by a sprightly and engaging elderly genteel lady sleuth, Daisy Dillingham, one of a series of well-drawn women characters who appear in the Bristow-Manning detective novels. At one point Daisy pronounces: "Men always see the obvious. You'll run around putting two and two together and making your own chesty fours out of them. Sometimes two and two make-twenty-two." And the novel's jaw-dropping conclusion proves that she is right. Gwen Bristow and Bruce Manning may have only moonlighted in mystery for but a short while, but vintage mystery fans are fortunate that they did.

Curtis Evans

PART ONE

CHAPTER ONE

THE wind whipped and snarled around Paradise Island, bending the palm trees like plumes and driving the whitecaps hissing across the beach. Off the west promontory the sun paused angrily above the tumbling sea, flooding the island with an ominous red light before which the shadows were black and sharp. The windows were like squares of fire along the side of the Peacock Club, and under the threatening sunset the golf course looked almost purple. The sails of the sloops that were scurrying back to the mainland were snapping in the wind, as though in spite of the threat that sent them flying to a safer harbor. The boats were waving a gallant goodby to the brightest spot of all the playground that edges the Gulf of Mexico.

Paradise Island was glamorous and far-fabled; one of the many dots that speckle the Gulf off the Louisiana-Mississippi coastline, it had been a jungle fifteen years ago, when Brett Allison had turned up from nowhere with money in his pocket and a vision of fortune in his head. He had bought the island for next to nothing, and had cleared its matted tangle, keeping his vision intact. Trees fell, brush burned and swamps were drained as the jungle made way for stables, wharfs, cottages, a golf course, tennis courts, shooting ranges, gaming rooms and the hotel—the Peacock Club. And now from tip to tip of the island life had a gay swiftness, with Brett Allison in the background, master of all the bright details that made Paradise Island what it had become: a glittering resort twelve miles from land, where he governed alone.

He had made himself one of the most famous hosts in America. But not even Brett Allison's deft authority could forestall the rising of a storm. When the first warnings appeared his stewards had blandly ordered racing sloops to take his guests to the mainland before dark, and had as blandly accepted the fact that several of them elected to stay. Very well, had come the word from Alison's walled-in house behind the Peacock Club; Paradise Island had never failed to make its guests comfortable, and if they chose to brave the storm, the resources of the island were theirs to command. Meanwhile the wind was rising, promising a battle between earth and the heavens; Mr. Allison hoped they would enjoy the spectacle.

From an aeroplane Paradise Island looked like a horseshoe nailed with palms. Cottages cuddled among the trees on each side and a channel between the points widened into a bay that filled the curve. Back from the bay the Peacock Club, built to withstand tropical storms, stood closed with jaunty security against the wind.

The sun slanted across the lounge room of the club-house and made a bright spot on the floor just in front of Major Jack Raymond, who sat by the fireplace, meditatively puffing at a cigar. It was a good, comfortable cigar, short and stocky like the Major himself, but the Major at this moment looked less like a contented connoisseur of tobacco than like an impatient gentleman who smokes to keep from fidgeting. Now and then he glanced out with snug approbation, as though he had ordered the storm and was well pleased at its preliminary disorder.

His cigar was half ash before the doors of the lounge room opened. The Major started and sat up expectantly, for the opening of the doors signalled the entrance of a lean young man in golf tweeds, who came glowering over to meet the Major's alert query.

"What luck, Andrew?"

Andrew kicked a chair closer to the Major's and slumped into it.

"I don't know," he answered curtly. "She's staying."

"Good."

The Major was gruffly approving, as though resolved to stampede over Andrew's sullenness. Andrew lit a cigarette and threw the match down with impotent distaste.

"Where's Barclay?" he demanded.

"His boat's aground off the keys. He went down with Brett Allison's tug to get it free—" the Major smiled—"and at the same time to look over the tug. He'll be gone about an hour."

Andrew crossed his long arms on his knees and stared morosely out of the window.

"Nervous, Andrew?" the Major asked.

"No. It's not that."

There was a crease between Andrew's eyebrows, and his black eyes, which ordinarily had a frank twinkle, were glumly narrowed. The Major studied him with a tinge of uncertainty.

Andrew's appointment to the commission organized by Federal authorities to stop drug traffic through the port of New Orleans had delighted him until he found that his job was to trap a young girl into admitting that she was the mysterious woman of the government reports. The commission had been in existence three years, but Andrew was not made part of it till six months ago, when Tommy Sanders was killed. Sanders, an aviator with a brilliant war record, had crashed his plane into Barataria Bay. Department of Commerce inspectors had said that they could find no evidence of foul play and no suggestion of a failure in the machine, and their only theory was that this pilot had fallen asleep and that his plane had dipped into a dive. It was then that Linton Barclay and Major Raymond had come to Andrew; had told him how they had been appointed to do the work which Federal officers were apparently unable to do, and how they had followed the insidious trail for three years, discovering many of the lesser men in the organization but always failing to identify the leaders behind it.

The Major drew long puffs of his cigar and was silent, till Andrew, as if to distract attention from himself, asked, "What do you think of the storm?"

"It's fine," the Major answered readily. "Gives us a clear field. Nearly everybody has gone to the mainland, including most of Allison's servants. There are only a few guests staying—you and I and Barclay, and Eva Shale and Judith Garon."

A trace of mischief showed on Andrew's set face. "Oh, no. The Cuppings are staying too."

"Damn!" the Major exploded softly. "That old fool."

Andrew was chuckling. "It's not the old fool. It's the young one—Imogen. She's telling everybody that she's 'never seen a tropical storm and wouldn't miss this one for the world and thinks it's going to be just too exciting.' They're moving from their cottage to the clubhouse."

The Major did not share Andrew's amusement. "They're both brainless."

"Well, they're here." Andrew lapsed into exasperation. "And with Imogen around, if we're wrong this time everybody from here to Honduras will know it. That puts Eva—"

The Major interrupted sternly. "Where does it put Eva? She's well able to take care of herself. Her palaver about criminals and penology—clever, but it's a front."

"You may be right." Andrew ran his hand wearily through his black hair. "But suppose you're wrong?"

"Nobody'll be hurt. Barclay and I agree that we won't bother her unless we're sure. That ought to satisfy you."

Andrew moved his chair back to escape the advancing sunlight. "I'm not worried about you and Barclay. It's something she said to me this afternoon." His face had grown suddenly bitter.

The Major regarded him with an odd mingling of inquiry, sympathy and triumph. He understood Andrew too well to think that he enjoyed spying on this girl, no matter what theories were advanced to justify it.

"I know it seems hard," he said after a pause. "But it's necessary, Andrew."

"Necessary?" countered Andrew. "You've got nothing on her."

"Maybe not," was the Major's non-committal reply. "What did she tell you?"

Andrew glanced uneasily around the lounge, but except for the telephone operator at her switchboard behind the front desk and a suave-faced gentleman who was examining the clubhouse records, there was no one else in the room.

"Well, it's a supposed confidence, made to a friend—" his words carried a sarcastic emphasis—"by a girl in a jam. You and Barclay will probably consider it a rare piece of sleuthing."

The Major's lips tightened on his cigar. "Nobody promised this would be a picnic."

"It isn't," said Andrew. Then, as if he had finally made up his mind to talk and wanted to get it done, he edged his chair close to the Major's and whispered rapidly for ten minutes. The Major listened, now and then giving a slow nod, as if all this were simply a sought-for confirmation of his own ideas.

"Anonymous letter!" he exclaimed when Andrew paused. "I knew that penology stuff was a front. Fine work, Andrew."

"Fine work," Andrew repeated. His voice was acrid. "Do I get measured for my medal now?"

The Major looked surprised. "Why, this proves she's playing us for suckers!"

Andrew answered with a left-handed smile.

The Major broke into a light, confident laugh. "I've had a hunch right along that the ring knew what we were doing." He put his hand on Andrew's knee and went on good-naturedly. "You know, there's nothing so refreshing as a hundred-per-cent chump, and at my age I know that there's nothing as easy to be a chump about as a good-looking girl. Barclay has a date with her this afternoon, and I'm going to prove to you that I'm right and you're wrong." Andrew's eyes were angry. As he still said nothing, the Major persisted.

"Here's the plan. We won't say anything to Barclay about this. They're going for a ride together, and she'll try this same gentle business of a confidence to a friend from a girl in a jam, or I'm wrong."

Andrew nodded with sudden optimism. "It's a bet."

He pushed back his chair and walked toward one of the long windows. The Major followed him.

"I hope you come around to seeing it my way, Andrew," he said in a voice that tried to be gentle and managed only to be a soft growl. "Hating the enemy isn't always easy."

Andrew started and flung open the window. The wind rushed in. "Listen!" Andrew exclaimed. "A plane. What do you think—"

"Ooooh! A plane!" chirped a voice behind them, and they turned to see young Mrs. Cupping, her cherub curls dancing as she ran down the staircase. "Isn't it just too thrilling? What sort of a plane do you think would dare to get out in a gale like this? Maybe it's an ocean flyer. Oh—Andrew, just *look* at it!"

She squeezed between them to look out, but Andrew and the Major were staring at the plane's disdainful course through the wind, as it wheeled over the bay and flirted its tail nonchalantly at the choppy waters below. The suave-faced gentleman who had been behind the desk was approaching the window.

"A plane?" he questioned. "In this wind?" He peered out. "Perhaps a mail plane off its course."

"Maybe it'll have to stay here all night," volunteered Imogen. "The poor pilot might be drunk. I knew one who always took a couple of drinks before he went up."

The plane hummed lazily in the mottled sky over the golf course, and its nose pointed with impudent scorn at the red storm-flag snapping from the roof of the Peacock Club. They could see now that it was a giant cabin plane, black and silver; as it lowered and its hum grew louder Imogen Cupping gave an excited little gasp and Andrew and the Major stared incredulously at each other, and suddenly the Major threw his cigar away and laughed.

"Nobody else in the world would do it. Let's go meet her. She's landing on the golf course."

"She would." Andrew had reached the door by this time, with the Major at his heels; as they slammed it shut and ran across to the eighteenth green the suave gentleman stared from the plane to Imogen's excited eyes.

"But who is it, Mrs. Cupping?"

Imogen puckered her pink lips and gave him a condescending look. "Anybody could tell that you haven't been here very long, Mr. Foster. *That's* Daisy Dillingham."

"She must be a very popular young woman," Mr. Foster suggested politely.

Imogen cocked up her green eyes and forgot the phraseology she had taken such pains to acquire since she stepped out of the chorus to wed an aging millionaire. "Listen," she said. "Daisy Dillingham is two years older than Adam. She's Andrew Dillingham's grandmother. She's the Who's Who and What's What of New Orleans and points South. And if she doesn't like this swell island Mr. Allison had better sink it, because nobody who's anybody will come here any more. That's who she is."

CHAPTER TWO

WITH a turn and a quick sideslip the plane nosed gently toward the fairway. Two caddies stared and grinned; the Scot to whom the greens were at once a glory and a shrine started forward in a black fury as the three wheels made a hop on the clipped grass and rolled toward the pin.

"It's Daisy Dillingham!" breathed an awesome caddie at his elbow. "Ain't that plane sump'n?"

But Fergus McPherson had no eye for marveling caddies and no ear for lordly names. As the silver propeller blades slowed and stopped he yelled his rage at this desecration of his citadel.

"And dinna ye know where the landin' field is, ye dolt?"

The pilot doffed his helmet and gave the Scot a mercurial grin as he stepped out of the forward cabin and dropped to the turf. Heedless of McPherson's epithets and the stares of the caddies he unhooked a three-step ladder and placed it under the door behind the wings. The door opened.

Andrew and Major Raymond, who had reached the plane's side in time to appreciate the wrath of McPherson, waved cheerily. "Welcome, duchess!" called the Major, and Andrew exclaimed, "My sainted grandmother! Daisy, you should be spanked."

The Major bowed like a cavalier and McPherson backed away, mumbling helpless imprecations, for there in the tiny doorway, her head bent to clear the top and her gold-headed cane grasped firmly in her right hand, stood Daisy Dillingham, whose word had opened the gates of tradition to a butcher's son and whose cane had thumped the tom-tom of many a social doom; Daisy Dillingham, who did as she pleased and said what she thought and who for sixty years had been adored and dreaded and obeyed. Coolly ignoring Andrew's proffered aid, she descended from her plane, surveyed the group, and bestowing a gracious smile upon the exasperated greenskeeper, she addressed her pilot.

"Sweet flying, Phipps. Take her back to town. I'll come in on the Major's boat."

The pilot saluted smartly, put down the last of four bags and scrambled back into the plane. Daisy linked an arm in the Major's and shook her cane at Andrew's grinning face.

"Thought you could run off and leave me at home knitting, did you? Not a bad-looking place, Paradise Island." She glanced around appreciatively.

"*What* are you doing here?" Andrew demanded.

Daisy dismissed his puzzlement with an impish grin. "You should know. Tell that youngster to bring my bags."

With a bow to McPherson she started across the fairway toward the main entrance of the Peacock Club, her full skirts whipping in the wind. Over Daisy's head Andrew gave the Major a look of helpless yielding.

"So this is Paradise." Daisy stopped before the wide entrance to the Peacock Club and nodded approvingly. Her jet-black eyes were sparkling. The Peacock Club was long and low, with a hint of rusticity that kept its exterior from being over-lavish. "Glad I came," she added complacently.

Andrew and the Major exchanged glances. "Stop trying to be mysterious," Andrew urged. "Why did you come?"

Daisy looked up at him and winked. "It's a secret," she retorted. "Besides, you're too young." She glanced back as her plane roared over the palms and headed for the sea, and they crossed the threshold.

Imogen Cupping tripped forward to twitter a greeting which Daisy acknowledged with a wave of her cane as she turned to the urbane and impeccable Mr. Warren, who released about her the efficiency of Paradise Island. A suite was ready and could be occupied now. Would Mrs. Dillingham take coffee? Tea, then, would be brought immediately. A glass of wine? Sherry cocktails? At once. A list of the other guests? Certainly. It was hoped that Mrs. Dillingham would be comfortable.

He saw her to the elevator. "You needn't come up," she said sharply. "I've got two escorts and a bellhop." Warren bowed and retired, and as the elevator doors closed, Daisy turned her impudent regard upon Andrew. "I've just heard about you, young man," she accused. "Playing gigolo. Ain't you 'shamed?"

"Not a bit," Andrew whispered. "I'm eminently fitted for the job. Ask the Major."

Major Raymond glanced meaningly at the bellhop and it was not until they were inside her suite that Daisy spoke again.

"Now, while I take off these shoes," she ordered, "suppose you tell me what's behind this scandal."

Andrew had recovered his good-humor. Daisy's wrath always delighted him.

"What scandal, pray?" asked the Major.

"Well, I was having lunch today with Mrs. Wales. She mentioned that Andrew was being very attentive to a young prison angel named Eva Shale. Of course I knew that—" she put up her hand—"and don't you stop me till I've finished. Mrs. Wales' daughter Laura said she had been in school with Miss Shale and after lunch Laura and I settled down to a little gossip."

Daisy's black eyes were snapping at her grandson. "I heard a great deal about Eva Shale. She seems to be a very interesting young woman, and I got to thinking over your many dates with her and realized what they meant. I thought I'd come over and see about it."

Andrew and the Major sat down, rather uncertainly. Major Raymond spoke. "Well, I thought—"

"You listen to me, Jack Raymond. I've known you for forty years and I've known Andrew since he was born and I've never noticed either of you doing any great inspirational thinking. Now tell me. What's the plot?"

The Major sighed and yielded. "An Eastern syndicate is going to buy Paradise Island," he told her. "A fellow named Foster is here now, closing the deal. We think the dope ring has smelt a rat, and are planning to pull out. It looks too as if Eva Shale might be in with Allison."

Daisy's cheeks puffed with indignation. "Nonsense," she derided.

The Major ducked to escape being hit by the shoe that she pulled off.

"Find my felt slippers, Andrew," ordered Daisy, kicking off the other shoe. "They're in the brown bag." She watched Andrew as he found the slippers, and as he apparently intended to volunteer nothing else, she asked shortly, "What about this Allison?"

"Brett Allison," said Andrew, bringing over the felt slippers and kneeling down to put them on his grandmother, "is the mainspring of the whole Paradise Island machine. He sits up in his house behind the club here and runs the whole works, but he isn't seen very often and nobody seems to know him. He's the great Paradise Island legend."

"Humph. No respect for legends. I'm one myself." Deep in her throat Daisy made a noise like a hen's cluck. Andrew grinned and tried to hide the grin by keeping his head bent, for he recognized both the noise and Daisy's general manner, and he knew they meant that Daisy was about to sally forth to battle. "Where's the girl—Eva Shale?"

Andrew had finished his job with the slippers, but he answered without looking up, in a voice that had become suddenly reluctant. "She and Judith Garon went out to the tarpon hole. They'll be back soon, if the wind keeps rising."

"Judith staying here tonight?" asked Daisy.

"Yes."

"What for? To be near Barclay? If they're such hearts, do you suppose Barclay has had her watching Eva in you-all's dope crusade?"

"Certainly not," returned the Major. "Barclay objected even to telling you."

"Cluck. He did, did he? Well, now that I know, I hope he can't object to my telling him I think you're all fools."

The Major scowled slightly. "We may be fools," he answered, shrugging his shoulders, "but the trail for some time has been pointing consistently to the Gulf as the avenue through which the drugs are coming in. We have a tip that a consignment was to arrive in New Orleans tonight. With the storm, that's impossible, and with Paradise Island nearly deserted, it's a pretty good time to make a search and an arrest—if Allison is planning to move his headquarters to a new location."

Daisy looked quizzically at Andrew, who was staring out of a window at the white-flecked sea.

"And does Barclay suspect that Eva is in with Allison?"

"Well, we know there's a woman involved," the Major answered, "and Eva Shale spends a great deal of time here. There's very little known about her. She has plenty of money, and it was Barclay's idea that we ought to get some more information on her. Scarcely anything is available through ordinary channels, so that angle of the inquiry was made Andrew's assignment."

"And so tonight, if you decide that Allison is involved, you're going to make an arrest?" Daisy was alert, like a lawyer examining a witness.

"No, we won't make the arrest. Regular agents will come over and act on our information. What we are trying to do is pin something on Allison."

She gave Andrew an ironic little smile. "It's not as bad as it might be, Andrew. You won't have to put handcuffs on her, at any rate."

"Rub hard, old girl," he said.

Daisy took a cigarette out of her handbag and for a minute she sat watching his grim young face through a cloud of smoke. Between Andrew and herself there was a bond of kinship that had nothing to do with the fact that he was the sixth Andrew Dillingham and she the present head of their line; it was rather a sense of temperamental unity that seemed to bring him closer to her than even her own children had ever been. Her voice was both sharp and sympathetic as she asked, "What have you found out, Andrew?"

Andrew was still contemplating the angry sea. "Just enough to make the Major want to shoot her before sundown."

"And is she in it?"

It was a question too imperative to admit of an evasion. "It looks bad," said the Major. "At any rate," he added, "she's got to be watched."

Daisy glanced at Andrew, but he was standing with his back to her.

"And you don't like it, Andrew?"

He wheeled suddenly. "Well, damn it, Daisy, do you? Fighting dope-smugglers is one thing, and spying on a girl like Eva Shale is another."

Daisy examined the head of her cane as though it were a queer museum piece. She was glad she had come.

"This gets better and better. Why has she got to be watched?"

Andrew sat down on a Louis XV chair that looked too delicate to hold his long person. "She talked to me about a letter—an anonymous letter."

Daisy nodded sagely.

"The Major said she was trying to pump me. She may have been."

Daisy smiled, for Andrew's mind was less remote from her than Andrew's years, and she knew that accepting any sort of confidence and then talking about it was not easy for him.

"Never mind," she said. "Ask her up for tea and I'll let her tell me about it."

"Afraid you can't do that," interposed the Major. "Andrew's not supposed to have told. She was asking for his advice."

"Look here, Jack. I traipsed over here for the single purpose of meeting Eva Shale so as to decide whether you two were about to be big heroes or big idiots. Andrew, tell Eva I want her up here for tea."

The Major studied his cigar. "Might not be a bad idea, at that."

"She won't come," said Andrew.

Daisy shrugged. "And why not?"

"Well, for one thing, she's not enthusiastic about making social contacts. I don't mean she snubs anybody. But she's difficult to know."

"If she's so standoffish, how'd you manage to see her every day? The Dillingham charm?"

"We like to do the same things," he answered. "We play golf and swim together."

Daisy gave an expressive scowl. So they played golf and went swimming together. And Laura Wales had said, "She's a first-class athlete and a splendid girl, really, but awfully provoking, if you get what I mean—morbid, I sometimes think." Daisy was very glad she had come.

"I see," she said dryly, and added, "you get her up here for tea with me, young man. Tell her your poor old grandmother is lonely, or some such nonsense. Bring her up and leave her with me. Who's that?"

Andrew had gone to the door in answer to a knock, and admitted a woman in a smart linen tailored suit. She carried a service-tray on which was a silver pitcher and four shallow long-stemmed glasses. She was a tall, rather harassed-looking woman, with an air of competence of which Daisy approved, and a suggestion of nervous energy that Daisy abominated.

"Your sherry cocktails, Mrs. Dillingham. With Mr. Allison's compliments."

"How considerate. Thank you."

"The tea-things are outside, Mrs. Dillingham. I'll bring them in."

She set down the tray and wheeled in the tea-table. "Is there something else I can do? I'm Mrs. Penn, the club manager. We're very short of waiters during a storm, and I thought you might be waiting for your tea. I'll fix the table."

Daisy was used to this sort of homage, and quite honestly enjoyed it. Mrs. Penn had briskly wheeled the tea-table into place, with the pitcher of sherry within Daisy's reach. She had taken the glasses into the bathroom, and Daisy could hear the splash of the ice-water over their rims.

Daisy took up the silver pitcher, sniffed at it with approbation, and turned back to Andrew.

"Now run along and get Eva Shale up here."

He acquiesced with a grim smile. "All right. I'll try."

"Try? You bring her. I want to see the victim of this conspiracy."

There was a soft crash on the carpet. They all jumped.

Mrs. Penn stood in the bedroom door, a look of hysterical dismay on her face. She had tilted the tray and dropped the glasses.

CHAPTER THREE

"Now don't be upset, Mrs. Penn. There's no spilt milk—or sherry—to cry over."

Daisy spoke with matter-of-fact cheerfulness, but she was puzzled; four broken glasses hardly seemed to justify the housekeeper's consternation. "Come into the bedroom and we'll find some tumblers," she added briskly, stepping over the fragments on the floor. "Pick up the pieces, Andrew." She closed the door and glanced at Mrs. Penn.

Though she could not guess the cause, she was not shocked at Mrs. Penn's nervousness; she knew that women executives who could handle business deals without a flutter often grew panicky over a minor domestic crisis. Mrs. Penn was quivering on the edge of hysteria. Even her suit seemed suddenly less crisp than before. Daisy chattered brightly.

"Won't hurt those men a bit to wait a couple of minutes for a drink. We can use those water-glasses. You're feeling better? Some people are terribly frightened when there's a storm."

Mrs. Penn caught eagerly at the proffered excuse. "Yes, storms always make me nervous. I hope I didn't startle you."

Daisy was busily unfastening her dress, but she was observing the lines of stern repression about the housekeeper's mouth. "Here, have a cigarette and get yourself together," she advised. "These storms aren't often as bad as they threaten to be."

Mrs. Penn declined the cigarette, but answered with professional reassurance. "Don't let me frighten you—I was foolish to be nervous. This building is perfectly safe. It has weathered worse blows than this."

"And you always stay?" Daisy was brushing her hair.

"Yes, it sets a good example to the servants, and besides, Mr. Allison pays a storm-bonus to all employees who stay. I have—" she hesitated—"a good deal of expense."

A slow flush crept over her cheeks. Daisy felt a troublesome foreboding. They had been talking about Eva Shale when Mrs. Penn dropped the glasses. She went on deliberately.

"I hope you don't mind if I change, do you? I'm expecting someone for tea—a Miss Shale. Do you know her?"

Mrs. Penn's face told Daisy exactly nothing. "Yes, I know her. She often stays here."

She stopped, and Daisy fancied there was a hint of constraint in her manner. But she could not be sure.

"Will you take these glasses into the other room?" she asked finally. "Tell them I'll be ready in just a minute."

Mrs. Penn had left when Daisy returned, and Andrew and the Major were sitting moodily over their cocktails. Her cane rapped sharply on the floor.

"Andrew Dillingham, I thought I'd sent you on an errand."

Andrew laughed resignedly. "What's the use? She'll only decline—with thanks."

"Nonsense. Go, and hurry. The tea will be cold and the cocktails hot."

Andrew pushed his chair away with such force that it fell over backward. He retrieved it and stood up.

"Daisy, I won't. It's bad enough as it is without inviting her up to meet my family. She knows you brought me up and how fond of you I am and if I tell her you want to meet her she'll think—oh, hell," he broke off, as he heard a knock at the door.

"Probably Mrs. Penn with another set of cocktail glasses," she said soothingly, and called, "Come in."

The door opened and Andrew's jaw dropped. A tall, brown young person in tan jodhpurs and a scarlet jacket came in, crossed the room with the swinging steps of the born athlete, held out a sunburnt hand to Daisy and exclaimed,

"So you're the Daisy Dillingham I've heard so much about. They told me you were here and I just ran in to get acquainted. I'm Eva Shale."

Andrew and the Major were nonplussed. Daisy shot a glance of sly mischief in their direction, put her own white hand into the hard brown one extended to her, smiled and responded.

"My dear, how good of you! I had just this minute suggested to Andrew that he introduce us. He and the Major were telling me they couldn't stay for tea, and I'm far too old and crotchety to be left alone. Must you really go too, Major? I'm so sorry."

"So am I," said Eva, "but after all, it's Daisy Dillingham I came to see, so I'm not crushed." She had a clear, challenging sort of voice. "If you happen to see Linton Barclay, will you tell him where I am?"

"I'll be glad to," promised the Major, and Daisy winced, wondering if Eva had guessed what was behind Barclay's attentions. She offered Eva a cocktail, while Andrew and the Major in obedience to Daisy's gesture spoke polite regrets. When they were gone Daisy turned back to her visitor.

"Brett Allison has more suitable crystal for cocktails," she explained as she held out sherry in a water-glass, "but when Mrs. Penn was here she jumped at a flash of lightning and zip went the cocktail glasses. Do you know Mrs. Penn?"

Eva smiled, and it was a delicious smile without a tinge of self-consciousness. "Indeed I do. She's rather a wonder. It's her management that makes the clubhouse so perfect. But I can't imagine her being scared of lightning."

Daisy offered her a cigarette and lit one for herself. "She was probably tired. The rush of getting everybody off at once."

"I suppose so. There's been quite an exodus. The dining room was full for lunch, and there'll be less than a dozen of us for dinner."

Daisy indicated the tea-table. "Speaking of dinner and things like that, will you pour the tea? For that honor, I'm going to call you Eva, and when you've poured, you'll have earned the right to call me Daisy."

Eva laughed. "Fine. We are getting acquainted, aren't we?"

She tossed her gloves, her riding-crop and her scarlet hat on the sofa and sat down behind the teapot. "Pardon the pants, will you, but I'm going to ride in a couple of minutes. Sugar?"

"Two lumps and cream. Thank God I'm too old to have to think of my figure."

Eva laughed again. She had a tantalizing laugh, with a quality of healthy excitement. "I take cream too. I don't think I could possibly get fat. I swim too much."

Daisy watched her with increasing approval. She liked the way Eva served tea. Any woman who could pour tea graciously and without making a ceremony of it found favor in Daisy's eyes.

Except for the tart modernity of her jodhpurs Eva might have been a warrior-queen out of a saga. She was tall—Daisy had noticed when she came in that she was nearly as tall as Andrew—and Daisy saw to her own surprise that she was blonde; years of wind and sun had tanned her like an Indian, but her eyes in her bronzed face were startlingly blue. Her hair was of that light shade of brown which can so easily be drab, but the long drench of sunshine had flecked it with gold, so that it had the colors of honey and amber, and brushed in vagabond tendrils over her sunburnt forehead. With a cool poise that Daisy liked at once, Eva poured cream into her own tea and took a scone.

"I've been wanting to meet you for ages," Eva said. "Is this your first visit to Paradise Island?"

"Probably my last. Paradise Island is no place for an old woman with a stick."

Eva twinkled merrily at her. "There's the Temple."

"The gambling-rooms? I might like that. I'm a rather remarkable crap-shooter."

"You can play anything in the Temple. Roulette, faro, dice, chemin de fer—I play lots in the evenings."

"You are here most of the time, aren't you?"

"Virtually live here all summer."

"You're staying through the storm?"

Eva frowned slightly. "I think so. I might go back tonight."

"But the boats are gone."

"I have my speedboat."

Daisy looked out. "You can't run a speedboat through that water. Brett Allison would lock you up for trying to blemish the reputation of Paradise Island with a suicide."

She had brought in Allison's name purposely, wondering how Eva would react to the mention of the man they believed was her secret associate, but Eva only smiled.

"Somehow, I rather think he wouldn't. Do you know Mr. Allison?"

"Does anybody?"

"I suppose not." Daisy still could not detect a trace of self-awareness in her manner. "But I've seen him. He looks rather jolly. I mean, he looks like the kind of man who might like to take a boat through a frisky sea himself, just to see how it felt. He has an electric launch that he handles like a professional. If he wasn't so touch-me-not, I think I could be good friends with him." She glanced out of the window. "I've taken my boat through worse water than that."

('And so,' thought Daisy, 'the subject has been changed. Allison's touch-me-not. That sounded almost deliberate.')

Daisy watched her as she refilled the cups. 'Hardly dope,' said Daisy to herself. 'Nothing vile and sneaky. Plenty of nerve, though. If it were whisky, I'd believe it. She'd have a lot of fun being a bootlegger.' But there was that anonymous letter Andrew had mentioned. Daisy decided to make Eva talk about herself.

"What do you do," she asked, "when you aren't swimming and golfing and riding?"

"Drive a speedboat, mostly." Eva put down her napkin and took a pack of cigarettes from the pocket of her jacket. "Don't you want to try one of these? I have them made for me?"

Daisy took one and looked thoughtfully at it.

Monogrammed cigarettes. Her own speedboat. Her exquisitely tailored habit. Virtually all summer on Paradise Island.

Evidently a staggering income from somewhere. That was one reason why they suspected her.

"I thought Andrew told me," she said, "that you spent your spare time studying penology."

"I do," Eva owned laughing. "But I don't say much about it, because people think it's freakish. It's a fascinating subject, really—the curious effect that being in prison has on people who commit crimes—do you think it's silly?"

"I can see how some people might call it an odd hobby."

"They do. But I love it. I'm getting up a casebook. Records of criminals who have become respectable citizens after leaving prison. It's lots of fun."

Daisy looked with an unjustifiable frown at the end of her excellent cigarette. Penology and the psychology of the prisoner. No accounting for the hobbies of the modern girl.

"How did you happen to take it up?" she asked.

"Just got interested."

Daisy was still frowning. She had begun to see what Andrew had meant when he called Eva difficult. Eva had ready chatter and an easy laugh, but she had a baffling quality of aloofness. In fact, Daisy had the not entirely agreeable sensation of being watched more closely than she was watching. There was nothing soft about this young person. Daisy decided to take the plunge.

"You're an orphan, aren't you?" she asked.

"Yes."

Eva's monosyllable was like a warning that she expected but would not welcome another question. She tucked up a wisp of her sun-gilded hair and lit another cigarette. Daisy looked at her, regretfully. Eva's curt reticence about herself amounted almost to sullenness. It was another reason why they suspected her.

Eva spoke abruptly. "I've been stalling for ten minutes. Didn't you wonder why I came hurrying up to see you?"

She was sitting very still, one brown hand closed on her knee, the other holding her glass so tightly that the fingertips were pink.

"Why, yes," said Daisy frankly. "I did."

"I came," said Eva, "to answer a lot of questions that you want to ask." She had become coldly defiant. But her defiance plainly conveyed, 'This is not a plea for understanding.' It was a refusal of sympathy before sympathy could be offered, as though she had carefully held up a shield to protect a nature so delicate as to be easily hurt.

For an instant Daisy was too appalled to reply. Then she said, "I'm not sure that I know what you mean, my dear."

"I mean," said Eva, "all the things you want to know. Why I haven't any people. Why I never mention even a cousin. Who I am. Where I get the money I spend. All that. So I'm going to tell you, and the answer is that I don't know any more about it than you do."

CHAPTER FOUR

EVA swung one leg over the arm of her chair and regarded Daisy with resolute impersonality. Her frosty blue eyes met Daisy's with a look that clearly said, 'Well, we've started. Let's go.'

It was a full minute before Daisy spoke. But when she did, neither her words nor her manner indicated that her minute of silence had been chaotic with uncertainty.

"I'm sure, my dear, that you don't have to tell me anything. Unless you want to."

"O, yes I do." Eva's tone was cynical. She put her cigarette into the jade ash-tray and lit another with the close attention of one who is settling one problem before tackling another.

Daisy did not answer. She knew she was on the verge of hearing something that Andrew's committee, with all its elaborate subtlety, had never heard; and yet her interest in it was less sharp than her feeling of pity for the girl opposite her. Eva flicked an imaginary speck of dust off the toe of her boot, straightened her tie and looked up. There was a hardness in her jaw and a cold steadiness in her eyes. As she began to speak, Daisy felt that each word was a blow dealt at her own inquisitiveness.

"I was brought up at St. Helen's Convent, just outside New Orleans."

Daisy nodded. St. Helen's was the most expensive boarding school for girls in the state. Evidently Eva's ample income was not of recent acquisition.

"They don't often take children under five at St. Helen's, but when I was three years old a woman brought me there, and told the Mother Superior that my parents were dead and that I had no relatives I could live with. She said she was my guardian and paid for the first half-year in advance. The Mother Superior was told to send all bills to a New York address. The money came regularly for my tuition and clothes and expenses, and as I grew older, for spending money. When I finished St. Helen's I went to college, and there was always plenty of money, once every quarter, and increasing every year. I still get it. Last year my income was twenty thousand dollars."

She stopped. Not once during her recital had her truculent eyes left Daisy.

"The New York address was a post-office box number." Eva's voice carried a hard bitterness. "I've written there, of course, since I've grown up, asking for an explanation. The only answer I received said that while my guardians were paying me my legitimate income, they were not at liberty to change the present arrangement."

Daisy thoughtfully looked at the set young face across the table. "It's very puzzling, my dear child," she admitted gently, "but not disgraceful."

Eva laughed shortly. "Try it sometime." She crossed her arms around her knee. "I remember things," she added briefly.

Daisy grimly smothered her compassion and looked for a flaw in the story.

"But how are the checks signed?"

"John Brownfield. He's quite inaccessible." She smiled as if guessing Daisy's thoughts. "I've tried to find him." She shrugged. "Well—I suppose I ought to thank heaven I've money enough to do as I please. I don't need anybody who doesn't need me."

She stopped again and looked out at the tumbling whitecaps.

"I suppose you're wondering," Eva went on at last, "why I told you this."

"I suppose," Daisy returned smiling, "because you needed somebody to talk to. It's a relief to get things said, once in a while."

Eva smiled too, but not in response to Daisy's unspoken overture. Her smile was both negative and harsh.

"No, it's not that," she said crisply. "I didn't want you to think that I've been trying to marry Andrew."

Daisy heard herself gasp. But if Eva's answer had been a surprise, Eva's sudden change of manner was even more so. She had turned suddenly to Daisy with a mischievous frankness.

"My dear girl," said Daisy with perfect honesty, "That never occurred to me. I leave guesses like that to Walter Winchell, my personal Cyrano."

"Really? I was told very definitely that you had come to Paradise Island to look over this ambitious young woman." There was a hint of banter in her eyes. "That's customary, isn't it?"

Eva's change of approach had been so swift, and her words so unexpected, that Daisy wanted to laugh.

"I don't mind putting all my cards on the table," Eva said, with a tinkle of laughter in her voice that Daisy thought charming. "When Judith Garon and I came back from fishing, that delightful Imogen Cupping told me you had arrived, and added that the reason was both obvious and expected. So I came right up to put your mind at ease."

Daisy yielded to her impulse and laughed frankly. "You're a brave girl, for I'm an old grump-grump and I growl when I feel like it."

"Oh, I know. People have told me. But I'd rather be growled at than growled about. Anyway," she finished decisively, "I'm not trying to marry Andrew."

Her bright nonchalance was both ludicrous and pathetic. Daisy could not be sure whether Eva was appallingly honest or possessed of serpentine subtlety; her own thoughts were turning cartwheels, and she vented her irritating uncertainty with several sharp raps of her cane.

"You listen to me, young impudence. When Andrew starts bothering about getting married, I hope I'll have sense enough to know my place."

Eva laughed. "And that place—?"

"Will certainly not be leaping from limb to limb of his bride's family tree. Imogen Cupping is one of those sweet persons who are more dangerous to the general welfare than all the bluenoses in Boston."

She felt that her own response had been inadequate, but she was too troubled to mind; Linton Barclay might call for Eva at any minute, and she had not heard the story of the anonymous letter that was torturing Andrew. So when Eva flicked the crumbs off her fingers with a carelessness that seemed to Daisy too airy to be genuine, and said, "Good. We'll consider that subject wiped off, then, but at least I'm glad I told you," Daisy plunged ahead with the remark,

"You've surprised me very much. I didn't guess it was that silly Imogen Cupping who had sent you up to see me. I rather thought you wanted to borrow a grandmother."

Eva gave her a quizzical look.

"Andrew said you had asked his advice today about a letter," Daisy went on. "He didn't go into particulars, but I gathered that it was something of a problem, and I thought perhaps I was going to help you settle it."

"Oh—that." Eva was studying the jade ash-tray. Between her eyes there appeared two opposing little wrinkles, curved outward like parentheses. She had straight brown eyebrows, but when she frowned they curled upward at the outer ends and lay like two question-marks above her eyes.

"Maybe I'd better tell you about it," she said after a pause. "Andrew seemed to be too startled to offer me any advice. This letter—anonymous—came five days ago." She was tearing a cigarette-stub to pieces. "The letter tells me to expect another letter, which should be at my home now. That's why I said I might go back tonight—I can't decide just what to do."

She hesitated like a diver about to plunge into cold water, then hurried on in sharp staccato sentences.

"The letter was typewritten. Postmarked New Orleans. The writer talked about this case-book I'm getting together. Very socialistic—called me a member of the privileged classes annoying under-dog convicts just for amusement. Said somebody ought to put a stop to rich women's doing this sort of vivisection, and then threatened to give me information that I'll either have to report to the police, with the risk of being shot by some gangster for talking, or else keep to myself and risk being accused of deliberately shielding a criminal, if the police ever find out that I know it."

Daisy smothered an exclamation. "Go on. What sort of information?"

"Well, the letter says that twenty years ago a convict escaped from a Canadian prison. He changed his name, came down to this part of the country, and has become rich and prominent. People think his money comes from reputable enterprises, but actually he's head of a criminal syndicate and has never been suspected."

Daisy was alert. "Did your correspondent give this man's name?"

"No. But he promised it. Tonight I'm to receive the second letter giving full details of his criminal career, past and present, and a rogues' gallery picture of him taken in Canada."

Daisy tried to keep a calm exterior. Eva's story as she told it had somehow sounded plausible.

"What was he convicted of, Eva?" she asked!

There was a knock on the door. They both started. Eva dropped her voice.

"Dope-smuggling," she answered.

Daisy nearly dropped her cane. The knock was repeated.

"And they say," Eva added rapidly, "he's still at it."

From the turmoil of her thoughts one realization blazed into Daisy's understanding—this was what Andrew had meant.

"My problem," Eva went on in a voice hardly above a whisper, "is whether to go back tonight and get the second letter and give it to the authorities, or to burn it unopened." She looked up with a daring twinkle. "And now, Grandmother Dillingham, settle that."

The knock came again. Daisy called, "Just a minute, please," and put her hand on Eva's arm. "I'd advise you," she whispered, "to do nothing so silly as take out a speedboat in this kind of weather. Sleep on it and talk to me tomorrow."

"Any reason?" There was a querying lift of Eva's eyebrows.

Daisy thought. 'Is this child trying to pump me, too?' She looked at Eva for an answer, but found only questioning and a tinge of amusement. This was too much. She looked toward the door and called clearly, "Come in!" and then as the door opened, "Linton Barclay! How are you?"

CHAPTER FIVE

LINTON Barclay was tall and heavy, with a purposeful air and a jovial voice; he looked like a man favored by tradition for large enterprises and obvious successes. There were shrewd little lines about his eyes (he was nearsighted, but too vain to wear glasses in public), and a suggestion of a smile about his mouth, but his lips were thin, and his most casual glance had the intensity characteristic of a man whose decisions, once made, are implacable. He crossed directly to Daisy, waving a greeting in Eva's direction.

"I just heard you were here, Mrs. Dillingham. I'm delighted to see you."

Daisy gave him her hand. "Have a cocktail?"

He bowed and smiled. "I have yet to refuse my first drink. But only one."

Daisy poured the cocktail and Barclay turned to Eva. Daisy was watching them both.

She had never been sure that she liked Linton Barclay, for in spite of his charm, his air of pitiless force made him a rather exhausting companion. Eva was pulling on her gloves reluctantly, as though she wished she had not been interrupted.

"The wind ought to make it good riding," Eva remarked, almost absently, and Barclay, in the overpowering fashion which demanded that everybody else's mood match his own, exclaimed,

"Couldn't be better. We'll have a long ride—the storm won't break till an hour or so after dark."

"The sky seems pretty heavy now," observed Eva, looking out of the window.

"The barometer's holding up," Barclay assured her. "We'll have loads of time. It will storm tonight and be clear by morning. We can all go back tomorrow on my boat."

"Don't count on me," she objected. "I've got my speedboat."

Barclay's big voice boomed. "We'll let one of my boys take your boat in. Of course you'll come with us."

Daisy fairly quivered as she suddenly realized what he was talking about—"Come with us." The captives and their captors. Brett Allison, and Eva—?

But Eva was jamming her bright red hat over her sunburnt hair, and laughingly shaking her head. Daisy wondered if she could know what Barclay meant and if that was her answer. But Eva was either ignorant of his purpose or defying it, for she took her riding-crop and said brightly,

"Thanks, but you'd better count me out. See you when I get back, Daisy."

"Good. You'll come up here?"

"Let's meet in the lounge instead," Barclay suggested. "How's that?"

"Fine. About six."

And with a brisk "Suits me," Barclay left with Eva. Daisy stood up with a vehemence that gave her a twinge in her bad knee, drank the rest of the sherry, broke three matches in an effort to light a cigarette and said "Damn!" to the opposite wall.

After an hour which she spent munching caviar sandwiches and trying to discover some sort of coherence in the riddle-some medley of facts, suggestions and surmises that had been presented to her, Daisy finally took up her cane and descended into the lounge. She saw Andrew. He was sitting by the fire-place, gloomily watching the backs of Mr. and Mrs. Cupping, who were going out by the main door. Imogen was tripping brightly along a step or two ahead of her husband, who looked like a well-fed cinnamon bear bravely endeavoring to keep the pace with an effervescent rabbit. Daisy gave Andrew's shoulder a tap with her cane and sat down.

"What goes on?"

He answered with an exasperated shrug. "I've been telling Imogen that she ought to mind her own business. She thought it was really somebody's duty to point out what a play for me Judith Garon was making, now that Barclay has deserted her for Eva Shale."

Daisy chuckled. "She's one of nature's pointer-outs. Is she right for a change?"

"I wasn't thinking about Judith. She's so resentful of Barclay's attentions to Eva that she's trying to kidnap anything available and under sixty. But Barclay *is* too attentive to Eva. Throws the line-of-duty bunk. If it is, he's certainly a slave to duty." Andrew glanced across to where Foster stood by the desk and lowered his voice. "Did she tell you about that letter?"

"Yes, but not voluntarily. She told me a lot of things."

"What?" Andrew was eager.

"More secrets," said Daisy. Then she added, "But I like her, somehow."

"Thanks," retorted Andrew. "So do I."

Daisy wanted to pull his hair and tell him to go right on liking her. But she couldn't yet—not until she was sure. "Where's the Major?" she asked after a moment.

"Keeping his eye on Allison, and seeing that no boat slips out of the north harbor. That's what they're figuring on. We know dope is to move across the Gulf tonight. It may be here—if it is we don't want to let it get away."

"I'd like to get a look at Allison," she said sharply.

"You will. You'll meet him here in the lounge and he'll bow with icy courtesy and say 'Good evening, Mrs. Dillingham.' Then, darling, he'll pass on, and all your piety and wit won't stop him."

"What's he like?" Daisy asked with a teasing smile.

Andrew's grin broadened. "You tell me. There he is."

CHAPTER SIX

IN SPITE of the wind that was pushing from outside, Brett Allison had closed the door behind him so silently that but for Andrew's chance look he might have entered and gone unobserved. He glanced toward Daisy, bowed gravely and crossed to where the clerk stood by the desk.

Allison was not tall, and he was slightly built; but though he had to look up to speak to Warren the most careless observer could hardly have failed to see that he was giving orders and his hearer receiving them, for there was about Brett Allison an air of dominance, as though having conceived Paradise Island he never lost the sense of being in the midst of his own creation. While he stood too far off for her to observe the details of his features, Daisy saw that he was dark, and his whole appearance had a hint of too fastidious elegance which she found hard to reconcile with his reputation. But Paradise Island was too completely Allison's work to be foreign to his temperament, and Daisy wondered if its brilliant gaiety might not be the projection of a secret ego within the enigmatic, over-polished recluse who ruled it.

"How old is he?" she asked Andrew.

"Forty. Maybe older."

"Where's he from?"

"I've no idea."

"Shall I speak to him?" she demanded, but before Andrew could answer her a gust of wind rushed past the doorway and Eva ran in, her cheeks tingling and her hair halfway down her back.

"Hello, Daisy!" she called as they went to meet her. "It's great out there. Oh, thanks." The last word was to Brett Allison, who had stepped forward to close the door.

For an instant his eyes rested on her—oddly, Daisy thought. An admiring glance at Eva's flushed face and tumbled hair would not have been surprising, but he had looked at her with an expression that conveyed not only admiration but something else—something curious and intent that Daisy could not fathom. Eva jerked off her scarlet hat and smiled at Andrew, who had come up to her.

"Wait a minute," he said. "I want to talk to you."

"Can't possibly. I'm blown all to pieces—can't you see?—and I've got to change in a hurry anyway." She smiled at Daisy. "Think I won't sleep on it, Daisy. I'm going back tonight."

"The water's pretty rough," Daisy admonished, but Eva laughed.

"Rats. I can do it in forty minutes, and the storm's at least two hours off."

Andrew ventured a protest, but she shook her head in merry disagreement and went toward the stairs.

"See you in a couple of minutes, after I've jumped into some more clothes."

Andrew caught up with her. "Where's Barclay?"

"The Major buttonholed him on the steps."

She waved over her shoulder and clattered upstairs. Andrew walked with Daisy back to the fireplace. She glanced toward the desk, but Allison had gone into Mrs. Penn's office. Andrew stared into the fire, and did not speak again till Barclay came in with Major Raymond. Barclay was grim.

"That must have been what she tried to tell me. About that letter, Andrew."

"She didn't say anything about it?" Andrew asked eagerly.

"I didn't give her a chance." He smiled apologetically at the other two. "The wind was so high that conversation was hard. Once when we slowed our horses she started to tell me something, but my mare shied and I forgot all about it."

The Major considered. "Can't you see her again this evening, and watch if she makes any attempt to sound you out?"

"She's taking her speedboat in to the mainland this evening," Andrew announced in a voice that tried hard not to be jubilant. "Leaving in a few minutes."

The Major whistled softly, but Barclay was undismayed. "She is, eh? Then I'll ask her to come by my cottage to have a drink before she leaves. Tell her you'll get a car, Major, and call for her there, to drive her to the wharf. Give her twenty minutes or so with me, and when you come I'll report on anything suspicious she says. Then we'll call the mainland and have her followed. Leave the letter to me. I'll get it if it exists. I think, though, it's a myth."

The Major nodded; Andrew thrust his clenched fists into his pockets.

"And what am I supposed to be doing all this time?"

"You watch her boat," Barclay advised. "It's over on the other side. Stay there until I get through talking to her, but don't let her see you when she goes aboard." He turned to the Major. "I don't understand this sudden impulse to run back to the mainland alone. I don't want them to get anything through on her boat."

Andrew made an unintelligible answer and started for the door. As he went out, Barclay beckoned to a bellhop, and when the boy had saluted and gone Barclay turned back to Daisy and the Major.

"Just sent the boy down for my bag," he explained.

The Major put a warning hand on his arm. "There's Allison. That fellow with him is Foster. He's the man from that Eastern crowd who are going to buy the Island."

As Allison and Foster came out of the office there was a bright greeting from the staircase and Eva came running down, crisp in white flannels, with a scarlet slicker flung over one arm.

"All ready," she called. "I'll have her tied up at Pass Christian before seven o'clock. See you all in the morning."

There was a jerk in Daisy's throat. Eva was so young, so rollicking, apparently so unconscious that there was anything more than friendly interest in their scrutiny. Daisy looked away from her, out of the window.

But neither Barclay nor the Major seemed to have any qualms. They had met her at the foot of the staircase.

"You'll have a chilly ride," Barclay was saying.

"It'll be fun."

"You'll need a drink before you go," he urged with his habitual cheery authority. "Come by my place first."

She glanced toward the window. "I'll have time, won't I?"

Daisy wanted to shout, "No! Hurry! Getaway!" But she knew coaching from the sidelines was barred.

"Of course." Barclay's big voice forbade a demur. "The storm's a long way off. Come by and I'll mix a couple of toddies."

"All right. Anybody else coming?" Eva looked toward Daisy, but Daisy shook her head.

"I'll pick you up later, Miss Shale," the Major was offering, "and drive you down to the wharf."

She smiled. "Thanks."

"Then let's go," Barclay said. "Here's the boy with my bag."

The bellhop came up with a small, smooth suitcase crowned

with a heavy bronze lock. He handed it to Barclay, together with a green-handled malacca cane.

The Major glanced at the cane with a smile. "I see you have your old luck-charm."

"Let's see it," said Daisy. "Are you superstitious, Mr. Barclay?" (If only she could get them to waste a little time! Eva might change her mind about going with Barclay to the cottage.)

"Very." Barclay laughed as he held out the cane. "I've carried it for years."

Barclay's stick had a square jade handle, fantastically carved, but hardly half an inch thick—so out of proportion to the malacca cane that its discrepancy could not fail to be noticed. "I like the handle," he added. "Not very practical for walking, but an exquisite piece of workmanship. My broker calls it my magic wand."

Daisy wondered if he were prophesying success in the evening's venture. She looked at a raised flower that decorated the flat end of the handle.

"It's beautiful," she agreed. "Italian?"

"Florentine." He glanced at Eva. "Do you like it?"

"It's lovely. I always thought luck-charms should be beautiful. So many of them aren't."

Daisy had the impression of something hideously taunting in Barclay's casual display of his luck-charm to Eva. She looked away and saw Brett Allison go out by the front door. But Eva, still apparently unconscious of any undercurrent to the conversation, spoke with bright impatience.

"We've got to be going."

"All right." Barclay smilingly picked up his bag.

"Goodby, everybody," Eva called over her shoulder. "Say a little prayer, Daisy, for us poor sailors on a night like this!"

She went out with Barclay. The Major, saying something about getting the car, left a moment later. Daisy moved over to the fireplace and sat down, her own cane across her knees, thinking.

The clerk and the telephone girl were the only other occupants of the lounge. There was a nice drowsiness about the fire, but it failed to lull the turbulence in Daisy's mind. "If I only had a kettle and a cat here," she said to herself, "I'd be a perfect picture of a useless old lady." She wondered if it would not have been better had she stayed at home. It was possible of course that Barclay and Major Raymond knew what they were doing—that Eva—

"And what is Daisy doing?" queried a gay voice over her shoulder. She looked up.

"Waiting for Whistler," she retorted, as Judith Garon, almost flamboyantly lovely in her clinging orange coat, came toward the fire.

"It's so nice to see you. Andrew told me you were here. When did you come?"

"This afternoon. Plane," said Daisy shortly. She had no great love for Judith, and just now would have preferred to be left alone.

But Judith had flung back her orange coat and was holding out her hands to the fire. "Where's Linton Barclay? Hasn't he come back from his ride?"

"Went down to his cottage with Eva Shale about twenty minutes ago. Said they were going to have a drink." Daisy spoke with a touch of amusement, for Barclay's desertion of Judith had been too recent and Judith's resentment at Eva too obvious not to escape attention less eager than that of Imogen Cupping. For an instant Judith did not answer; she took a rose from a vase on the mantel and touched it delicately to the end of her nose.

Judith looked thirty. That is, she looked like a woman who has had more adventures than any woman of thirty can possibly have had, but who manages to look thirty all the same. She was lush and lovely as a Southern midsummer, but to Daisy, contrasting her with the cool impersonality of Eva, it seemed that there was something about Judith that was over-rich, a suggestion of too brilliant sunshine and too many flowers, and voluptuousness gone ever so faintly stale. Judith tucked the flower into the ruby pin that fastened her blouse and said suddenly, "I promised to meet Mr. Foster. Think I'll go out. Like to come?"

"I'm going to sit by the fire," said Daisy, glad to be so easily relieved of Judith's too-sparkling presence. "You can run along and be robust by yourself."

"All right, darling. I'll see you for cocktails."

Judith walked out of sight toward the rear door.

Daisy thoughtfully twirled her cane and thought about Barclay and Eva Shale.

She had no doubt that given what he deemed a sufficient reason Barclay could be thoroughly cruel. He would be cruel and call it being efficient. That was probably one reason why Barclay's shipping brokerage ran itself so smoothly, so that his weekends were of the Friday-to-Tuesday sort, and he had time to lead civic movements and charity drives. When the Federal Government had consulted with the city officials about appointing an untouchable committee to trace the source of the drug traffic into New Orleans Barclay had been an obvious choice for chairman.

Barclay, mused Daisy, certainly did not look his age. She remembered that when he came to New Orleans from some vague place in the East, the year America entered the war, though past the age for active service Barclay had plunged tirelessly into the war excitement. Drives, crusades, committee after committee had gone briskly and efficiently over the top. But the war was long past—"Why, he must be at least fifty-five," Daisy thought. "Too old to be running about with that girl."

But he seemed to have won not only Eva's friendship but her confidence. Daisy scowled at the head of her cane. She had plenty of faith in her own judgment of human nature, and she reminded herself that all the evidence against Eva was circumstantial. She did not like Barclay's methods as regarded Eva, but she understood Major Raymond's condoning them. The Major's only son had died five years before in a sanitorium, a drug victim, and his horror of the traffic was such that to him no means that might stop it seemed too severe. But Daisy, as she thought of Eva, was less and less sure.

Suddenly she became conscious of the tumult outside. The wind gave a triumphant shriek, broke the top off a palm-tree and hurled it against the clubhouse wall. Sand and dead leaves spattered against the windows, the panes rattled and the hinges creaked their protest. The great oaks around the clubhouse bowed and groaned. Darkness and rain had swooped upon Paradise Island with savage swiftness. A flash of lightning showed her the raging sea and the long whirling tangles of gray moss, blown into crazy festoons.

The rain beat and poured and pounded, with fury louder than that of the wind. Lightning split the sky and quivered among the trees, and behind it crashed the thunder. Daisy smiled grimly. There was a splendid magnificence about the storm. To a venturesome watcher, the howl of the wind and the furious splendor of the sea were more spectacular than any charm of serenity and sunshine that the Gulf Islands could show.

Suddenly she thought of Eva.

They had all been so sure the storm was two hours away. They had forgotten the treachery of weather in the Gulf.

Daisy picked up her cane and hurried over to the switch-board. The telephone operator was plugging in answer to a light. "Order, please?" she said into the mouthpiece.

Daisy tapped her cane impatiently. She wanted to call and make sure Eva was safe on the island. She glanced at the clock. A quarter to seven. Eva had been gone from the clubhouse three-quarters of an hour.

The operator made a sudden choking sound. "My God! Murdered?" she gasped. "Murdered? What shall I do? Yes, sir—I'll tell him right away—of course, sir—"

She jerked out the plug and put both hands on her forehead, looking wildly around. Daisy had grasped her arm.

"What's happened?" she demanded. "Who's murdered? Where?"

The girl drew a short gasping breath. "I can't run this board— and I've got to call somebody—oh, Mr. Warren!"

The clerk had dashed out from behind the desk and was asking excited questions. The girl's hands fluttered toward Daisy in terrified appeal.

"What's happened?" Daisy demanded again.

"Oh—it's so awful—Mr. Barclay has been murdered."

PART TWO

CHAPTER SEVEN

LINTON Barclay was dead. Daisy stood still a minute, holding the head of her cane in a horrified grip. Foster, wrapped in a dripping slicker, had come into the lounge in time to hear the operator's last words, and was listening avidly to her jerky whispers. Warren stood hesitantly in the background. As they heard the belligerent rap of Daisy's cane they all started and ceased talking, and stared as though at an unfamiliar apparition.

"And what," demanded Daisy, "are you three whispering about? Who killed Linton Barclay?"

"I don't *know*, Mrs. Dillingham!" the operator exclaimed plaintively. She was on the verge of a whimper; Daisy, who had slight patience with girlish nerves, turned around disgustedly and faced Warren, whose front-desk manner had been sadly shattered. His countenance betrayed what to Daisy was an exasperating mixture of horror at the news and awe at her own warlike presence.

"Mr. Barclay's body has just been discovered in his cottage, Mrs. Dillingham," Warren informed her, jerking nervously at a heavy gold ring on the fourth finger of his right hand. "Apparently he has been stabbed. A most regrettable affair—I assure you we shall do everything in our power to make our guests—"

"Who found him?"

"Major Raymond. He just telephoned. Miss Meade, our operator—"

"Where's Brett Allison? I suppose he's the man to be told, isn't he? Or are you managing things?"

"Miss Meade phoned him, Mrs. Dillingham," Warren assured her eagerly.

"When did you phone him?" asked Foster. He had put aside his raincoat and returned to the desk.

"I phoned him the *minute* I could," Felicia Meade protested in an aggrieved tone. "He said he'd be *right* over."

Daisy clucked and looked her three companions up and down with a survey that disposed of them as entirely inadequate to handle such a situation as this. A bolt of lightning split the black sky beyond the windows and the thunder crashed around the clubhouse; Felicia Meade shuddered, and even the impassive Foster gave a start. The noise of the rain was like a tattoo on gigantic drums. For a moment they said nothing, listening to the howling and creaking of the storm, then the main door of the lounge room opened and Brett Allison entered.

He appeared neither hasty nor flurried. Ignoring the cascade of words that immediately poured upon him from Warren and the telephone girl, he carefully closed the door upon the storm, shook a spatter of raindrops from his tweed cap, loosened the upper buttons of his black oilskin raincoat and bowed to Daisy and Foster with the quiet, impersonal deference with which he invariably greeted guests whom he chanced to meet on Paradise Island.

"Good evening, Mrs. Dillingham."

The greeting was at once the epitome of detached politeness and a warning to come no nearer. It was the first time she had heard him speak, and she observed that his voice was low and strangely soft, with something of the haunting quality of an echo. Daisy rested both hands on the head of her cane and watched him.

"One moment, Warren, if you please. Miss Meade, I believe you were the first to receive word of what has happened?"

"Yes, sir, I guess I was." Felicia answered him with the tremulous complacence that comes of having been granted a well-deserved spot downstage. "I was just sitting here, waiting for calls, when Major Raymond telephoned. He said he was in Mr. Barclay's place—that's Noah's Cottage, you know, the one that's built like a ship, down by Adam's Inlet—and that he had found Mr. Barclay murdered."

"Did he give you any details?"

Brett Allison was neither curt nor nervous; he was simply gathering the facts of an important matter that must be attended to. Daisy looked with approval at his incisive profile.

"No, sir, he just said that he'd found Mr. Barclay's body—that Mr. Barclay had been stabbed. I called your house right away."

"You did quite right, Miss Meade. Warren, will you tell McPherson what has happened, and ask him to come over here? He should be around the locker room at the golf course. Miss Meade, was there anyone else here when you received the Major's message?"

"Just Mr. Warren, sir, and Mrs. Dillingham. Mr. Foster came in a minute ago."

Foster smiled. "Just in time to keep Miss Meade from fainting, I think."

Felicia pouted, but Allison was addressing Daisy. "Mrs. Dillingham, you can corroborate Miss Meade's testimony as to the time when Major Raymond called, if it should be necessary?"

"I can," Daisy returned tersely. "Quarter to seven."

He gave her a smile of assent. "It was about ten minutes of seven when I received the message. Have you any idea of the whereabouts of the other guests, Mrs. Dillingham?"

"Unfortunately," said Daisy, "I haven't. My grandson went out before it began to rain, and I haven't seen him since. So did the Cuppings. Mrs. Garon went out a few minutes after Mr. Barclay left."

"And Miss Shale?"

"Miss Shale?" Daisy stopped suddenly. Her hands tightened over the head of her cane. "Miss Shale," she replied, "left the clubhouse with Linton Barclay about six o'clock."

Her words sounded strange in her ears. Before Allison could speak there was a shrill exclamation from Felicia Meade.

"She was in the cottage! I forgot to tell you—I was so excited—"

"What, Miss Meade?" Allison spoke crisply. Daisy, fairly stricken with apprehension, took a couple of steps closer to the switchboard.

"What are you talking about, girl? How do you know she was there?"

"I'm sorry I forgot about it. That's how Major Raymond found the body. Miss Shale called him. She said she was at Mr. Barclay's cottage, and for me to tell the Major to hurry."

"Did she say why she wanted him to hurry?" Allison asked.

"No, sir. She just said, 'This is Eva Shale. Tell Major Raymond to come for me now. Please ask him to hurry.' So I rang the Major's suite and gave him the message, and the next time I talked to him it was when he called to say he had found Mr. Barclay dead."

For an instant Allison did not speak. The pupils of his eyes had contracted to pin-points. Warren and McPherson came in, and Allison turned to McPherson and spoke quickly.

"Warren told you what happened?"

"Yes, sir, yes indeed." McPherson nodded solemnly. "I heard the bad tidings. It'll prove an ill thing for the island, I ween, sir." With a glance at Daisy, McPherson shook his head slowly, as if to convey that trouble had started with that lady's arrival.

But Allison manifested little interest in the reactions of his golf pro. "Ring the cottage, Miss Meade," he ordered, "and let me speak to Major Raymond. McPherson, radio the mainland police at once. Then get the servants together in the caddy house. Find out where they were between six o'clock and six-forty-five. If any of them can't prove their stories have them wait until I come back. Check up on all the boats that were here today and those that are still here. Have all the doors of the clubhouse locked except the front entrance. Miss Meade, make a record of the time when each of the guests returns to the clubhouse, and ask them to wait here for me. Foster, I have a car outside. You and I had better go down to the cottage. Warren will drive us."

Foster, who had been observing Allison's methods approvingly, nodded. "Glad to," was all he said.

"I'll go too," said Daisy, "if you don't mind." Allison frowned slightly at her demand. "That isn't necessary, Mrs. Dillingham."

"Maybe not. But expedient."

Warren, who seemed to have recovered from his first shock, had put on his front-desk manner again. "Really, Mrs. Dillingham—" he began deprecatingly, but Daisy cut him short.

"Don't argue with me. I'm going down to see where this man was murdered. You'll need a woman along, or you men will think all you've got to do is hand Eva Shale over to the coroner with the body." She gave the floor a thump with her cane.

Brett Allison's mouth was grave, but there were faint little crinkles of comprehension at the corners of his eyes. "Perhaps you are right, Mrs. Dillingham."

"Right? Of course I'm right. Men always see the obvious. You'll run around putting two and two together and making your own chesty fours out of them. Sometimes two and two make twenty-two."

"We'll take Mrs. Dillingham along, Warren." Allison's smile gave place to his habitual gravity. "It will probably be wise to have a witness not connected with the club. McPherson, bring a raincoat for Mrs. Dillingham."

McPherson's expression took on an additional dourness as he went into the office and brought out a long dark slicker.

"I'll be at the caddy house," he told Allison, but as he went out he cast a black look upon Daisy.

"Major Raymond on the line, Mr. Allison," put in the operator.

"Thank you." Allison took up the receiver. "Major Raymond? This is Brett Allison. Please stay where you are. I will come down immediately. Don't let anyone into the house until I get there. Yes? I see. Ask her to stay, please."

Foster had helped Daisy swathe herself in the crackling folds of the long raincoat, and as Allison put down the receiver she tucked her cane under her arm and marched out ahead of him. There was a screech of wind as she entered the veranda, and she could see the rain beating furiously around his car. He stepped from behind her and opened the door. Warren took the wheel, and Daisy found herself seated between Allison and Foster.

The engine screamed a protest of the angry night and started. Allison drew a silver case from his pocket.

"Do you smoke, Mrs. Dillingham?"

"Constantly."

He struck a match for her and lit another cigarette for himself. She gave him a monosyllabic word of thanks, realizing that her voice sounded waspish, but her thoughts were in a tumult. Eva Shale was in Barclay's cottage. Barclay was dead—murdered. Daisy set her jaw grimly.

The rain streamed down the windows. The end of Allison's cigarette made a red spark in the darkness. He said nothing. The lightning flashes came swiftly, and she studied his expressionless profile against the greenish flares. Wrapped in his loose black oilskin, he had still about him a certain monkish elegance as he looked out into the rain. Daisy slowly began to analyze the impression he gave her. It was not elegance that made him remote, nor sternness, nor gravity; it was—she sought for the right word—it was *completeness*, his air of having so organized his life that it was as separate from its surroundings as a sun dial.

Outside, the headlights turned the rain into a silver spray. The wind roared up from the fenders and the tires sizzed along the wet concrete.

Once Foster spoke. "This man Barclay—did you know him well, Allison?"

"He came here very seldom," Allison answered. "More often this last month than ever before."

"This is bad business," said Foster.

"Terrible," agreed Allison.

They both lapsed into silence again. Neither of them seemed to have any intention of saying more, but there were things Daisy intended to find out.

"Did the Major say," she asked, "how long Linton Barclay had been dead?"

"No. Just that he was dead when he found him."

Allison's clipped, even syllables came with strange smoothness through the howl of the storm.

"And Eva Shale," Daisy persisted, "had been there all along?"

"Apparently."

Daisy's spine straightened. "She's due for trouble, then."

"It's lucky she didn't get off the island before Major Raymond found the body," Foster remarked.

Allison did not answer. The car swung around to Abel's Bridge, which crossed the inlet, and stopped in front of Noah's Cottage.

Noah's Cottage was built more like a yacht than like an ark. It had many windows, all of them portholes, looking as if they should have opened upon a deck instead of a porch; indeed, the porch itself looked like a deck, for it was so placed that the steps ran up alongside of the house like a ship's ladder. A boarded rail ran around it and two life-preservers leaned on each side of the front door.

The door opened into a foyer, rectangular in shape; its every detail, from the two portholes looking into the companionway between the two back rooms to the brass ship's clock on the wall, combined to give a nautical illusion, intensified by the beat of the rain outside.

"There are two rooms, besides the bath and kitchenette," Allison explained. "On the right is the bedroom and bath, on the left the kitchenette and living room. All rooms can be entered from the back through the companionway. There's a door leading to it from the rear of the house."

Daisy was hardly listening. She was hurriedly freeing herself from her luminous raincoat, with the intention of finding Eva Shale before the two men behind her had time to demand an explanation of Eva's position, with their automatic accusations; but she had no chance to do so, for as she flung her coat across a chair the door to the living room opened and she saw Eva standing on the threshold.

In her white flannel boating dress, Eva looked ready for a summer sail. For an instant she stood in the doorway without speaking, her hands in the pockets of her jacket and her stern blue eyes looking at the others as though daring them to ask her why she was there; then her eyes rested queryingly on Brett Allison.

"Major Raymond told you I was here?"

She spoke without a quaver. Daisy stood still, watching her closely; she had not thought to ask why Daisy had come. Allison had gone up to Eva. To Daisy's surprise, he was neither questioning nor accusing; he simply answered,

"He did. Have you seen the body?"

"Yes," said Eva, and she nodded toward the other door. "In there."

Allison, his hand on the handle of the bedroom door, turned and spoke over his shoulder.

"Will you gentlemen come with me? You need not bother unless you wish, Mrs. Dillingham."

"Humph. I've seen more dead men than the lot of you. Of course, I'll go in." Daisy patted Eva's arm reassuringly. "Do you want to come in, child? You might as well."

Allison gave them both an intent look, but made no protest. Daisy suddenly marveled at his impassivity; curious, she thought, although Allison was hardly an inch taller than Eva and considerably smaller than Foster and Warren, whatever position he occupied in a room immediately became the foreground. She felt that she had never seen a man whose presence so completely forbade the idea of chaos. His hand closed on the doorknob, but before he could turn it the door burst open in his face and the Major exploded his gruff presence upon them.

"So you finally got here. Well, he's dead, all right." The Major's brown eyes were hard; they brushed past Eva and Daisy and looked again at Allison. "We'd better radio the police and not touch a thing."

"I've had a message sent," Allison returned. It was almost a rebuke. "The storm may hold them up. We may as well go in."

Daisy grinned as she linked her arm in Eva's. Men and their everlasting rules! Well, the police would have to be ducks to get to the scene of the crime tonight.

Allison was talking to the Major. "You're sure he was dead when you got here?"

"Beyond a doubt." The Major nodded with a decisiveness that did not disguise the fact that he felt shaky. "No pulse at all," he added with a suppressed shudder. "He was stretched out just as you'll see him there."

"Did you touch anything in the room?"

"Certainly not." The Major's brusque brevity seemed to imply his dislike of this sort of catechism. "I came out immediately and called Miss Shale."

"She was here?"

"Yes. In the other room when I *arrived*." The Major glanced at Eva, and went on, "Then I rang the clubhouse."

"Which telephone did you use?"

"Why, the one in the living room."

"Thank you, Major Raymond. The police will ask you for the details when they arrive."

Allison spoke tersely. The Major gave an almost impercep-tible shrug. "Undoubtedly," he retorted, and looked again at Eva.

"I didn't kill him, Mr. Allison!" she exclaimed desperately. She had been standing at Daisy's side, her hands clenching and opening. Her voice was harsh.

Allison answered quietly. "We'll discuss that later, Miss Shale."

"Don't you think," came a soft suggestion from Foster, "that we had better look at the body?"

"Yes," agreed Allison. "Will you come in with me?" He opened the door. For an instant Daisy had thought that he was about to say something else, but whatever it was that had broken through his impassive mask was gone. He glanced past Daisy and Eva to the stern figure of Major Raymond, then beckoned to Foster and Warren. They crossed the threshold.

For a moment none of them spoke. The room where the dead man lay was like a pit of silence in the midst of the clatter of the storm. It was a large, brightly-lit bedroom, furnished and fitted like a ship's cabin. The body of Linton Barclay sprawled across the floor, between the bed and the door to the foyer, his eyes staring hollowly at them. One arm was flung over his head and the other fantastically doubled under him. He had not changed from his riding habit, and on the front of his white soft shirt was a small tear and around it an uneven stain of blood.

There was a sound in Eva's throat that was something between a sob and a gasp of horror. Daisy slipped an arm around her.

"Steady, girl. This is no time to be feminine."

Eva quivered into Daisy's arms as if struggling desperately for a sense of protection; the bravado with which she had met them crumbled suddenly away from her and she buried her face in her hands. "They'll never believe me!" she exclaimed in a frantic whisper. "I was here all the time—but I didn't do it."

"Some of us will believe you, my child." Daisy's eyes sought the Major's. He stood with Foster and Allison, his back to them, looking down at the body on the floor. Warren was officiously examining the windows.

"He must have died the instant he was struck, Allison," Foster was saying. "Doesn't look as if there was a struggle."

"Notice that tear in his shirt, where the knife hit him," said the Major. "It's not much more than a quarter of an inch long."

"Like a rapier wound." Allison's voice sounded mechanical, as if something else was engaging his notice. "Seems to have been making a drink."

He indicated the cellarette, where they saw a flask of whisky and a bowl of fruit and sugar half crushed.

The pestle lay on the floor. "Apparently," he suggested, "whoever did it surprised him."

The Major looked at Eva. She had moved a step away from Daisy and was standing with her back to the door watching them with more arrogance than fear. "Miss Shale," he asked, "were you in here while Mr. Barclay was mixing this drink?"

The muscles of her sunburnt throat quivered faintly above the open white collar of her blouse. "No," she said flatly, "I wasn't."

"Why on earth should she have been?" Daisy demanded. "Anybody can make a toddy alone."

Major Raymond replied with sarcastic politeness. "I was merely wondering why he should have mixed it here instead of in the kitchenette."

"There may have been any one of a dozen reasons," Daisy rejoined with more asperity than tact. "There's no ice here—he probably intended taking it into the kitchenette when he had crushed the sugar."

The Major shook his head. "I'd like to know how he happened to have fruit juice and sugar in his bedroom."

"He brought the things from the kitchenette," explained Eva.

The Major wheeled abruptly. "He did? You're sure you didn't help him carry them in? Sure you didn't have an ice-pick in your hand? That you weren't just about to chop some ice when it happened? Where's the ice-pick kept—do you know, Allison?"

"I'm sorry," returned Allison's even voice. "I don't. We have electric refrigeration in all the cottages."

Daisy wanted to laugh.

The Major cleared his throat. "We must look closely for a knife. I was too shocked to make much of an examination when I came in."

Foster gave his palms a business-like rub. "We'd better leave that for the police and lock up this place, Mr. Allison. After all, it's going to be bad enough as it is."

"You're right," Allison returned quietly.

—"And," said the Major, "we'd better put someone on guard to keep people away. We can't run the risk of destroying any footprints there may be outside."

Allison gave the streaming windows a glance that was faintly derisive.

"In this rain? I hardly think there's much use in guarding footprints, Major Raymond."

Giving the Major no time to express his annoyance Daisy walked over to where Barclay's body was lying and picked up the malacca cane from the floor. "Ever seen this before?"

"I've seen it," said Eva, and Daisy beamed with pride at the steadiness with which she spoke. "Mr. Barclay showed it to all of us in the clubhouse this evening."

Daisy held it out. Allison glanced at it and nodded; Foster smiled patiently at this interruption by a meddlesome old woman; the Major's sternness relaxed in a faint smile of recognition of Daisy's characteristic brisk interference. Daisy shook the cane implacably.

"It's conceivable," she said, "that Barclay was attacked and snatched up this cane to defend himself. He'd hardly have done that if his assailant had been a woman. Now, all of you, use what brains you've got. The police are stupid enough, God knows, without any added inspiration."

Brett Allison nodded slowly. "Very good, Mrs. Dillingham, but you've probably smudged whatever fingerprints there are on that handle."

"Next thing you know," snapped Daisy, "you'll be calling me an accessory after the act. Nobody can photograph fingerprints on a carved handle. What do you think fingerprints are—trademarks?" She laid the cane carefully back where she had found it. "Linton Barclay was my grandson's friend," she went on more mildly. "I've had him to dinner. I'd like to know who killed him. But the murderer can't get off Paradise Island tonight, and we'll do a whole lot better by protecting our own lives than by trying to make new records as conclusion-jumpers."

Foster made a gesture of affirmation. "You are quite right, Mrs. Dillingham."

Allison nodded agreement. He spoke to Warren. "Warren, will you lock all the windows and doors of this room?" He held the door open for Eva, and as she passed him Daisy saw their eyes meet.

Daisy stiffened, for the look he gave Eva was so intent as to be almost a signal. But Eva apparently had not noticed, or if she had, her own eyes had given no answer. Sternly Daisy tried to hold back a rush of suspicion. An hour ago she had been inclined to discard the theory that Eva and Brett Allison were allies; now, she could not tell. His curious look at Eva was past in an instant, but in that instant it had been borne to Daisy by some indefinable subterranean channel that in Brett Allison Eva had a champion.

The next moment they were all in the foyer again, and Foster had taken up a scarlet raincoat that lay across a chair. "Is this yours, Miss Shale?"

Eva nodded, and he held it for her. The Major, oddly quiet now, offered Daisy the stiff dark raincoat she had worn from the clubhouse, and as she pulled the coat around her, he whispered,

"I hope you haven't misunderstood me, Daisy. I think she—"

"I understand you mighty well," she cut in, and started toward the door.

"Isn't anybody going to ask me what I know about it?" Eva exclaimed. She was holding her raincoat together with a savage grip.

"We aren't going to talk about anything," replied Daisy, with a look at Allison, "till we get away from this place. Come along." She put her arm around Eva and they went out on the porch. From inside she heard Allison call,

"Warren! Lock the bedroom door. Stay here till I send someone to relieve you. Don't let anyone in except on written orders from me."

Warren demurred. It was plain that the assignment was hardly to his liking, but Allison was implacable. Daisy heard Warren's ungracious "O.K., Chief."

"Are we going back now?" asked Eva.

"Yes. Don't worry."

Eva's arm slipped through hers. Daisy took her hand.

Allison opened the front door. The Major and Foster came out. "If you must telephone, Warren," Allison was saying over his shoulder, "use the phone in the living room."

"I sure will," Warren's voice answered. "You'll send a couple of men down to stay with me?"

"As soon as I can." Allison closed the door behind him, and they began their drive back to the clubhouse in silence. Allison drove the car, and Eva sat in the back between the Major and Daisy. The Major lit a cigar and offered one to Allison, who refused it. Eva took a cigarette case from her pocket.

"Daisy?" asked Eva.

"Thanks."

There were three points of light to break the darkness between the lightning flashes. But for that, thought Daisy, the rides were the same. Again the headlights picked up the rain and turned it into a splatter of silver; the wind rumbled under the fenders, the tires sizzed along the wet road. Outside the storm hurled its pandemonium upon the island; inside the car the silence was almost tangible. Suddenly Allison gave an exclamation; the car lurched, and there was the pull of brakes. By a flash of lightning Daisy could just make out a figure halted by the side of the road. Allison reached inside his raincoat, and the light from the cigarettes glowed on the blue steel of an automatic. He opened the door.

"Who is it?" he called.

The figure moved closer into the range of the head-lights. "It's only me—Andrew Dillingham. I've just heard about it."

"Oh—*Andrew!*" Eva cried. Then she sank back upon the seat. "Please, Daisy," she whispered tensely, "don't let Major Raymond say anything silly."

Daisy smiled to herself. "He won't. Don't you."

Andrew had climbed into the front seat and squeezed himself between Foster and Allison. He turned to speak to them, but Daisy interposed. "I've got the jitters, Andrew. Not a word about this till I get back by the fire."

He nodded and lit a cigarette. They were silent till the car stopped in front of the clubhouse and they went in.

The lounge room, warm and bright and normal, cheered them all, in spite of the frightened questions that poured upon them from Judith Garon and the Cuppings, who had been detained there by Felicia. Allison tossed the raincoats upon a sofa and sat down by the center table. The others hurried around him as though grateful for a calm focus around which to center their own uncertainty. Daisy thoughtfully surveyed the group.

It was plain to her that except for the telephone girl, every person in the room had recently been out in the rain.

CHAPTER EIGHT

"WILL you all take chairs here, please?" said Brett Allison.

He stood by the big table in the center of the lounge, a slight but strangely imperative figure in his impeccable dinner-jacket, regarding the others with eyes that were frostily blue under plumy black eyebrows. His chill authority swept them into order. Nobody spoke; Daisy and Eva obediently took the seats Andrew and the Major brought forward for them. Brett Allison was still standing. His eyes moved over the rest of the group.

"Of course you all know," he said, as he filled a large and incongruous briar pipe with dark yellow-flecked tobacco, "that Linton Barclay has been murdered."

"You're damn right we know it, sir!" Tracy Cupping was on his feet, the long ends of his white moustache trembling with rage. "What we want to know now is what steps have been taken to guard us from the murderer? I demand immediate—"

"Will you be good enough to let me finish, Mr. Cupping?" Brett Allison's voice cut like a thread across the blurred thickness of Cupping's indignation. Cupping spluttered and stared and stopped talking.

Allison did not raise his voice. "Mr. Cupping, whatever it is you are demanding will be granted to you as soon as possible. If it is the right to return to the mainland tonight—"

A clap of thunder crashed over the roof and finished his sentence. His hearers jumped nervously. Imogen squeaked. With a furious look in her direction, Cupping sat down on the edge of his chair as if ready to spring up again any minute. Allison put a match to his pipe and puffed calmly.

Daisy looked at the group around her. They were a curious company, she thought, to be starting out to find a murderer. Brett Allison, quiet, grave and immaculate, was like a bridge expert explaining contract. At his right was Judith Garon, her beautiful dark eyes turned to Brett with an expression of supercilious inquiry. By her was Tracy Cupping, red-faced and angry, proclaiming by his frequent growls that decent people didn't go and get themselves murdered. Imogen looked small and unusually quiet, as if being involved in a murder inquiry was a rare responsibility. Major Raymond sat at the end of the table, facing Brett Allison. His mouth was set in an accusing line, and there was a trenchant crease between his eyebrows. Foster was at Daisy's left, opposite the Cuppings; he was cool and attentive, watching Allison closely as if resolved not to miss a word of what was being said. On the other side of Daisy was Eva. She had her arms folded across her breast, and her lowered head hid her truculent eyes. Andrew had one hand on the arm of Eva's chair, as though trying to be near her, and holding back for fear that she would draw away from him.

Allison was speaking. "The police on the mainland have just answered my radio. Beans?"

"Yessir." A small, brown, rather grubby young gentleman sprang up from a corner like an alert spaniel. "Here y'are."

Allison unfolded the paper Beans offered him. "Beans is the wireless operator," he explained. "He received this message while I was in Mr. Barclay's cottage." He read:

'Unable reach island till storm abates this appoints you my deputy meanwhile wire names of all persons on island and detain everyone till we arrive.

'MORRISON.'

"Mr. Morrison," he added, "is the district attorney of Hancock County, Mississippi. Beans, McPherson will give you the list. Send it to Mr. Morrison, and take any further instructions."

"Yessir." Beans looked at Eva almost shyly. "Howdy, Miss Shale," he said as he walked off.

There was an odd dignity in Beans' exit. Eva smiled faintly. "Beans was my first case," she said to Daisy. "I took him out of the Waifs' Home and sent him to a wireless school."

Daisy nodded and grinned. Beans' impudent countenance had plainly declared that no matter what they said he was ready to roll up his sleeves and fight for Miss Shale.

Allison was speaking again. His manner suggested neither diffidence nor over-assurance; it was rather as if he had had long training in the art of supervising a crisis and took this one as part of his routine. He reminded Daisy of a croupier spinning the little ivory ball without any great interest in where it dropped.

"There are two courses open to us," he was saying. "We can all go to bed and wait for the police and newspaper reporters to arrive in the morning, or we can review the circumstances of this evening and take whatever steps seem necessary to protect ourselves."

Cupping was on his feet again. "Mr. Allison, of course you know why I'm here, and so do some of the others." He looked sharply at Foster. "I came here yesterday with the view of entering a second bid for Paradise Island."

Foster smiled slightly, as if to say, 'So that's it, is it?'

"I just wanted to say," barked Cupping, "that I've not changed my mind, but I'd like to ask that nobody mentions that fact at this time to the papers or the police."

Imogen was watching her husband with the same scared quietness. Her head jerked around as Allison answered,

"I'm afraid I can't promise anything of the sort, Mr. Cupping. It would be very poor policy to withhold anything."

"I should say so!" Foster vehemently struck the table. "I represent the International Hotel Syndicate, and we wish to hide nothing of our transactions. Our option, whether we exercise it or not, can be made public at any time, Mr. Allison."

Cupping snorted. "I want it understood that I have not entered a formal bid. I've got a gentleman's dislike of messy publicity for both myself and Mrs. Cupping. We do not wish to be prominent in the newspapers, sir."

As he sat down a teasing smile crept over Judith's lips. "You had enough of being prominent in the papers before you got married, didn't you, darling?" she murmured to Imogen, but before Imogen could do more than pout angrily Allison was giving a characteristically suave reply.

"There's nothing we can do to keep the names of those present from the newspapers," he said. "The police will give them out."

"Police be damned!" exploded Cupping. "My lawyer will take care of them."

"But there may be lots of danger," fluttered Imogen, "right this minute!"

Outside the storm howled. The panes of the long windows were like slabs of onyx fitfully discolored by the blue-green flares. Allison was still standing. His blue eyes, bright and hard as ice, met Daisy's, and it was as if they told her that this was but the latest of a long series of tumults from which he had come, triumphant in his own inscrutable way. Daisy gave him a smile that was like a handshake.

"There may be some danger, Mrs. Cupping," he said, "although there is no reason to believe that the person who killed Mr. Barclay intended to kill anyone else. As for unwelcome publicity—the more definite information we can give to the reporters, the less we are likely to be subjected to newspaper innuendoes."

Imogen smothered a nervous titter and reached for a cigarette. Judith's lovely eyes narrowed between their provocatively beaded lashes, but Brett continued as though quite unaware that his suggestion had carried a threat. "If we can find out who killed Barclay before the police arrive," he finished, "we will all escape a great deal of annoyance."

('A treasure hunt,' thought Daisy, 'with reputations in the pot.')

"But you can't stop the papers," Cupping growled.

"That's right," said Andrew. "You can't."

Eva's fingers dug into her arms. Her head was still turned and her eyes cast down.

"What's your plan, if any, Mr. Allison?" Daisy inquired sharply.

"I propose that we start the investigation ourselves tonight, and begin by gathering all possible information."

Andrew looked up suddenly. "Are you taking that message from the district attorney as authority to act, Mr. Allison?"

"Yes—for all of us to act." Brett answered with cool irony. "Murder is rarely subtle. I think we've a good chance to find the person who killed Barclay before he can cover up his tracks."

"Good plan," said Daisy stoutly. "I'm for it. Go ahead."

"A very good plan," agreed Foster. "Our idea is to avoid as much unpleasant publicity as possible." He laced and unlaced his hands like a man who has just said something of justifiable importance.

Cupping cleared his throat. "I don't think it'll work. We can't run around in this storm chasing a gang of murderers all over the island."

"I hardly believe we shall have to bother with chasing murderers," Allison offered with mild sarcasm. "The probability is that one of us here knows the reason why Linton Barclay was killed, as well as who killed him."

In spite of the whip of the storm it was as if a dead hush had fallen over the room. They looked at each other, fearfully. Andrew threw a quick glance at the Major, who sat silently puffing at one of his stubby cigars. Daisy turned to Eva. But Eva's head was still bent, and her arms still folded. Only Judith seemed to have retained her poise. She was whispering teasingly to Imogen.

"It sounds fearful, doesn't it?" said Judith. "But you'll probably like it, darling. The young and innocent always enjoy these things."

"Cluck," went Daisy. "Go on, Brett Allison. Start your investigating." There was a murmur of approval and Daisy patted Eva's shoulder. "What do you think, child?"

Eva looked up slowly. With a half-puzzled, half-defiant gesture she pushed a lock of light hair off her forehead.

"What difference does it make? Tonight—or tomorrow—it's all the same."

Daisy clucked by way of retort. But Eva was looking at Brett Allison, and Daisy found that she herself as well was looking at him—expectantly; and it was a strange sensation, for it had been a long time since Daisy had permitted somebody else to handle a situation for her. In spite of his quiet assurance, she was not even yet sure that he should handle it—there was still all that Andrew had told her this afternoon—and an instant later she knew that Andrew had not forgotten it either, for he was speaking to Allison almost curtly.

"Just a minute, Mr. Allison," he said. "I agree with the plan, but I don't think this investigation should be in your hands."

"Why?" asked Brett Allison. His voice was cold—it almost carried a challenge.

"Because," said Andrew, "Major Raymond was Linton Barclay's associate in his work, and he may be the one of us who knows what led to his death."

"I don't think so," cut in Major Raymond, and Daisy caught the meaning glance with which he silenced Andrew. "Mr. Barclay and I were associated in a business affair, but since Mr. Allison has been empowered to act, and probably feels the responsibility for his guest's death, I think it will be wise to let him go ahead."

"Well—if it suits you it suits me," Andrew acquiesced. He sat down again.

Judith, who had half stood up, sat down with a flutter of such indecision that Daisy wanted to laugh. "Barclay's associate, Andrew?" Judith asked in a voice that tried to be casual and managed only to add to the general bewilderment. "I didn't know that."

The undertone of comments around the table had become a hubbub. Brett looked calmly around, and the others grew suddenly silent. With perfect self-possession he examined the smouldering ashes in his pipe.

He was so much like an actor doing a long-rehearsed scene that the others looked like amateurs who had forgotten their parts. Daisy listened eagerly for his next remark.

"Very well," said Allison. "Then we are agreed—everyone is to tell everything he knows. I shall be in charge."

There were murmurs of assent. Andrew sat forward, half facing Eva, and he looked from her to Allison as though daring him to accuse her. The others were watching Allison. Foster lit a cigar and settled back as if ready for a long siege. Allison waited an instant, the elegant, untroubled gambler who had made Paradise Island a legend, plainly telling them all that he was dealing and that he would run the game. He turned to Felicia Meade, who was waiting like a scary little sentinel by her switchboard.

"Miss Meade, you have McPherson's reports?"

"Yes, Mr. Allison." She brought him a sheaf of papers.

"Thank you." He glanced over them, and turned to explain his earlier instructions to McPherson. "All the boats that were here today, except your own and Mr. Barclay's, have unquestionably left the island," he added after a glance at the reports. "Miss Meade, you were with Mr. McPherson when he questioned the servants?"

"Yes, sir. They could all tell where they had been from five o'clock on."

"I see." As he turned back to the group Imogen, who was whispering excitedly to her husband, stopped and subsided like a bad girl caught talking in school. "Mr. Barclay left the clubhouse this afternoon about six. There were several of you here then—Mrs. Dillingham, Mr. Foster, Major Raymond—did anyone else see him go out?"

"I did," said Felicia Meade, "but I didn't notice what time it was."

Eva lifted her head with a jerk. "Mr. Barclay went out with me, Mr. Allison."

His expression did not change. "Do you remember what time it was?"

"Yes." Eva's voice was metallic. "It was two minutes past six when we went out. I looked at my watch. I was planning to leave before seven."

"Thank you, Miss Shale." Allison glanced at his papers. "I asked McPherson—"

"Pardon me, Mr. Allison." Judith Garon was lying lazily back in her chair, and behind the veil of smoke from her cigarette her eyes were sardonically questioning. "Don't you think it might clarify everything if Eva told us what happened after she and Linton Barclay left the clubhouse?"

('What a long tail our cat has,' thought Daisy.)

Eva shuddered and Andrew gave a start of sudden horrified comprehension. Again his hand closed around the arm of her chair. With a characteristic ignoring of the reactions in front of him, Allison answered,

"Yes, but Major Raymond will be our first witness, if he doesn't mind. Before that, however, we'll take a look at McPherson's report on the servants."

"As you like," said the Major. He threw a sharp look at Eva. There was a stony self-assurance in his manner. Daisy could almost hear him add, "And if you think you're going to out-manoeuvre me, Brett Allison, you've got another guess coming."

Brett bowed and went on imperturbably. "I asked McPherson to find out what the employees of the clubhouse were doing between six o'clock and six-forty-five. McPherson reports that they were all engaged in their usual duties or recreations, and that all of them have supported alibis except—" He turned as a tense-looking woman came out of the office.

It was Mrs. Penn. She seemed older, Daisy thought, and her air of competence was gone. She came up to the table as though facing a jury, and stood rigidly looking from one to another of them as if begging for reassurance. The skirt of her suit was spattered with mud.

"Mr. McPherson said you wanted me, Mr. Allison," she ventured tremulously.

"Yes. Sit down, Mrs. Penn. Mrs. Penn is the club manager," he explained. "Her statement of how she spent her time from about half-past five till after the death of Mr. Barclay is unfortunately without corroboration."

"But I don't know anything about it, Mr. Allison," she began eagerly. "I'm sure—"

"One moment, Mrs. Penn. We shall be glad to hear what you have to say in a little while. Miss Meade."

Felicia came back from her switchboard. "Yes, sir?"

"I believe you and Warren were together in the lounge office from the time I left the clubhouse till I received your telephone call?"

"Yes, sir." Felicia was plainly relieved.

"Telephone Warren that I am sending two of the stable boys to take his place. Have him come back here—I may need him later on."

"Yes, sir. Anything else?"

"That's all."

Brett turned back to the reports and spoke again to the impatient circle of his guests.

"These reports dispose of everyone except ourselves and Barclay's crew. I'll speak to them later. I can personally answer for the radio operator, as I can see his sending-room from my bedroom."

"And who, sir," demanded Cupping, "can personally answer for you?"

Allison smiled. "I am afraid no one but myself. I made an inspection of the piers at five o'clock. After tying up my launch, I came to the clubhouse and was here till about six, when I went to my house. I was still there when the telephone operator called. My house servants have gone to the mainland, so you will have to include me in your list of suspicious characters."

Daisy saw the look that passed between Andrew and the Major. 'Consider yourself included, Mr. Allison,' she thought grimly.

Cupping sat back as if immensely pleased at this information. "Nothing personal, Mr. Allison," he rumbled complacently. "Just puts us all in the same fix, eh?"

Allison smiled again, this time with a sort of sardonic acquiescence. "Every one of us, Mr. Cupping, with the single exception—" he bowed toward Daisy—"of Mrs. Dillingham."

CHAPTER NINE

BRETT Allison turned to the Major with a deference that yielded nothing of his authority.

"Now, Major Raymond, will you tell us just what happened when you went to Mr. Barclay's cottage?"

"Certainly," the Major returned gruffly. "When Mr. Barclay and Miss Shale left for the cottage—" he was looking directly at Eva, but she had rested her forehead on her hand, as if unable to face his accusing eyes—"I went out to the garage and asked your chauffeur to bring an automobile to the clubhouse. I suppose you want an outline of my actions from then till I called for Miss Shale?"

Allison nodded.

"I came back to the clubhouse, entering by a side door. Mrs. Garon can confirm that. I met her going out."

"Just a minute, sir," ordered Cupping. He faced Judith. "And where were *you* going, ma'am?"

"*Not* to Mr. Barclay's," she answered sweetly, but Allison cut off Cupping's indignant retort.

"One story at a time, if you please. Major Raymond?"

"I went directly to my room. I looked over some reports there until the telephone operator rang to say Miss Shale was in a hurry for me to call her. I left the clubhouse and drove to Mr.

Barclay's cottage." The Major's eyes were on Eva, but she had still not looked up. Her hand still hid her eyes, but Daisy could see that her lips were pressed into a thin line, and the hand that lay in her lap was clenched rigidly. The Major continued.

"I went into the cottage by the front door. As I entered, the door slammed behind me, as though another door had opened and caused a draft, and I thought I heard someone going through the companionway between the bedroom and living room. I called 'Miss Shale!' and went toward the living room door. Miss Shale's voice answered, 'Is that you, Major Raymond?' and she opened the living room door and invited me inside. That's correct, isn't it, Miss Shale?"

He was malignantly polite. Eva lifted her head slowly. "Yes, I called you," she said, and looked down again.

"I said," the Major went on, "'you can't get back to the mainland tonight. It has already started to rain.' She nodded but said nothing. I asked her where Barclay was, and she told me he was in the bedroom. I excused myself and crossed the foyer into the bedroom and found him dead."

Andrew spoke quickly when the Major paused. "Were there any windows open in the bedroom?"

The Major considered. "No. I am sure I should have noticed if there were, because it was raining hard and there was a high wind."

"Did you notice as you drove up whether or not the lights were on in both the rooms?" asked Daisy.

"I didn't notice from the outside. But the light was on in the bedroom when I opened the door."

"And the companionway between?" she asked.

"Yes, but the light there is very dim. I remember looking there as I came in, because one of the little portholes between the companionway and the foyer was open."

Brett Allison took his pipe out of his mouth. He had listened with an interest that could be measured only by the intentness with which his eyes had followed the Major's every change of expression. Neither Brett's face nor his manner conveyed what his reactions might be, and his voice when he spoke was as soft and even as before.

"Did you go into Mr. Barclay's room without knocking, Major Raymond?"

Brett's laconic impassivity had the effect of putting the Major on the defensive. "I knocked several times," he answered, "and called, but when I had no answer I concluded that he could not hear me because of the noise of the storm, and opened the door."

"Yet Miss Shale heard you when you called her name the first time."

"That hardly seems important, Mr. Allison."

"Possibly not." Allison replaced his pipe.

Foster interposed suavely. "What happened after you found the body, Major?"

"After determining that Barclay was dead, I went back into the living room and asked Miss Shale what she knew about it."

Eva sat up. Her hand went to her lips as if to hold back an angry exclamation. Andrew was looking at her, his eyes holding a desperate plea for reassurance, but she did not turn to him. She listened to the Major, who had not paused.

"She said she knew nothing. I told her I didn't believe her."

Eva was white. Daisy could see the scene—the Major's horrified report and his accusation; Eva's quivering protests. She glanced at Andrew, and saw by the sudden tightening of his whole body that he could see it, too.

"I told Miss Shale that if she didn't already know Barclay was dead she could find out by crossing the foyer. At first she refused, but then said she would go. I went with her. In the bedroom I asked her a few questions."

Foster nodded several times, as if he understood. Daisy understood, too. It was not hard to imagine the Major banging the door behind him and brusquely demanding across Barclay's dead body that Eva confess to murder. Eva gave a long silent shudder.

"Barbarous!" broke suddenly from Andrew. "A few questions. Any questions, any pretext to keep her in that room and break her nerve!" Eva turned slowly toward him with incredulous gratitude. The Major started indignantly. But Andrew had not stopped. "And after this astonishing bit of third degree, I suppose you sat down and waited for her to confess?"

"No," returned the Major with a tolerance that was evidently a concession to Andrew's youth. "Miss Shale insisted that someone must have entered the cottage and killed Barclay while she waited for him in the living room. I called the clubhouse, and told her not to make any attempt to leave the cottage, then I went back into the bedroom to get the scene fixed in my mind. It was only a few minutes later that Mr. Allison arrived with the others."

"A very clear account, Major," Foster murmured.

Cupping was mopping his bald spot. "Just as I said," he rumbled, "just as I said."

"Just as you said what?" asked Daisy.

"All in the same boat. Everybody. Even Major Raymond." He tucked his handkerchief into his pocket and patted it as though grateful for having kept that bit of property safe in the disaster. "My word, but we'll all have a hard time convincing the police."

Daisy had a sensation of puzzled dismay.

"What *are* you talking about?" she demanded.

"Yes, what do you mean?" Imogen whispered fearfully.

"Something profound, undoubtedly," murmured Judith.

Foster was leaning across the table, regarding Cupping with a slow light of comprehension dawning on his face. "Why, of course, Cupping's right! Don't you see, Major Raymond? It would have been very simple for you to have gone directly into Barclay's bedroom and put a knife into him, and then to have stepped back into the foyer and called Miss Shale."

There were gasps of amazement. The Major had gotten heavily to his feet. The corners of his mouth twitched with repressed fury.

"You are insinuating, Mr. Foster, that *I* killed Linton Barclay?" His voice fairly shook.

Foster made a disclaiming gesture. "Oh, no—I am insinuating nothing."

"What Mr. Foster means, Major Raymond," said Brett Allison—as deferentially as though he were adjusting a bill for a complaining guest—"is merely that up to this point we have only your word."

His cool, clipped sentence ended in a shocked silence. The Major set his jaw and sat down. Cupping nodded blandly as if his own excellent judgment had at last received due consideration. Foster shrugged and re-lit his cigar. Imogen shivered and looked dismally at everybody in turn, as if wondering why somebody didn't say something cheerful. Judith drew a long bored breath, like a woman yearning to escape from a tiresome after-dinner speaker. Daisy glanced at Eva and Andrew; she saw that for the first time since they had gathered around the table Eva had lost her rigid apathy and was smiling, a normal eager smile of relief. Andrew stared a moment at Brett Allison, and slowly his tense features relaxed; then, frankly and openly, he grinned.

Impulsively Daisy laid her hand on Eva's arm. "Don't be too frightened, child," she whispered.

Eva gave her head a gallant little shake. "Thanks, Daisy." But there were tiny beads of perspiration on her forehead.

"Just a moment, Mr. Allison," said the Major. He had recovered his self-control. "What Mr. Foster says is absurd."

Mrs. Penn had turned her chair and was watching them all with strained, almost terrified attention. It was the same strain that had been in her face when she broke the cocktail glasses. The Major appeared not to notice her. "I had been in the cottage less than ten seconds when I called Miss Shale," he was saying.

"Miss Shale," said Brett Allison, "did you hear Major Raymond open the front door?" His eyes were on her with a strange earnestness.

Eva shook her head. One hand was twisting nervously at a button on her jacket. "No, I didn't."

"It's hardly to be expected that you would have," Judith murmured gently.

There was an angry cough from Mrs. Penn, but Judith continued to smile her serene little smile. Brett paid no attention to the interruption.

"At what time did you leave the clubhouse, Major Raymond?" he asked.

"As soon as I got the operator's call. I didn't look at the clock."

"Mhm," said Foster, and knit his brows. "And how long did it take you to get to the cottage?"

"Oh, I don't know. Not long."

Both Daisy and Andrew were watching the Major intently. These were very different from his usual decisive answers. The Major was plainly hesitating.

Brett had turned again to Eva. "Do you remember, Miss Shale, how long it was after you called that Major Raymond arrived?"

Something in Brett's unruffled voice or his earnest eyes gave Eva added courage. "No, I don't remember, Mr. Allison," she answered clearly. "I called the clubhouse just before it began to rain. It was raining hard when he came."

Cupping cleared his throat. "Which tells us, my dear young lady, exactly nothing. The rain started like a cannon. Ahem. What I'd like to ask my friend the Major—"

"Yes?" the Major rapped impatiently.

Cupping peered at him affably. "Of course, only a matter of form, sir, but did you drive, ah, directly from the clubhouse to the cottage? What I mean, sir, is, did you come down the short road by the bridle path, or did you by any chance go the other way, around the golf course?"

The Major knocked the ashes off his cigar before he answered. Daisy scowled. He did not often require time before replying to direct questions.

"Let me explain," began the Major. "I started down the short road, then I saw that the storm was about to break, and remembering Miss Shale's insistent determination to take her speedboat in tonight, I decided not to arrive at the cottage till it was plainly too late for her to go. I thought it a very dangerous plan."

('Too smooth,' said Daisy to herself, 'too smooth.' She shook her head. 'He could bluff his way out, but he can't oil his way out. Not like him.')

"—and so," the Major was saying, "where the road forms a T with the bridle path, I turned off and drove around the golf course. I drove around—oh, say five or six minutes, then when it started to rain I turned again, drove over the bridge and to the cottage." Andrew's eyes had narrowed to slits. "Then we're to understand, Major, that you *wanted* Miss Shale to stay on Paradise Island tonight?"

The hand on his knee was doubled into a fist. Eva turned a puzzled look on him and then on the Major. They heard Judith's satiny voice.

"Could you tell us, Major, just why it was so important to you that Eva shouldn't leave?"

"Certainly. I didn't want her to be killing herself."

Cupping was tapping his fingertips together. His eyes were wide in a simple stare.

"Well, we're all in the same boat, all in the same boat, eh, ha-ha!" he cackled. "All of us out of the clubhouse at the time the beastly thing was done, and now good old Major Raymond explaining how he was being chauffeur and guardian angel at the same time! Really amazing, Mr. Foster, eh?"

"I don't think it's amazing at all," Imogen said with mournful petulance. "I think it's just dreadful. Are we going to have to sit around here all night, Mr. Allison?"

Daisy did not hear Allison's reply, for at that moment she felt a paper thrust into her hand under the edge of the table. She glanced to either side of her, but the others seemed to be listening to Brett. Daisy spread out the scrap on her knees. It was a note in the Major's handwriting.

"Don't let Andrew talk too much and keep your eyes on Allison. The chances are that he uncovered what Barclay was doing here, and either had Eva Shale do the murder or did it himself. The more he talks the more he's likely to give away. Watch him."

Daisy felt something jerk in her throat. She looked at Brett Allison, who was telling Imogen that he would declare a recess in the inquiry as soon as it seemed necessary, in a crisply polite fashion at which Imogen's marshmallow face crumpled more sulkily than ever. Daisy tried to see Brett Allison as a dope smuggler who had just killed a man to protect his traffic. As she listened to Brett's even voice and watched his compelling blue eyes the characterization seemed strangely incongruous.

"—I trust, Mrs. Cupping, that we'll be able to take time out after we've heard Miss Shale." He turned to Eva. The eyes of the others followed him. But Eva, white and determined, revealed nothing except a grim self-control. Daisy looked back at Brett. His face was inscrutable as a mask; he stood oddly at ease compared with the tenseness of his listeners. His left hand still held McPherson's reports, and in his right he held his rough briar pipe between his long fastidious fingers.

"Miss Shale," he said, and his low voice was as assured as his attitude, "you heard what Major Raymond told us about his discovery of Mr. Barclay's body. What he said was correct?"

"Yes," answered Eva. The word came clearly, without a tremor, but the knuckles of her locked hands were white with tension. Andrew leaned over.

"Go on, Eva!" His voice broke abruptly into the tight interest that was centered on her. "Tell them what happened. They'll believe you."

"No, they won't," she returned wearily. "But I'll tell them."

She stood up, very still and straight; with her soft white dress and her ruffled sun-streaked hair she looked like a sailor about to go out in a gale. She had thrust her hands into her jacket pockets, and she looked from Brett Allison to the others with a steadiness that dared them to disbelieve her.

"I went to Linton Barclay's cottage on my way to the wharf. I thought I could make the mainland before the storm broke."

Judith tilted a querying eyebrow. "Would you mind telling us, my dear, why it was so necessary for you to get away?"

"She's telling you all you've got any business knowing," Andrew exclaimed.

"It was very important," said Eva steadily. "I thought the storm would hold off longer than it did, and that I'd have plenty of time. The rough sea didn't bother me. I've handled a boat in all sorts of weather. When we got to the cottage Mr. Barclay gave me a map of the sound and asked me to wait a few minutes while he fixed a drink. He went out."

"And then what happened?" asked Brett Allison.

"Nothing happened!" she exclaimed desperately. "Not where I was. That's what I'm trying to tell you. I simply sat there, thinking, and suddenly I noticed that the wind had risen. So I phoned the operator to tell the Major to hurry down for me. I still thought that if I rushed out I might be able to make the trip. Then the storm broke."

She stopped an instant.

"If you want to know how Linton Barclay could be murdered without my hearing anything, listen."

They listened. The creaking of the trees outside, the rain, the thunder, the yelp of the wind around the clubhouse explained better than Eva could have done why in Linton Barclay's tiny cottage she might have heard nothing but the mad revolt of the storm.

"It was even louder then. Thunder every few seconds. The door of the living room where I sat was closed, there was a passage between that and the bedroom, and the bedroom door, I suppose, was closed too."

She drew a long breath. Daisy, leaning on the head of her cane, looked up at Eva's set face and wondered what it was that had made her resolve to read her mysterious letter tonight. But what Eva said offered no explanation.

"At first I thought I could make it anyway. But after a few minutes I knew I couldn't. A storm like this would swamp my boat in five minutes. So I sat there and listened to the wind and the thunder and called myself several kinds of an idiot for not making up my mind to go in this afternoon."

She stopped again. She had told her story clearly, without a quaver; now she stood gathering her courage to face their doubts.

"While I was there, somebody came in and killed Linton Barclay. I didn't hear. I didn't hear anything but the storm."

"This is terrible!" chirruped Imogen. "Eva, darling, why did you have to go to Pass Christian?"

"Oh, be still!" cut in Andrew rudely. "Eva, you don't have to tell!"

Eva looked down at her own reflection on the polished top of the table.

"Miss Shale," said Brett Allison, and it was as if he had spoken her name as a prelude to asking whether she took White Rock or ginger ale—"you wish to add nothing else to what the Major has told us?"

"No. If I'd had anything else to tell I'd have told him—when we stood there with that dead body lying on the floor between us and he shouted questions at me—trying to make me say I had done it."

She stopped again. Her blue eyes flashed defiantly. For an instant there was silence, then a flash of lightning glittered at the windows and the thunder clapped over the island.

"Did Linton Barclay say anything to you today, Miss Shale," asked Foster, "to indicate that he might be in danger?"

"No—nothing that I noticed."

Major Raymond leaned toward her with searching appraisal.

"He didn't talk to you on the way to the cottage about a— letter, perhaps?"

Eva drew a step back. Her eyes turned slowly to Andrew and then to Daisy, and in them was neither fear nor dismay, but only a bitter, unbelieving hurt. It was as if she had cried out, 'How could you? Oh, how could you?' Then she looked back at her questioner.

"No," she answered coldly, "we did not discuss any letters."

Andrew's hands closed and opened; the look he sent the Major was hot with fury. Eva's tense self-control snapped. With a hard, choking little cry she crumpled back into her chair.

"Isn't there a decent person anywhere?" She had covered her face, and her words broke wildly through her sobs. "I didn't kill that man! I didn't! I know you think I did—all of you—but I don't know any more about it than—"

"Eva!" exclaimed Andrew. He was standing, his hands on her shoulders. "Of course you didn't kill him. I believe you."

She jerked up her head. "Oh, you do, do you?"

Daisy bent over her, speaking with a gentleness that was strangely out of habit. She did not hear the excited voices of the others; like Andrew, she was thinking only that in spite of the Major's devastating question Eva must keep her self-control and not give way to the fear that looks so much like guilt, for confident as she had become that Eva had not killed Linton Barclay, she knew as well as the rest of them that Eva's ambiguous position was still unconvincing. Out of the turmoil she heard Brett Allison speak.

"Then that's all, Miss Shale?"

There was a mildness in his voice that Daisy had not heard there before. She wanted to cheer. Strangely and inexplicably, but indubitably, Brett Allison believed what Eva had said.

Eva looked up with a regretful smile. "That's all. I'm sorry."

"Very well." Allison smiled, and in his smile was confidence and reassurance. He turned to the others. "I am going to suggest that we take a half-hour intermission. When we resume, I shall ask that all of us tell what we were doing between six and six-forty-five."

"Seems to me," mumbled Cupping, "that's a matter for the police."

"For the present, Mr. Cupping, I represent the police."

"But what's the idea of giving us all the third degree, sir? Seems to me we've all got embarrassment enough as it is. We can't get away, sir—might as well be in jail."

"Oh, be quiet, Tracy!" Imogen's pink and white face was puckered with annoyance.

"I'll thank you to let go of my sleeve, Mrs. Cupping! What I want to know is—"

"Oh, sit down, Tracy Cupping," ordered Daisy, and like many women who have little respect for their auditors she spoke with authority and Cupping obeyed. Allison glanced at her with mingled thanks and amusement. But Cupping was not silenced.

"It's going to be bad enough without making it any worse. All this damned publicity—"

"Publicity?" echoed Judith sweetly. "You shouldn't mind that. You haven't anything to hide, have you?"

"Of course not! But that doesn't prevent having one's name splashed all over the front pages—"

"Oh, no?" she asked with her creeping smile. "But that isn't what bothers me."

"Then what does? Let me tell you, my dear lady, it ought to! By the time the papers get through with their insinuations you'll—"

"Oh, you think so, do you?" She sprang up, her black eyes flaming. "Maybe you won't be so damned sure, my dear Mr. Cupping, that the papers won't have plenty to tell about your own family! Why don't you look at your wife?"

Cupping's jaw dropped. Daisy stared at Imogen. Cupping spluttered; then, like all the rest of them, he stared too. Imogen's pink face grew scarlet; her lips quivered; she gasped something angry and incoherent, and suddenly she burst into tears. Cupping was purple.

"What do you mean? 'Look at my wife'?"

"Not a thing," answered Judith coolly above Imogen's sobs, "except that one can't help noticing what she was wearing when she came back into the clubhouse after her pleasant little stroll in the rain. It's lying there on the sofa—Linton Barclay's raincoat."

Tracy Cupping stared down at Imogen's bent golden head with the look of a man who has been slapped across the mouth.

Judith stood regarding them with supercilious triumph. Eva had started violently, and now leaned forward, her hands grasping the arms of her chair. They could all see a blue leather windbreaker lying on the sofa. For an instant nobody spoke; then Daisy heard a wordless sound like an audible shrug, and she became aware that Mrs. Penn had gone over to the fireplace, where she stood with her hands behind her, curling her lips angrily at Judith's clear profile.

Suddenly Imogen began to speak, her words tumbling out in a nervous torrent.

"Well, I won't admit a thing! And I think you're a horrid woman! And I won't—"

"But if you don't care to talk to us," Foster interrupted, "I suppose you won't mind explaining to the police?"

"And the reporters?" Judith murmured in an undertone.

Tracy Cupping's face was almost gray. Daisy was impulsively sorry for him and for the way Judith's blow had gone home.

"Of course, Mrs. Cupping," Brett was saying quietly, "we have no way to force you to tell us how you happened to be wearing Linton Barclay's raincoat when you came in. However, if you don't care to tell us, you must remember that it will be necessary for us to tell the police."

"You aren't being very fair, Imogen," Andrew put In. "We've all agreed to tell everything we know."

"Oh, you think I'm scared, do you?" flared Imogen. "Well, I'm not! You all *want* me to tell what I know, do you? You *want* me to tell, Andrew?"

"Certainly I do. Eva told everything she knew."

Imogen's big eyes, green as pea-soup, narrowed maliciously. "Well, we'll see."

She laughed, a thin, cutting little laugh. "All right, then, I'll tell. It just happens that I was in Mr. Barclay's cottage when he was murdered. He was murdered by a woman in a red raincoat and when he spoke to her just before she killed him he called her Eva."

PART THREE

CHAPTER TEN

ANDREW had walked up the staircase at Eva's side, appealing without effect to her stony profile. As she turned to go down the corridor toward her room he caught her elbows savagely and forced her to face him.

"Please, Andrew!" she exclaimed.

"You listen to me," said Andrew. "I'm the only person on this island, except Daisy, who wouldn't be willing to see you go on trial tomorrow for killing Linton Barclay. You've got to trust me."

"Well, I don't." Eva put her hands behind her and stood looking directly into his eyes. "I did trust you. I didn't mind your telling Daisy about that letter. But for you to go around making it common property—"

"I didn't make it common property. I had a reason for telling Major Raymond. I had to tell him."

"Maybe you think you did. But Andrew—" her face softened and her dark blue eyes became almost pitifully appealing—"Andrew, I've had so much to stand tonight—"

"I know. That's why I've got to make you understand that you can count on me."

"I did think I could," she said, and he winced. She went on. "I do want to be fair, Andrew. Maybe you didn't understand, but I'd rather give everything I own than have to tell all those people why it was so horribly important to me to read that second letter tonight. I knew the water was dangerous. But I simply had to go."

A dark flush of apprehension had spread over his features.

"You mean you were afraid of that letter? And you won't tell me why?"

"I can't, Andrew. Please don't ask me. I was afraid of it, and I still am. There's another reason. I've lost the first letter."

He started. "Somebody has been in your room?"

"I think so. When I went up after my ride with Barclay I looked for it, to show to you and Daisy. It wasn't there. I'm sure I brought it with me—I haven't let it get out of my hand-bag since it came."

Andrew looked at her intently. "Eva, listen. You can't tell me why you were afraid of what you might see in that second letter. I can't tell you why I told the Major about it. But I do trust you, Eva—and you got to trust me, too. It means more than I can explain."

Abruptly she held out her hand. "All right, Andrew."

He took her hand in his and pressed it. "Thanks, Eva."

She smiled bravely over her shoulder as she went into her room. Andrew ran down to where Daisy was waiting for him by the fireplace.

"It's all right," he told her. "I mean between Eva and me. But the rest is more tangled up than ever." He told her what Eva had said. Daisy twirled her cane thoughtfully.

"Somebody went into her room? Andrew—I wonder—"

She broke off as she saw the Major approaching. He had been talking to Allison and Cupping.

"Mrs. Cupping has just sent word that she won't be down for half an hour. Allison and Foster are going to give the servants a final check-up. Allison says McPherson may have overlooked something relative to Mrs. Penn." The Major shrugged, imply-ing that he put little faith in the sincerity of what Allison might say. "He's increasing the guard at the house and is going to send

Warren down to get the engineer and pilot of Barclay's boat, so we can question them."

Daisy had stood up. "Shall we go upstairs while Imogen makes up her mind what to wear in her big scene? There's a question or two I'd like to ask you both."

"All right," agreed the Major. They crossed to the staircase and went up. None of them spoke till they were in Daisy's suite. As the Major closed the door behind him he broke their silence.

"Daisy, I know you've taken a fancy to this Shale girl, and I'm afraid you have, too, Andrew." He paused and studied them. "So you won't like it when I insist that there's no doubt of her being concerned in Barclay's death."

Andrew had not sat down. He took a step nearer the Major. "Rot. All the evidence against her is circumstantial."

"Worse than that," snapped Daisy. "It's a horrible example of what happens when a couple of middle-aged fools and a boy are made detectives by Act of Congress, or whatever it was."

She thumped her cane. "The rest of them are no more use than you are, Jack. That Foster with his smiles and bows. Like most hotel men. When they rent you a room and bath they want to give you the bath." She glared at the Major. "Brett Allison's got some sense. At least he's not barking around that he's a watchdog of decency. Circumstantial! Of course the evidence is circumstantial. It's the innuendo, not the evidence, that's direct."

"You forget," the Major argued, "that Eva Shale was under suspicion before the murder, and that it was Barclay who suspected her."

Daisy snorted. "Under suspicion by Barclay and you! That means less than Andrew's faith in her. Age explains them both. Credulity and incredulity. One at the cradle end, the other at the grave. Cluck."

"Andrew swore to do his best to carry on in Sanders' place," the Major continued. "Sanders was killed just after he had wired us that he had found out a vital detail. His death may have been an accident. But Barclay was murdered just as we seemed on the verge of getting the necessary evidence against Brett Allison, and Allison has placed himself directly in the way of our finding out who killed him. Your prejudices are beside the point, Daisy."

Andrew kicked a chair out of place and confronted the Major. "Eva Shale didn't kill him."

"Then why is Allison trying so obviously to protect her?"

"He's simply trying to keep you and the rest of them from hounding her out of her senses."

"Or," said the Major, "he killed Barclay himself, and she knows it."

"Brett Allison," Daisy inserted, "looks about as much like a murderous dope-racketeer as Tracy Cupping looks like the Prince of Wales."

"Which is not proof of the innocence of either of them," the Major retorted tersely.

"What made you take so long to get to Barclay's cottage?" Andrew demanded.

"I wanted to give Barclay time to finish talking to her. Her message that I was to hurry sounded as if she was too eager to get away. I don't doubt that she was—because when Mrs. Cupping tells us what she saw in the cottage there'll be little doubt that Barclay was killed by a woman."

"Then doesn't that let Allison out?" Daisy asked.

"Not entirely. A man in a loose oilskin might be mistaken for a woman, and we've got a pretty good motive for suspecting Allison."

"What is your 'pretty good motive,' then?" she snapped. "If lightning had struck Barclay you'd probably have a 'pretty good motive' for suspecting Jupiter."

The Major smiled ruefully. "The dope comes through the Gulf, Daisy. We know that. There must be a supply base."

"But Allison doesn't need to smuggle," countered Daisy. "He has lots of patronage here. His prices are the nearest thing to piracy allowed by law."

"That's the point," the Major explained. "His patronage. Paradise Island would make an ideal landing-place for contraband drugs. Nobody thinks of searching any private yacht that lands here, and once here, it would be easy to get drugs to the mainland, because Paradise Island is only twelve miles from the coast of Mississippi."

"Too perfect," she snapped. "He'd have been suspected before. It's a pat musical-comedy setting."

"He *has* been suspected before." The Major smiled and then grew serious. He had always evidenced deep respect for Daisy's ideas. "The island has been searched once. It was done like this. Brett Allison invested a great deal of his capital in liquor and wines just before Prohibition went into effect. He had permits for it, and frankly declared his intention of giving it to his guests. Figured at pre-Prohibition prices, it's not a considerable amount to spend for good will."

"No wonder he has such a big trade," she murmured, and he went on.

"Federal agents have never gotten any evidence of a sale. All liquor is served with Mr. Allison's compliments, and as Paradise Island is his property, it's perfectly legal. But when this dope-smuggling came up they used the device of checking up his permits to go over the island and see what was going on."

"And—?" she prompted.

"They found nothing. Allison smiled and bowed and showed them over the place, and when they hinted that his guidance was superfluous he retired and let them alone. As usual their results were nil. There have been a good many arrests—peddlers, handlers, men who stored the stuff—but none of them could talk. Not loyalty," he answered her incredulous exclamation. "They didn't know. Here's a typical case. The arrested man said he got his instructions every week from a woman who telephoned. She simply gave him an address and a name—'2210 Joan Street—See Henry.' He'd see Henry and Henry would give him his consignment of cocaine or heroin or opium. Every week it was a different address and a different name. Undercover men were told that Henry got his stuff in the same fashion, but in wholesale lots, and at the same time the name he was to use that week. We followed the trail step by step, and always, just before we got to the source, the trail ended."

"And the woman is young?" she asked frowning.

"She sounds young."

"Sounds young? You've been reading voice-with-the-smile ads. She might be an old harpy—as old as I am."

Andrew, who had been watching the rain streaming down the window-panes, turned and spoke.

"It has been coming from here, or from very near here. So tonight, with Allison off his guard and the island virtually deserted, our plan was to detain him and make a search."

Daisy sat thinking a few minutes. Then she hit the floor savagely with her cane.

"You're wrong. All of you. Dead wrong. This place. His way of living. All wrong."

"About Allison?" asked Andrew.

"Certainly. It sounds like Gilbert and Sullivan. A gorgeous island. Resort of the gilded minority. A monastic figure. Loneliness, silence, mystery in the midst of the whooping throng. It doesn't work." She gave her head a vigorous shake. "Look for your dope smuggler in a skyscraper, a man everybody knows, not one who stays shut up here for the whole obvious-minded police force to point at and ask, 'What's his racket?'"

"You may be right," the Major agreed thoughtfully, "but unless we were getting too warm for the ring's comfort, why should Linton Barclay be killed just when we were closing in on Allison?"

"If they killed Barclay," said Andrew suddenly, "do you think they might have been responsible for Tommy Sanders' death?"

"I don't know. Sanders made his last report to Barclay, saying that he was going to check up once more, and on the flight that was finally to prove his theory he died. We were never able to prove his idea, but we found no evidence that the dope ring had anything to do with his death."

Andrew was unconvinced. "Stick to Allison as much as you like. But if I had to pick a murderer tonight it wouldn't be Allison. I'd choose Foster."

"Foster?" Daisy repeated. "I wonder?"

"He's bothered about something. He's trying hard to agree with everybody and keep things tangled." Andrew smiled. "He even made out a pretty good case against you, Major."

"Another fool," growled the Major, "trying to manage other people's business."

"Think so?" demanded Daisy. "Andrew may have an idea for a change. What are you going to do about it?"

Andrew had started for the door. "I'm going to send a radiogram to Washington and ask the Federal Administrator what the International Hotel Syndicate really is. I'll meet you downstairs. If I don't get back before the others come down, don't say anything about where I've gone."

CHAPTER ELEVEN

AFTER Andrew and the Major had left, still adamant in their opposing convictions, Daisy straightened her collar before the mirror and mused upon what fools men were. They had minds to which the world seemed divided into layers as definite as the layers of a chocolate cake; either something was or it wasn't, and they paid no attention to the bending of truth to circumstance or the subtle shadings that changed right into wrong and wrong into something not so bad after all.

Daisy's years had brought to her no mistrust of youth and no yearning for the peace of a chimney-corner. She used a reasonable amount of makeup and she had no aversion to highballs except when they were made with a minimum of ice. She had given up dancing only when her bad knee made it necessary, and she had a fairly comprehensive idea of what had constituted a breezy book from the eighties onward. She had seen war, flood, fire and pestilence, but personal and individual murder under her very nose was a new experience. She found thinking about it not only wearisome, but fruitless. So after thirty minutes alone, she went back to the lounge.

They were all there. Imogen had changed into a bubbly frock of sea-green chiffon, and her hair, yellow as flypaper, was caught into little cherubic ringlets. She sat by the table chattering with many gestures to her husband, who was gloomily enduring it. Judith still wore her knitted orange suit, but she had taken time to change to a darker lipstick and add a suggestion of violet shadow to her eyelids; with her bright dress and rippling dark hair she was as provocative as a beautiful and languorous gypsy. Foster was bending over her chair, talking and evidently admiring.

Eva had not changed. She had flung her white jacket across the back of her chair, where it made a soft background for her tanned face and sun-streaked hair; her bare arms showed brown and hard against her dress. Andrew was talking to her, but she seemed to be answering in monosyllables, as though in her determination not to ask for understanding she had shut herself in too tight to see it when it was offered.

Brett Allison was speaking to the Major. Though they were not far off, Daisy could not hear Brett's voice, but she watched him, wondering if there was any possible cataclysm that could crack his suave assurance. She looked at him thoughtfully—his blue eyes, with their sharp contrast to his black hair, the imperious lift of his chin, and the steady delicate fingers that held his briar pipe—and she felt a conviction that his ironic calm had been learned in a bitter school; that Brett Allison, when he came out of his guarded castle to take command of a situation that might but for him have been chaotic, had been adequate because he already had knowledge of desperation. She had a rare sensation of respect.

Mrs. Penn sat apart from the others, idly watching the fire. Daisy spoke to her.

"What has happened?"

Mrs. Penn answered with a sort of apathy. "Major Raymond just asked where you were. Mrs. Cupping says she has finally made up her mind to tell everything she remembers."

'—or can think of,' Daisy mentally added, but aloud she only thanked Mrs. Penn and went back to her place at the table. Eva turned and smiled.

"You're feeling better, my dear?" Daisy asked.

"Much better. Mr. Allison sent me up a tray. I'd forgotten how hungry I was."

"Mr. Allison is always considerate," said Foster's voice behind, them. There was a benign mischievousness about him; Daisy was absurdly reminded of a frolicsome bishop who had been in love with her fifty years ago, and who under her tutelage had naughtily learned to dance a waltz-quadrille. Beans, the radio operator, strolled out of a corner and deposited his cheerful person by Brett's chair. He blinked his beady eyes and beamed at Eva.

"Howdy, Miss Shale. Want anything?"

Eva smiled back. "Not a thing, thanks."

"If you do, just lemme know." He glared at the others as though yearning for a chance to fight.

Brett Allison came to the head of the table. "And now, Mrs. Cupping," he said clearly, "we shall be glad to hear just what happened while you were at Mr. Barclay's cottage."

Imogen poked out her lower lip. Fortified by her ripply new dress, she was being cute. Daisy would have loved to spank her.

"Well, you needn't talk to me as if I was a criminal." She shrugged a dimpled shoulder. "I just happened to be near Mr. Barclay's cottage when it began to rain."

"Suppose you tell us," said Brett, "how you happened to be there."

"Good heavens, you sound as if I was loitering around looking for a chance to steal his pocketbook! I was just taking a walk."

"Alone?" asked Major Raymond.

"Yes, I was all by myself. You see—" Imogen was feeling the spotlight thrill—"I had been playing tennis with Tracy, but the wind got pretty high, so we came back to the clubhouse. We saw you here in the lounge, Andrew."

"Yes, I remember."

"Then we went out and walked around for awhile, and I suggested to Tracy that we might go down and see if our boat was tied up tight, for it was blowing awfully hard then."

"Your boat is anchored in Lilith's Inlet, I believe?" Brett asked.

"Yes, that's right. Close to Adam's Inlet. So appropriate, I thought—that is, after Tracy explained it to me. I didn't know who Lilith was. She isn't in Genesis, is she?"

"Did Mr. Cupping go down to the wharf with you?" asked Andrew with a trace of impatience.

"No, when we had gotten as far as the bridle path he said he wanted to go by the golf club to speak to the pro, so I went on down and saw the boat. Then I thought I'd walk to the point off the inlet and see if any more boats were leaving. Then, while I was walking, it started to rain. You know how suddenly the rain started—long before anybody thought it would."

"Go on," said Brett as she looked around for confirmation.

"Well, it had gotten dark all of a sudden, and I was getting cold and wet—I had on a light flannel coat, and the rain had soaked it the first minute—and through the trees I saw a light in Mr. Barclay's cottage. I thought I could call the clubhouse from there and have them send a car for me. So I began to run. The rain was pelting and I was all wet when I got there, and I was so glad to get to a shelter that I didn't think about ringing—I just opened the door and walked in."

"There are three doors to the cottage," said Brett, "the front door opening into the foyer and the two back doors from the living room and passage. Which one did you use?"

"The front door," said Imogen importantly.

"Did you see anyone?" asked Andrew.

"Not then, I didn't." She was getting mysterious. "You see, I was so out of breath I couldn't have said a word if I had seen anybody, so I just dropped into a chair by the door and panted. You'd have thought the Indians had been chasing me," she added with a giggle. "I thought I'd just rest a minute and then knock on the living room door and ask Mr. Barclay if I might use his telephone. The rain and the thunder were making an awful racket and I was a little bit scared—thunderstorms always make me nervous. And then—" she hesitated.

"I suppose I'd better explain. You know how that cottage is built—like a ship. There are two portholes in the wall between the foyer and the passage, so anybody in the foyer can see anybody in the passage. Well, I don't know just how long I had been there, because at first I was so breathless from running that I wasn't noticing much, and anyway the light in the passage was rather dim, but after awhile I saw Mr. Barclay in the passage. Oh—this is really pretty awful, isn't it?"

"You're sure it was Mr. Barclay?" Daisy asked shortly. Imogen's histrionics were getting bothersome.

"Well, it must have been Mr. Barclay. I didn't see his face, but you can tell who a person is from his back, can't you, if you know him very well?"

"And you knew Mr. Barclay *very* well, didn't you?" asked Judith silkily.

"Of course I did. He was an old friend. I think it's just terrible that he had to die like that—"

"Yes, Imogen, it is very tragic," said Daisy. "But you were telling us you saw him in the passage."

"Well, I'm sure I'm going just as fast as I can. But it's all so dreadful, you know—I never thought I'd be involved in a tragedy like this—almost an eyewitness, so to speak—" she dabbed at her eyes as if just reminded of them.

"You said," Brett Allison put in inexorably, "that you saw Mr. Barclay in the passage. Did you speak to him?"

"No—you see he wasn't alone. There was a woman with him."

"A woman?" exclaimed Eva. She had been listening with tense interest. "A woman?"

"Yes," snapped Imogen, "and don't you forget I didn't want to tell them."

"Did you recognize this woman?" Brett asked with weary insistence.

"Not then. I didn't know who she was. I couldn't see her face, you see—their heads were both above the level of the port-holes—but she had on a red raincoat, and it was open in front and I could see that she had on a white dress underneath."

She offered this with a triumphant flourish. Their eyes all turned to Eva in her white flannel boating suit, and then to the scarlet slicker she had tossed on the sofa when she came in. Eva sprang up and went to the sofa.

"Like this, Imogen?" she asked. There was more defiance than fear in her manner. "It was a slicker like this?"

Imogen nodded brightly. "Just like that."

"And like *this*?" she had put the raincoat on, and now stood before them all, her head thrown back. "The woman you saw looked like this?"

"Yes, just like that."

Eva took off the red raincoat. It fell in a heap on the floor. "I hope you know what you're talking about," she flung over her shoulder as she went back to her place by Andrew, "because I don't."

"Please go on, Mrs. Cupping," said Brett Allison. One of his slender, fastidious hands was absently playing with his tobac-co-pouch.

"Well, I'll try. I don't know how long they had been standing in the passage before I looked up and saw them, but as soon as I saw them I thought I'd call Mr. Barclay. I couldn't hear whether or not he was talking to this woman with him, but I thought I'd call and tell him I wanted to go in the living room and use his phone. But just as I was about to get up Mr. Barclay opened the bedroom door and they both went in. And then—" she spread out her little hands in a helpless gesture and looked around for sympathy—"and then, I didn't know *what* I ought to do. It was an awfully embarrassing predicament. I mean it really was. Imagine my situation. There was Mr. Barclay and that woman in his bedroom, and there was me, just sitting in the foyer not knowing what to do. And there was the storm outside. If it hadn't been for the storm I'd have gone straight out and said nothing about it to anybody, of course, because I never was one to gossip and I'm sure I don't want to get anybody into trouble—but as I said, thunder and lightning always did scare me to death—and the longer I stayed there the worse I felt."

"Could you hear them talking?" Brett asked dryly.

"Oh, no—you don't think I'd listen, do you? Besides, I couldn't have heard anything—the rain and the wind and the thunder were so loud—though of course once or twice I thought I heard voices from the bedroom, very indistinctly. I couldn't have understood anything they said even if I'd been trying to listen. I wanted to leave, and I went to the window and just as I looked out a branch broke off one of the palm trees, and then there was a flash of lightning, and I got too frightened to move, so I went back and sat down, praying that the rain would hold up so I could leave before they knew I was there, and I kept wondering who the woman was, and then all of a sudden I remembered that Eva Shale had a red raincoat and I was so horrified I didn't know what to think—"

"I suppose it never occurred to you," Andrew interrupted harshly, "that there might be two red raincoats on Paradise Island?"

"Of *course* it did," she answered with an injured air. "And I couldn't believe it was Eva. But while I was sitting there wondering, all of a sudden the door opened. The door between the bedroom and the foyer, I mean. And I nearly jumped down my own throat, I was so startled."

"Who opened the door?" asked Andrew. He was holding both Eva's hands in one of his, and looked past her to Imogen, fairly quivering with anger.

"I couldn't see. Whoever opened it was behind it. But I heard Mr. Barclay say 'You're a fool, Eva! You can't bluff me.' He sounded terribly angry."

Andrew had sprung to his feet. "You are sure he called her Eva? You'd better be careful of what you're saying, Mrs. Cupping."

"I don't like being addressed in that tone of voice, and I'm perfectly sure he called her Eva." Imogen pursed her pink mouth.

"Look out how you talk to my wife, young man!" thundered Cupping.

"I'm not—"

"Sit down, Andrew," Major Raymond interposed crisply. "You wanted Eva to hear the evidence against her."

"I'm hearing it," said Eva wearily. "Andrew—please let her finish."

"But I don't see why Mrs. Cupping should continue," barked Mrs. Cupping's husband, "if she's going to be insulted every other minute."

"Nobody has insulted Mrs. Cupping," said Brett. He spoke calmly, but he was turning the tobacco-pouch around and around, as though seeking an outlet for his exasperation. "Will you finish your story, Mrs. Cupping?"

Imogen sighed dramatically. Andrew had sat down, but he was leaning forward glaring as though eager to silence her for good. Judith was blowing smoke rings with an air of relish.

"Well, he said, 'You're a fool, Eva! You can't bluff me.' And the door slammed shut. Then I was more frightened than ever, because he sounded pretty mad, and I knew it was just Providence that had kept him from coming beyond the door and seeing me, and I knew if they did come out of the bedroom and see me they'd think I was listening, and I never did go around eavesdropping and I don't want anybody to think I do. So I decided to get out, storm or no storm, and I saw that blue wind-breaker of Mr. Barclay's hanging on the coat-rack and I thought I'd wear it and send it back after I'd gotten to the clubhouse, and Mr. Barclay would never, never guess that I had known about Eva's being in his room. So just as I put it on I heard something fall. I thought he'd gotten terribly angry or maybe was drunk and had knocked her down. My heart jumped up in my mouth and I got out of the cottage and ran back to the clubhouse as fast as I could. And when I got here they told me Mr. Barclay had been murdered."

She lifted her eyes and gave a long sigh. "So I knew then what it meant, the noise I heard. Can you *imagine* the state I've been in?"

CHAPTER TWELVE

EVA was sitting very still, her chin cupped in her hands. She did not look at Andrew or at Daisy; it was as though she had realized that her denial of Imogen's story would only give it emphasis. Daisy watched Andrew's hard-set profile, and wondered what he was thinking; she looked at Brett Allison, but his head was bent over the sheaf of notes in his hand. Imogen was whisper-ing to her husband; she looked like a kitten cuddling up to a big bad-tempered dog. The Major was frowning at the floor. Judith, leaning back in an attitude of boredom, was idly snapping and unsnapping the catch of her handbag. Mrs. Penn sat staring glumly at nothing. They were all silent; Daisy felt herself in the midst of a vague, terrifying world in which the only certainties were negative. She was sure Eva had not killed Linton Barclay, but she could be sure of nothing else, and she had no idea how to snatch Eva from under the landslide of evidence that was moving upon her.

Daisy pitied her desperately. Eva had been so secure, so self-reliant—why was it that tragedy seemed so often to select such sparkling victims? Eva was staring ahead of her with a chilly defiance that seemed to be challenging anyone who should dare to offer her pity. Daisy thought suddenly that it was as if she had buckled herself into this impenetrable armor because she was conscious that underneath it she was more fragile than any of them had suspected.

Studying Andrew's taciturn grimness, Daisy wished that he and Eva did not belong to this brittle young generation, for she wanted to take them both in her arms and offer them the solace of her understanding. But she did not dare to break down the wall behind which Eva had taken refuge. If she fought for Eva now it must be from outside, for she sensed that stripped of her hard young pride Eva would feel herself helpless. Daisy looked again at Brett Allison, and broke the bleak silence that had followed Imogen's story.

"Mr. Allison," she said, "did Miss Meade set down the time that Imogen returned to the clubhouse?"

Brett glanced at the notes in his hand. His fine-cut features were shadowed with weariness.

"Yes. She came in at five minutes after seven."

"That's about right," Imogen confirmed. "I was a nervous wreck when I got here."

"And I hope," thundered Tracy Cupping, "that Mrs. Garon is satisfied and will keep her insulting insinuations to herself."

"Oh, well—" said Judith airily. She turned and gave Foster a softly catlike smile, as if to ask 'What's the use?'

Cupping jerked at his walrus moustache and was about to retort when Brett's voice clipped smoothly across his irritation. "Miss Shale, should you like to comment on Mrs. Cupping's story? Or should you prefer to wait?"

"I don't know what she's talking about," said Eva flatly.

"I'm sure, Miss Shale," exclaimed Cupping, "that you don't think my wife would have made up such a story."

"No," said Judith creamily. "It would take a great deal of imagination to make up all of it."

Cupping started furiously. "And just what, madam, do you mean by that?"

"Not a single thing, Mr. Cupping. I can't see why you're always insisting that I mean more than I say." She regarded him with poisonously docile eyes. Daisy indulged in four mental 'damns' and an audible cluck.

"Pardon me, ma'am, but—"

"One always allows for age, Mr. Cupping." Judith smiled indulgently.

Brett Allison spoke with a calmness more potent than all Cupping's blustering. "Mrs. Garon, you have not yet allowed us to ask whether there is anyone else who wants to comment on Mrs. Cupping's story."

"Sorry, Mr. Allison." Judith slid back into her velvet silence.

"Look here, Imogen," Daisy put in crisply. "You said you went down to see if there were any more boats going out. Did you see any?"

Imogen put a finger to her forehead and screwed up her face as though in deep thought. "I didn't get very far before the rain started. And then I wasn't looking for boats."

"I think this incident is entirely finished," said Tracy Cupping. His mottled nose was red and purple with excitement. "I want you all to know that I have absolute faith in my wife and her story. The only explanation due now is from the other person who seems to have been involved." He looked at Eva.

She did not move. "I told you I didn't know anything about it. Imogen says she saw me go into Mr. Barclay's bedroom. She couldn't have, because I didn't go in there."

She spoke like a child reciting a memorized lesson. It was as though the shock she had received had blunted all her power of thought till she could do nothing but repeat her simple denial.

"As I said before," exclaimed Andrew, "there might possibly be another woman on Paradise Island who owns a red raincoat!"

Brett smiled his bitterly ironic smile. "I was about to remark, Mr. Dillingham, that there are perhaps forty red raincoats on Paradise Island. They are part of the regulation uniform provided for the maids employed here."

Andrew sprang up. "Then the servants—"

"The servants are provided with alibis," put in Foster, and Brett added,

"There are only four women servants on the island tonight, and they were all busy at the time of the murder."

Andrew was looking at Mrs. Penn. She returned his gaze steadily. "I don't wear a maid's uniform, Mr. Dillingham." Her mouth snapped shut.

Brett was still smiling. "Anyone who wanted to borrow a red raincoat," he said evenly, "could have taken one from the staff's cloakroom under the back stairs."

"However—" Judith began silkily. She paused and stroked her chin. Brett's smile did not waver.

"Yes, Mrs. Garon?"

"It does seem rather strange," commented Judith with a sardonic tilt of her black eyebrows, "that nobody has suggested that it might not have been merely the rain that sent Imogen running to Linton Barclay's cottage or merely simple curiosity that made her so eager to wait and see what happened when she got there."

Imogen gave a startled little cry and Cupping leaped to his feet. "Look here, Allison! I demand that you either throw this woman out or make her keep quiet about my wife! I don't care who has been murdered, or who—"

"But I do, Mr. Cupping," said Judith with a plaintive sweetness. "Mr. Barclay was an old and very dear friend of mine, and I am naturally concerned about—"

"Mrs. Garon," said Allison quietly, "if you have any reason to believe that you know anything about who killed Mr. Barclay, we shall be glad to hear you. Your opinions on other subjects are of no interest to us tonight."

('He talks like a mechanical man,' thought Daisy. She had small liking for stilted courtesy.)

"If I could only say what I'm trying to say without being interrupted so often—" Judith's sigh made Daisy cluck disgustedly—"I might be able to make myself clear. What I mean is that when Imogen was on the front row of the chorus of 'Candy Man' Mr. Barclay knew her very well, and in view of that, and also because she seems so well acquainted with the geography of the cottage, I can't help wondering if she might not have gone through the bedroom and the passage herself and come out by the back door—"

"If you were a man," exclaimed Cupping, red in his wrath, "I'd thrash you till you couldn't move! I know positively that my wife went into Linton Barclay's cottage by the front door and came out by the front door! I know Eva Shale was in the cottage then. Now will you be quiet?"

Andrew was on his feet. "How do you know that, Cupping?"

Cupping's face turned from red to a sick lavender. He looked down and blinked uncomfortably.

"Come on, Cupping," Andrew insisted. "Tell us. How do you know?"

Cupping jerked his head up. "Because I followed her," he said defiantly.

"Tracy!" cried Imogen.

"Yes, I did. A man married to a girl thirty years younger than he is can't help acting like a fool sometimes. And if you think it's amusing, you're wrong, every damn one of you!"

CHAPTER THIRTEEN

BEANS whistled. "That cottage would make a swell place for a cigar store," he said under his breath. "Everybody goes by there."

Brett raised his hand for silence. "You say you saw Mrs. Cupping go in the front door of Barclay's cottage?"

"Yes," answered Cupping, with threatening righteousness.

Imogen was glowering. Cupping stirred uncomfortably. Daisy marked up a three-base hit for Judith.

"And it's my theory," Cupping amended loudly, "that whoever murdered Linton Barclay had robbery for a motive."

('Anything will do,' thought Daisy, 'except what that old codger probably still calls the eternal triangle.')

Foster was looking up with mischievous amusement. "So you're in the same boat with the rest of us, Mr. Cupping! I only meant to suggest," he added hastily as Cupping began to splutter, "that we must not forget Mrs. Cupping's account of the woman who quarreled with Mr. Barclay."

"Oh, he's going to eliminate the woman angle now," Judith suggested softly. "Aren't you, Mr. Cupping? You see, it depends on who the woman is."

Cupping turned his back to her and addressed himself to Brett. "We have not even tried to find out if Barclay was robbed."

"Well, *I* didn't steal anything from him," Judith put in with venomous meekness, "and thank goodness," she added clearly to Foster, "he wasn't trying to steal anything from me."

"If Major Raymond was associated with Mr. Barclay in a business deal," suggested Foster, "maybe he can tell us whether or not Barclay had anything with him worth stealing."

('So now,' Daisy told herself, 'we turn the game into cops and robbers. Convenient for Cupping.') The Major shrugged. "He usually carried a good deal of cash."

Brett looked at the report in his hand. "We'll go into the robbery theory shortly. According to Miss Meade, Mr. Cupping, you returned to the clubhouse ten minutes after your wife."

"Yes—she was here when I got in." Cupping thrust his hands into his pockets. He was struggling for poise and doing pretty well under the circumstances, Daisy thought.

"And while you were out, you saw Mrs. Cupping both enter and leave Barclay's cottage."

"I said," answered Cupping meticulously, "that I saw her enter. I didn't exactly see her leave, but I know she left by the front door—that is, I know it by what's already been said by the others."

"Did you come directly here from the cottage?" Brett asked.

"I—er—yes, I did. Yes." Cupping swallowed. "But I must say, sir, that I think all these embarrassing questions are beside the point. My conviction has been and still is that somebody tried to rob Barclay and Barclay got killed trying to protect his property. I can't see the use of all this prying into my affairs, sir." He was fairly squirming under Imogen's furious regard.

Daisy cocked up an eyebrow and wondered what was hidden in the Cupping woodpile, but her reflection was interrupted by Brett's voice. "We shall be glad to consider your theory, Mr. Cupping. We can go down to the cottage and see if Mr. Barclay had any valuable property there." He glanced understanding^ from Imogen to Cupping, and Cupping, sighing with relief at this prospect of a chance to smooth down Imogen's resentment, sat down. Foster spoke to Brett.

"If we're going to take time out," he suggested good-humoredly, "have you any objection to my sending a radiogram to my New York office?"

"Not if you dictate it here," Brett answered dryly. "I am keeping Beans here," he added, "because a little while ago he sent a private message. While we have no right to ask him for the details of that message, we can prevent anyone else from communicating with the mainland unless we know the nature of the communication."

"A message?"

"Who sent it?"

"I don't like that at all."

There was a gurgling excitement around the table, and Daisy sent an impudent glance at Andrew, rejoicing that his expression did not betray him. Beans looked archly mysterious as if fully cognizant of his dignity as the holder of an important secret.

Foster nodded. "I've no objection to your hearing what I have to say. I'll be glad to dictate here." He turned to the others. "It might be well if I give you the details of our option. Mr. Allison has contracted to sell us Paradise Island at a specific price. In order to get that price we must take up our option before September 17, which is tomorrow. That's right, isn't it, Mr. Allison?"

Brett nodded affirmation.

"It is a peculiar sort of option, however," Foster continued. "It provides that if another formal bid is made to Mr. Allison for the purchase of Paradise Island before September 17, Mr. Allison has the right to conduct an auction between ourselves and any other interested parties. You see, this option is a year old, and the International did not want to tie Mr. Allison up for so long a period on an option. In fact—" Foster smiled affably—"Mr. Allison would not be tied up for so long a period. Now, Beans, if you are ready, I'll be glad to dictate my message."

Daisy glanced at Cupping, who she knew had evinced more than a passing interest in Paradise Island, but he was fidgeting uncomfortably under Imogen's whispered recital of her injured feelings at having a husband who followed her about, and was apparently oblivious to business concerns.

"Okay, shoot." Beans' voice broke her reverie. He held a pencil poised over a grubby envelope.

Foster studied the ceiling and dictated.

"Mr. J. Coblin, INTTEL, (that's the cable address)— Linton Barclay, prominent civic leader, found murdered Paradise Island cottage tonight. Any instructions?— FOSTER."

Beans finished writing and looked up.

"All right, Beans," said Allison. "You may send it."

"You'd better wait for an answer," Foster advised as Beans got up to leave, "if that's agreeable to Mr. Allison."

"Certainly. But it's understood that no one will attempt to send any other messages without our knowledge." As the others nodded he went on. "And now, perhaps we had better take a look at the cottage and see if there is anything there to bear out Mr. Cupping's theory of robbery."

"Good idea," approved Andrew. "I'd like to go with you."

"Fine. First I want a few minutes to go over these reports. We'll resume, say, in a half-hour."

Imogen was already on her way to the staircase, with her husband sheepishly following a step behind. Judith gave herself a lazy stretch and got up. Allison went toward the fireplace, where he stood leaning against the mantel, his eyes on the papers in his hand.

Daisy and Andrew had both turned to Eva. She had relaxed her tight muscles and lay back in her chair like a tired child.

Andrew bent over her. "Eva—you *can* prove to them Imogen was lying, can't you?"

"I don't know," she answered exhaustedly. "I—I'm scared, Andrew."

"Eva," he said earnestly, "I'm not asking you any questions. But if there's anything you haven't told Brett Allison, tell him. It's safer."

She sat up. "Andrew—please—you do believe me when I say I don't know who killed him?"

"Yes," said Andrew.

She sank back with a little sob of relief. "Oh, you *are* so good! Daisy, do you believe me, too?"

Daisy sat on the chair-arm and ran her hand across Eva's rumpled light brown hair. "Of course I believe you, silly. But our problem is to make other people believe you, too—not the rest of them here, but the detectives who are going to come in the morning. They won't be looking for anything but a good scapegoat. That's why you've got to make them understand that that idiotic Cupping girl didn't see you."

"She didn't," said Eva. "I don't know who it was that she saw. There *must* be another woman whose name is Eva."

Andrew put his hands on her shoulders. "Don't worry. We'll make it come out all right. But if there's anything you haven't told Brett Allison, tell him."

Eva looked intently at a fold in Daisy's skirt. "I haven't done anything I'm ashamed of, Andrew," she said in a low voice.

"I know you haven't." Plainly the last shade of his doubt of her was gone.

Daisy moved away, guessing that they had rather be left alone. Eva looked up. Her eyes met Andrew's. For a moment neither of them spoke or moved. Then, suddenly, Andrew took her face between his hands and kissed her.

She started back from him as if she had been struck. "Please, Andrew!"

He was holding both her hands tightly in his. "I've been such a damned fool, Eva! I might have known it before this, but I didn't—it had to take all this mess tonight to make me understand how much I care for you. I can't let them do anything to you now!"

She stood up and slowly withdrew her hands. Suddenly she turned and looked around for Daisy.

"Daisy," she called, "come here."

Daisy came back. "You wanted me?"

"Yes." Eva looked from her to Andrew. She was holding one hand of each of them. "Daisy, you heard what Andrew said to me?"

"Yes, dear. I couldn't help hearing."

Eva glanced around to see if they were being observed. Daisy followed her eyes, and saw that Brett Allison, standing by the fireplace, appeared to be studying the papers in his hand with an inscrutable attention. Eva's voice dropped lower.

"Andrew, I want Daisy to hear this because I think perhaps she'll understand it better than you can. Ever since I've known you I've tried not to let myself love you. Because you see, I know the grand Dillingham tradition—and I can't share it."

"Don't be an idiot!" he exclaimed. "Eva, my dear,—I don't know who your grandfathers were and I don't give a damn. I can't—"

But before he could finish she had broken away and was running toward the stairs, choking back a dry little sob in her throat. Andrew started to follow her, but he had taken only a step or two when she was out of sight, and they heard the faint sound of a door closing overhead. Daisy caught his wrist.

"Let her be alone now, Andrew."

He turned on his heel. "I've got to talk to her, Daisy. There's a lot of things I have to say."

"They'll keep. Let her cry a bit. Tears are very humanizing." She looked at him with grave earnestness. "Do you love her, Andrew?"

"I love her more than I ever thought I could love anything on earth. And if she bangs doors on me because I'm Andrew Dillingham, I'll pull them down and make her understand how much I love her."

Daisy smiled leniently. "Don't start making grand declarations now, darling. If you love her, find out who put that knife into Linton Barclay."

He grasped both her hands so tightly that she winced. "You know she didn't do it, don't you?"

"Of course she didn't. But she's going to trial for it unless we can prove somebody else did."

There was a step behind them, and Andrew let go of her hands. "May I interrupt you a moment?" asked Brett Allison. "We are ready to go down to Barclay's cottage. Major Raymond is coming with us."

Andrew answered with quick eagerness, evidently glad to find an immediate outlet for his energy. "Fine. Where is he?"

"He's waiting. In my office."

"I'll get him." Andrew picked up his slicker. Brett smiled at Daisy, his quietly deferential smile. "We'll be back soon, Mrs. Dillingham."

"I hope so," she said shortly. Her cane thumped. "Brett Allison, do you think Eva Shale killed that man?"

Allison's blue eyes regarded her thoughtfully. He was only an inch or two taller than Daisy herself, but she had the feeling of standing before an overpowering presence.

"No," he answered with grave emphasis, "I don't."

"Then hurry up," exclaimed Daisy, "and find out who did."

"I am doing my best, Mrs. Dillingham," he said. "I'm trying to spare everyone, except the murderer."

"I believe you are," she agreed impulsively. "But you're up against a tough job."

He smiled again, a curiously introspective sort of smile. "It's not the most agreeable sort of occupation. But I'll be through playing detective in a little while." For a moment she stood looking intently into his eyes. They were sincere, understanding eyes, thought Daisy, but there was a strange tiredness about them, as if they were the eyes of one for whom life held no more surprises. She looked from his eyes to his delicate, sensitive hands. They did not match, those eyes and those hands. Daisy wondered what it was that had broken the continuity of his life. She guessed that it had been a wound he had dealt to himself; nothing, she was sure, could have struck him so deeply except through the failure of his own inner reserves.

Brett broke their silence. "Here are Andrew and the Major," he observed, "all dressed up for the weather."

"Don't miss anything," she advised them, and as they went out she crossed over to the fireplace, where Mrs. Penn sat stiffly regarding the bright ashes. Daisy put on a log and stood by the hearth a moment, wondering if anything was to be gained by talking to Mrs. Penn. The efficient lady-manager seemed in no mood for words; she simply sat there, twisting her old-fashioned wedding ring.

100 | GWEN BRISTOW & BRUCE MANNING

"I hope you're going to be able to give us some help, Mrs. Penn," Daisy said with brisk invitation.

Mrs. Penn started. "I don't know anything about Mr. Barclay, Mrs. Dillingham."

"But you must have seen him a good deal—I believe he used to come over here often."

"Yes, he did, lately. He and Mrs. Garon."

"They were very good friends, weren't they?"

"They were together a great deal. Friendship seems hardly the term." Mrs. Penn's face plainly added that those who ran hotels saw a great many things that others merely suspected.

Daisy whiffed an idea from afar. "I don't believe you like Mrs. Garon very much, Mrs. Penn."

"I hardly know her. She comes here and I work here." Her shrug suggested the gulf between a guest and a paid hostess.

Daisy laughed. "Judith has always been hard to get along with. She's somewhat disillusioned, I'm afraid."

"Disillusioned?" Mrs. Penn repeated, and gave Daisy a sarcastic smile. "She's been worse than disillusioned since Barclay started seeing so much of Miss Shale."

"Really?" Daisy prodded.

Mrs. Penn looked up incredulously. "Haven't you noticed?"

"Noticed what?" Daisy asked innocently.

"Her efforts to annex Mr. Dillingham."

Daisy clucked. "She's middle-aged compared with Andrew."

Mrs. Penn smiled with increasing relish. This bit of gossip was evidently proving a welcome break in the evening's strain. "She's evidently not yet disillusioned about that, then. But she's not the first woman who tried using a young man's attentions to help her keep an old one in line."

"Do you know, I really think that must have been it." Daisy nodded profoundly over the head of her cane. She wanted to keep Mrs. Penn talking—this gossip might prove more pregnant than even the shrewd hotel manager guessed. "So Mrs. Garon is really resentful toward Miss Shale?"

"She certainly is," Mrs. Penn declared vigorously. "I'm not trying to suggest that she killed Mr. Barclay in a fit of jealousy. But I think there've been times when she'd have liked to. She loathed Miss Shale." Mrs. Penn stopped suddenly, as if she had said too much. She nervously took out her handkerchief and wiped her lips. "Please don't quote me," she pleaded. "Mr. Allison might not like it."

Daisy watched the fire for a minute, wondering if there was anything else Mrs. Penn could be induced to tell. But Mrs. Penn seemed to repent saying what she had. She sat quite still, looking into the fire and twisting her ring. Plainly she had said all she was going to say on the subject of Judith Garon. Daisy thought of Brett Allison and the Major's dope-smuggling suspicion.

"How do you like Mr. Allison?" she ventured.

"Mr. Allison? He's a splendid man." Mrs. Penn was obviously relieved at the change of topic. "Not the over-friendly sort, but very fair and sympathetic. All his employees adore him."

"I wonder," suggested Daisy, "what he does to amuse himself. He seems to lead a lonely sort of life, don't you think?"

"I don't know. Of course, he's very busy. At night he's usually in the office behind the gambling rooms. He passes on all the credits and things like that. I usually confer with him after dinner. He's seldom around the club in the daytime. He usually takes his launch out or stays in his house."

"What servants has he?"

"Only two Japanese boys. They've gone to shore tonight." She smiled slightly. "Nice of him, wasn't it, to give Mr. Cupping a chance to get himself back into his wife's good graces before he had to tell his story in public! But he's like that. I've always thought—"

The opening of the door interrupted her. Allison entered with a suitcase, and the Major and Andrew followed him, carrying between them a bundle wrapped in tarpaulin, which they set on the big table in the middle of the lounge. Major Raymond beckoned to Daisy.

"Re-enter the woman in red," he said in a grave undertone.

"What do you mean?"

"Look at this." He held out his hand. "We found it on the floor by Barclay's body. There can be no doubt about it—it came from a red raincoat."

In the palm of his hand lay a red bone button. Clinging to it was a thin piece of waterproofed red cloth.

"This means," the Major went on decisively, "that Imogen was right. A woman in a red raincoat did kill Linton Barclay."

CHAPTER FOURTEEN

BEFORE Daisy could answer there was a step on the staircase behind her, and Judith Garon came toward them, serenely beautiful in a sheath of black satin, with a great flower of crimson velvet catching the drapery at her waistline. She carried a long ebony cigarette-holder, and a thin line of blue smoke trailed behind her.

"What have you been uprooting, Major?" she inquired with faint and subtle mockery, as though she was humoring a little boy who had just found a new marble. "More mysteries?"

"Barclay's effects," he returned briefly, closing his hand over the red button.

"Yes? Anything thrilling?"

"That's to be determined."

Judith draped herself along the sofa. "He's very mysterious, isn't he, Daisy?"

Daisy did not answer. Her eyes and the Major's had turned toward the staircase, where they saw Eva, still wearing her white flannel boating-dress and her flat white oxfords. She passed them with a faint smile and sat down at her old place by the table, where Brett and Foster were unwrapping the tarpaulin bundle. Daisy saw Brett speak to her with unobtrusive gentleness, and Eva answered gratefully. Daisy was almost feverishly thankful for Brett's kind attitude, and as she walked to the fire-place, where Andrew stood looking moodily down at the logs, she saw that he had noticed it, too, for he glanced up with a low "Lord, he's being decent to her!"

The Cuppings appeared on the stairs, Tracy truculent behind his walrus moustache, Imogen cool and fluttering in her sea-green chiffon, her golden hair fluffed around her head like a baby's curls. Cupping thumped across to Brett.

"I suppose you are waiting to proceed with this inquisition?" he demanded, a vengeful scowl on his forehead.

Amusement struggled with accustomed impersonal urbanity on Brett's face. "Yes, if you please. Won't you sit down, Mr. Cupping? And you, Mrs. Cupping?"

As Brett drew up a chair for Imogen, Cupping jerked at another for himself and fairly flopped upon it. Brett addressed the others.

"If you will be good enough to join us, we can go on."

('And on,' thought Daisy, 'and on and on, until I scream!')

They came back to their places by the table. Andrew spoke in a low voice to Eva. Her hand gave his a furtive touch and her chin quivered, but before he could make even an answering gesture she had drawn away again.

"I'm not a bit tired," she said, and smiled bravely. Daisy looked thoughtfully at Judith and Imogen, waiting in charming characteristic attitudes—Judith shining and gracious, her beautiful face smilingly ironic under the sleek black coronet of her hair; Imogen clasping her little dimpled hands in her lap, her green eyes lifted to Brett, and her whole attitude suggesting ingenuous entreaty, like a child begging for another chocolate cream. Daisy looked back at Eva, calmly and sincerely defying them all, and thought how different they were—Judith and Imogen so conscious that any woman is better able to cope with a situation if she is dressed for it, and Eva refusing even the meager aid of an appealing gown. Brett Allison had begun to speak.

"As you see," he was saying, "we have wrapped up all the articles that might possibly bear fingerprints. I shall urge all of you to be careful to touch none of these unless it is absolutely necessary. Major Raymond, have you unlocked the suitcase?"

"Yes." The Major pushed up the top and showed a green lacquered box that took up nearly half the space inside the Gladstone bag. "But I thought it better not to open this box until we were all together."

"You were quite right. Will you show us what you found by Mr. Barclay's body?"

"Yes—first I should like to ask Miss Shale about the coat she wore when she went to the cottage." Major Raymond spoke steadily, but there was an underlying menace in his look as he turned to Eva.

"What about it, Major?" she answered. "It's on the chair over there."

Daisy could hear Andrew's sharp breath as the Major asked, "Are the buttons on it red or black?" Eva smiled slightly. "It fastens with metal clasps. Why?"

The Major bit his lip. ('Bang goes another theory,' Daisy thought with relief.)

"Because we found this on the floor near where Linton Barclay's body is lying." He held up the red button. "This bit of rubberized cloth on the back plainly shows that the button was ripped from a red raincoat. Our theory of how it happened to be there is this." He held up his hands as if to ward off a blow. "Barclay sees the knife coming at him. He raises his hands, but the blade gets through his guard. As it strikes him, he falls forward and his hands catch at the coat of the murderer. He clutches and then collapses, and slides to the floor. The pull on the coat as he falls rips out the button."

"Do you take this as evidence," asked Foster, "that Barclay was killed by a woman?"

"It isn't conclusive evidence, of course," Major Raymond began, but Cupping broke in,

"It certainly confirms Mrs. Cupping's story. I hope you'll all have the decency to stop doubting her now."

"And," added Foster, "it knocks your own theory into the well-known cocked hat."

"Anyway," Imogen twittered with a satisfied nod, "a man would look pretty silly in a bright red raincoat."

"I'm not quite satisfied," Daisy persisted. "*Could* a woman have killed him? I thought it took a good deal of strength to stab a man."

Judith tilted an eyebrow at the firm muscles of Eva's arms. "Some women are more athletic now than they were when you were young, Daisy."

"Permit me to point out, Mrs. Garon," said Brett, "that even a not very muscular woman could have committed this crime. The knife that made the wound was very thin and narrow—in fact, the surface cut is less than an inch long. If the blade were sharp and finely pointed, it would be possible for even a small woman to drive it home."

"I see," said Judith. "Very simple, isn't it?"

"Did you find the knife?" Daisy asked with a waspishness intended for Judith. The Major shook his head, and Daisy went on. "No matter how important that red button seems, I should think your theory of a woman murderer is weak because a knife was used. I know a lot of females that dress and act like savages, but I don't know any that top it off by carrying a knife around."

"The knife is important," agreed Brett, "but it's logical to suppose that the murderer got rid of it. There's enough water around to make that easy. So, for the present, we'll have to consider the button an important clue." He took the button from the Major and wrapped it in his handkerchief. "Now, as there seems to be no evidence of robbery, I believe we should hear the rest of Mr. Cupping's story. Mr. Cupping, just what did you do after you and Mrs. Cupping left the clubhouse this afternoon?"

Cupping shuffled his feet uneasily and cleared his throat.

"Well, after we'd gone a little way, I remembered that I was to meet McPherson tomorrow for a golf lesson, and I thought I'd better call it off, because the rain would make the course too soft. So I started back toward the golf lockers and took the short cut from the bridle path around the far end of the inlet, and I suppose you know that from there you can see the front door of the cottage where Barclay was staying."

Brett nodded. "Yes, I know."

Cupping hesitated, and took time out to settle his tie. But his audience was waiting impatiently, and as there seemed nothing to do but continue, he hemmed and plunged in.

"To be sure, I just mentioned that the cottage is visible from there so as to make things plainer. I wasn't thinking about Barclay at all. I was just walking around the far end of the inlet, meaning to go over to the golf course, when I saw Mrs. Cupping around the other side. I saw she was walking out toward the end of the wharf, and I waved at her, but she didn't seem to see me."

"I *didn't* see you," Imogen broke in petulantly.

"No, no, my dear, I know you didn't," he soothed her. "Well, just about a couple of minutes after that it started to rain. Naturally I abandoned my plan of going over to the golf course, and turned right around to come back here to the clubhouse as fast as I could. I could just make out Mrs. Cupping running back along the other side of the inlet, and I thought I would hurry back to where the paths joined and jump out and surprise her."

Judith politely smothered a giggle.

Cupping paused and a peevish wrinkle corroded his brow; then, switching his attention to the rest of them as if to stamp Judith as beneath his notice, he went on.

"Well, Mrs. Cupping was running and she reached the joining of the paths before I could. I'm rather—er—heavily built, and I've got—" he smiled benignly—"'some disadvantage of years. Perhaps it was the shortness of breath when trying to run that—er—made me conscious of this—er—disadvantage of years as compared to my wife. At any rate, I saw with distinct surprise and—shall I say, absolute lack of reason—that she did not go toward the clubhouse, but turned aside and hurried toward Barclay's cottage, and I saw her go in."

"It was a perfectly reasonable thing to do," said Imogen snappishly.

"Yes, my dear, quite. Quite. I am afraid I made myself look a bit foolish."

('And you'll pay for it, my dear walrus,' Daisy commented silently.)

Imogen flicked her chiffon handkerchief across her nose in a disdainful fashion which indicated that he certainly would. Cupping tugged at his moustache and continued apologetically.

"Well, as I said, I am afraid I was not very reasonable. But after all—" he smiled on her with a bashful attempt at conciliation—"after all, I have a very deep affection for my dear wife, and at the moment, in my surprise, I recalled that Mr. Barclay had been very well acquainted with Mrs. Cupping before her marriage—"

('Men are such fools,' Daisy reflected. 'He makes it worse and worse. She'll never forgive him.')

"I *do* seem to have heard something of the sort," Judith contributed absently.

Imogen shot her a look like a poisoned arrow, and Cupping hurriedly went on talking.

"As I said, I was surprised to see Mrs. Cupping enter Mr. Barclay's cottage, for I knew she thought I was over on the other side of the island."

"It didn't occur to you," asked Major Raymond, "that she might be simply getting out of the rain?"

Cupping cleared his throat awkwardly. "Well—yes and—no. You see—"

He was floundering badly. Imogen's wrath was adding to his confusion.

"I'm afraid I've changed my mind—I don't think it's necessary to tell this story," blurted Cupping, as if gripped with sudden scary resolution. "It's preposterous. I'm a man of some position in the community—everybody will know that I've had nothing to do with this thing."

Foster pushed back his chair. "Then I'm going to bed. I presume this means we wait for the police and let Mr. Cupping tell them what he saw at the cottage?"

"Just a minute," ordered Brett, and there was biting determination in his low voice. "Mr. Cupping may or may not finish his story, as he sees fit. But I think he will finish it, when he understands that we are trying to spare Mrs. Cupping the necessity of a most unpleasant sort of police inquiry."

"What are you talking about?" Cupping exclaimed fiercely. "Why should she—more than anybody else?"

Imogen curled back her upper lip. "He's just trying to be smart."

Brett smiled with caustic politeness. "One does not have to be smart, Mrs. Cupping, to predict that the police will think it strange that you went out this evening without any sort of raincoat, when Mr. Cupping, who was with you, wore his."

Imogen gasped. "I didn't bring any raincoat from home. I really didn't. Did I, Tracy?"

Brett intervened before Cupping could reply. "The police are likely to say, Mrs. Cupping, that when you went out and saw that the storm was about to break you might easily have returned by the back entrance and taken a raincoat from the servants' cloakroom, and that if you did—now remember, this is merely a prediction of police psychology—you might have decided that with a button missing this raincoat might be noticed when you came in, particularly if you knew that the missing button would be found near the body of Linton Barclay."

"This is outrageous!" shouted Cupping. "I protest—"

Daisy snorted and rapped her cane. "Be quiet, Tracy Cupping. Mr. Allison is right. He's merely trying to tell you what you're in for when the police and newspaper hounds get here." She sat back with a look of exasperation. "If you've got the sense that an impartial Maker is supposed to give all men at birth, you'll tell us what happened down there and maybe save your face."

Judith smothered a yawn. "Then what is it?" she inquired politely—"to bed or not to bed?" She smiled at Foster. "I'm perfectly willing to wait for the police. You see, I brought my raincoat, and it's brown."

"I think Mr. Cupping will go on," said Major Raymond. "I think he understands that the general attitude, while it may not be unanimous—" he looked at Judith—"is that we will do everything we can to spare Mrs. Cupping from embarrassment."

"Thanks, Major." Cupping glanced nervously at Imogen, who was wiping her eyes with an air of pained innocence. "Maybe it will help us all, if I tell the little I know about this."

Foster nodded, and Judith murmured, "Well, go on." Cupping gave a sigh of acquiescence.

"I walked toward the cottage as fast as I could, and went around to the back." He cleared his throat again, gave his unwieldly shoulders a shake, and looked down. "I—I looked in the back windows."

"Were the shades up?" asked Brett.

Cupping looked sadly at his pouting wife and answered, "Well, you see, that was what bothered me. Mrs. Cupping and I stayed in that cottage one weekend not so long ago, so it happened I knew where the bedroom was. And as I was going toward the cottage, after Mrs. Cupping had gone in by the front door, I saw Barclay pull down the shades of the bedroom windows. He jerked them down as if he was in a hurry and was afraid of being seen. That was why I hurried around to the back—I hoped I could get there before he could pull down the back shades and I could see—er—into the room."

He stopped and swallowed. Imogen turned up her hands with a helpless gesture and looked around as though inquiring of everybody present what in heaven's name a girl could do with such a nuisance of a husband. Daisy nearly giggled. The idea of Tracy Cupping in the role of Peeping Tom was almost too much for her equanimity.

"Could you see into the bedroom?" asked Brett.

"No, the back shades were down too by the time I got there. So I—er—stood there in the rain, and I don't mind telling you that I was feeling pretty bad. Then I saw that one of the other shades was up. It was a back window of the living room. I walked over and looked in."

Andrew galvanized to attention. "And you saw—?"

"I saw Eva Shale in the living room."

Eva was twisting her fingers together nervously. Her breath came quickly. "Please go on! What was I doing?"

"Why, ma'am, you were just sitting at a desk. I could see the side of your face. You were looking down at something."

"So you know she was in the living room!" Andrew exclaimed. "You know she wasn't in the bedroom with Barclay. Why didn't you tell us before?"

"Now, now, don't get yourself all excited, young man. All I know about Miss Shale is that she was in the cottage. I don't know whether she went into the bedroom or not. And I didn't tell you before because I don't like to own up that I've been thinking unjustly of my wife, sir, because my own peace of mind, believe it or not, means something to me."

"Do go on, Tracy!" Imogen exclaimed pettishly. "When you saw Eva in the cottage you knew you'd been an idiot to be following me."

"Of course I did, my dear, of course I did. I knew if there was another young lady in the cottage besides you it was perfectly all right. To be sure, I should have known it all the time. Certainly I should."

Daisy's impatience was getting the better of her. "What did you do then, Mr. Cupping? Did you go into the cottage?"

"No, madam, I did not. Perhaps you, being a lady, will not understand this, but I am sure the gentlemen will when I say that I was extremely eager not to have Mrs. Cupping know that I had entertained unworthy suspicions of her, even for a moment. I stood there by the window for a moment or two, undecided as to what I should do, then I realized that at any moment Miss Shale might look up and see me and ask why I seemed to be spying on her, so I moved along the side of the house out of sight of the window and stood there trying to think, till my teeth began to chatter with the cold and I knew I ought to be getting under a roof somewhere, so I walked around to the front of the cottage. There is a sort of pagoda opposite the cottage, across the road, and I took shelter there. I did not go into the cottage because I did not want Mrs. Cupping to know I had followed her, and I could think of no other reason to explain my presence in that neighborhood. I kept hoping the rain would hold up a little so I could get back to the clubhouse and make it appear as if I had come in from the golf course. After a while I saw a car drive up."

"What time was this?" asked Daisy.

"Madam, I assure you I was not thinking of the time. The car stopped in front of the cottage and Major Raymond went in. I assumed that he had called to take Mr. Barclay to the clubhouse for dinner and I expected at every moment to see them all come out. Presently the second car drove up and when I saw Mr. Allison, Mr. Foster, Mrs. Dillingham and the chauffeur get out, I supposed that Barclay had invited you all down for cocktails before dinner, and that my own presence, soaking wet and in a not very pleasant frame of mind, would be hardly welcome, so I walked back through the rain to the clubhouse. Upon arriving here, I received the shocking news that Barclay had been murdered while I stood outside." Cupping mopped his neck under his collar.

"I'm afraid I'm inexcusably stupid, Mr. Cupping," said Judith, as he paused, "but I still don't quite understand how you can be so sure that Imogen didn't—er—go through the bedroom and out of the cottage by a back door." She lifted her eyes to him in delicate mockery.

"Mrs. Garon, I have my wife's word!"

"Yes, of course, but you said awhile ago that you were positive she had left by the front door." Cupping fairly puffed with rage. "Although explaining myself further to a woman with your kind of mind is beneath me, Mrs. Garon, I shall attempt to answer you. My wife did not leave while I was standing in the pagoda, for if she had I should have seen her, and we have the testimony of Mr. Allison and the others that she was not there when they arrived. She reached the clubhouse some time before I did. It is therefore impossible not to accept the fact that she left the cottage by the front door while I was waiting at the back."

Andrew, grimly intent, interposed before Judith could answer. "Mr. Cupping, how long were you at the back of the cottage?"

"I have said, sir, that my agitation was such that I took no account of time."

"Then we'll put it this way. Mrs. Cupping says that while she sat in the foyer she saw Barclay and an unidentified woman go into Barclay's bedroom. So it must have been just after this that you saw Barclay pull down the bedroom shades. Then you walked around to the back of the house and saw Eva Shale alone in the living room."

Eva sat upright. A light of unspeakable gratitude broke over her face. She caught her lower lip between her teeth as though to force back a sob of relief.

They all started to attention. Daisy wanted to shout. Of course Andrew was going to be able to do it!

"Very well," Andrew was saying. "Now listen to this." Every syllable was like a hammer driving in the evidence more securely. "Mrs. Cupping says she left the house after she heard a body fall in the bedroom. If she left by the front door before you reached the pagoda, as it seems apparent that she did, then the woman who was in Barclay's bedroom could not have been Eva Shale."

Cupping scowled as though in profound consideration. "Well, it does look like that."

Judith rested her chin lightly on her hand and looked at Andrew as though he were a performing monkey.

"However, Andrew," Major Raymond reminded him after a moment, "it needn't necessarily have been like that."

"What do you mean?"

"Cupping says he left the window through which he was so conveniently observing Miss Shale, and waited awhile at the back of the house, not watching anything that might have been going on inside. All this time-testimony is very confusing. He doesn't remember how long he stood there. Isn't it conceivable that Barclay might have gone in and drawn the shades before he called Miss Shale? Then he might have gone back into the living room and asked her to help him with the drinks. They might then have crossed the passage to the bedroom together, when Imogen saw them."

Andrew's effort to control his anger had drawn a white line around his lips. "Cupping," he exclaimed, not quite steadily, "how was Eva dressed when you saw her?"

"Let me see, sir. Just as she is now, I believe. Anyway, something white."

"Are you sure," asked Major Raymond, "that she didn't have on the red slicker?"

Cupping thought for a moment. "I'm not sure. I didn't notice her clothes much."

"But why should she be wearing a raincoat in the house?" Andrew demanded.

"She may have been getting ready to leave for the mainland," answered the Major. "Barclay might have told her later why he wanted her to stay."

('The fat's in the fire now,' thought Daisy, looking up.)

"I didn't wear the raincoat in the house," Eva began, but Cupping had already caught at the Major's last remark.

"And why did Barclay want her to stay on the island?" he was asking. "And for that matter, Miss Shale, why did you want to leave?"

"You'll have both the answers in good time," growled the Major.

Cupping's face flushed. He struck the table with his fist. "And I insist, sir—"

His insistence was halted by a gesture from Brett. "We are getting away from the point, Mr. Cupping." He turned to the Major. "Major Raymond, Mr. Cupping could have waited at the back of the cottage, out of sight of the window, for only a very few minutes. According to your theory during this time Mr. Barclay called Miss Shale into the bedroom, she rose, put on her raincoat, accompanied him there, quarreled with him and killed him, and Mrs. Cupping, hearing the body fall, left the house, all while Mr. Cupping was standing irresolutely in the rain. If all this occurred, Miss Shale must have committed the murder after being in the bedroom only about thirty seconds. Mrs. Cupping, you saw Barclay go into the bedroom with a woman. How long after that was it that you heard the body fall?"

Imogen pursed up her lips in an effort at concentration. "Oh, I couldn't say, really. But I'm sure it was longer than a minute or two. That's such a very little while, isn't it?"

"Thank you, Mrs. Cupping." Brett glanced reassuringly at Andrew.

Andrew glanced triumphantly at Eva; her eyes were on Brett, with incredulous gratitude. Daisy hurried to press the advantage Brett had given them.

"Mr. Cupping," she put in, "you said that after you saw us get out of the car at Mr. Barclay's, you started back to the clubhouse. Did you see anyone on your way here?"

"Yes, certainly I did."

"Was it Imogen?"

"No, I don't think so. I don't know who it was and I'd rather not say when I'm not sure," he returned judicially. "I'm trying to be fair to everyone."

"Then could you tell us," Daisy persisted, "whether it was a man or a woman?"

"Well, ma'am, after all that has been told, I suppose I could. It was a woman."

"Where did you see her?"

"Well, ma'am, I came back by way of the bridle path, because the trees don't grow near the path and I'm always careful to avoid trees when there is lightning. Just before the path crosses the main road leading to the clubhouse, I could just make out a woman in front of me."

"Did you try to overtake her?" asked Daisy.

"No, ma'am, I didn't. I had decided that I'd been foolish enough for one night. I wanted to be alone."

"Did this woman come to the clubhouse?"

"Yes, ma'am, she did. But then I knew it couldn't be Mrs. Cupping, because she went around to the back end, towards the servants' quarters, and of course I thought nothing about it at the time, but now that my wife has reported there was a woman in his room I remember it, particularly when Mr. Allison told about the servants he said there was only one of the employees who couldn't give any alibi—"

There was a cry from Mrs. Penn. She jerked up from her chair, frantically wringing her hands.

"I don't know anything about it!" she cried. "I swear I don't know anything about it!"

Brett laid a quietening hand on her shoulder. "There's no need to be so frightened, Mrs. Penn. All we want you to do is tell us about the errand that took you outside."

But Mrs. Penn was sobbing wildly. "I don't know anything about it at all! I did go to see Mr. Barclay. But not to kill him! Mrs. Garon knows I went to see him. She'll tell you why. Mr. Allison—" she pointed an accusing finger at Judith—"it's time she told the truth!"

PART FOUR

CHAPTER FIFTEEN

IN SPITE of Brett's efforts to calm her, Mrs. Penn's sobs rose as relentlessly as the storm. Barclay's name and Judith's broke through her hysteria, and occasionally Eva's, but it was evident that it would be impossible to obtain any coherent statement from her yet. Daisy's eyes turned queryingly to Judith. She sat looking coolly at Mrs. Penn, but Daisy saw a faint quiver of the ebony cigarette-holder between her fingers. Ignoring their startled scrutiny, she tapped her cigarette on the end of the ash-stand.

"I'm sure I don't know what she means," she said acidly. "I haven't seen Mrs. Penn since four o'clock this afternoon."

Andrew, who had beckoned Felicia Meade from her place by the front desk, spoke in a low voice to Brett.

"Don't you think you might send her out? Miss Meade can give her some aspirin or ammonia or whatever it is they give people, and we can talk to her when she's quieter."

"Excellent," Brett approved. "Miss Meade, will you take care of Mrs. Penn?"

Daisy watched Mrs. Penn go toward the door with Felicia, and looked back at Brett, marveling at his self-control. Though he was plainly exasperated there was a flicker of amusement in his eyes as they met hers.

"Do women often get like that?" he asked her.

"Not all of them," she answered. "Sometimes their conniption fits are thrown when they can't think of any other way to cover up their own or somebody else's foolishness."

"I am afraid," said Brett, "that I find it more frightening than murder."

"That's what you're supposed to do," she retorted.

Mrs. Penn had about-faced suddenly on the threshold of the office. "Don't you worry, Miss Shale," she said clearly. "No matter what happens, don't worry."

She shut the door behind her. Eva looked quizzically at Brett Allison.

"Why's she so interested in me?"

Brett paused on his way back to the head of the table. "I suppose she knows a nice girl when she sees one. Won't you sit down, Mr. Cupping? Please don't follow Mrs. Penn—I'll have her brought back when she's calmer. I'm sure she'll tell us anything she knows about this, for Mrs. Penn is a thoroughly trustworthy woman. Meanwhile, it would be well if those of us who have not yet told where we were at the time of Mr. Barclay's death would do so now."

"Just put me down," said Judith, spreading out a petal of the crimson velvet flower at her girdle, "as another of those people who were out taking a walk."

"And where did you walk, ma'am?" inquired Cupping. "This is a very important matter, you know."

Judith smiled lazily. "Strange as it may seem," she returned, "I didn't go near Mr. Barclay's and I missed all the excitement. I walked over toward the other end of the island, and got caught in the rain."

"I suppose," suggested Brett, faintly sarcastic, "that you were alone?"

"In uninterrupted solitude, I regret to say. I was looking for Mr. Foster. You remember I promised to show you the oyster-reef markings, Mr. Foster?"

Foster nodded. "That's right. We were talking about red-fish," he explained to the others. "I said I might go fishing tomorrow evening, and Mrs. Garon offered to show me a place where there were some bull-reds."

"And where were you, Foster?" Brett asked.

Foster smiled at Judith. "I walked over toward the sand-dunes looking for the reef Mrs. Garon had told me about."

"You were looking for Judith," said Andrew, "and she was looking for you. Strange you didn't meet."

Foster made a deprecating gesture. "I'm not very familiar with the geography of Paradise Island. Mrs. Garon had described the position of the reef off the dunes, but I wasn't quite sure of it. I looked for it, but when the rain started I hurried back to the clubhouse."

"As I did," said Judith imperturbably. "Reached here out of breath, wet, tired and thoroughly uncomfortable."

"You don't look as if you were ever thoroughly uncomfortable in your life," said Daisy.

Brett smothered a smile. "And where were you, Mr. Dillingham?"

"I was down at the wharf where Eva's boat is, waiting for her."

"When did you last see Barclay?"

"Just before he went out with Eva. The Major and Barclay and I met here in the lounge for a conference."

Brett caught inquiringly at the last word. "A conference? About what?"

"I'd rather not say."

"Just a minute!" interrupted Tracy Cupping. "Allison, I don't think you should permit any hems and haws. Now, young man, what were you and Barclay talking about?"

"I really think you ought to make him tell, Mr. Allison," said Imogen in an aggrieved tone. "I think everybody ought to tell the whole truth. I'm sure I did."

"Major Raymond?" queried Brett. "Do you agree with Mr. Dillingham that this subject has no bearing on Barclay's death?"

"Frankly," answered the Major, "I am afraid it may have. But I agree with Andrew that it might better be discussed with the official authorities."

"Well, I don't!" thundered Cupping. "You were both eager enough to listen while I told all I knew about this affair, at the cost, sir, of very great embarrassment to myself and my wife! Indeed, sir—"

Brett had re-lit his pipe, and leaned back with ironic patience to wait till Cupping's bluster had spent itself. Eva put her hand on Daisy's arm uneasily.

"What's all this about, Daisy?"

"I think Mr. Allison will make them tell," Daisy whispered back. "Wait till that old walrus gets tired."

Silenced but not satisfied, Eva glanced at Andrew. He sat stubbornly, his eyes on Brett Allison. Daisy sighed, reflecting on the sad hopelessness of her convincing her grandson and her friend that she was right when she insisted that their suspicion of Brett was absurd. Cupping's oration was interrupted by the entrance of a servant.

"Warren is here, Mr. Allison, with the men from Mr. Barclay's boat."

"Thank you," said Brett. "Will you ask them to wait a minute or two?" As the man went out Brett took a key-ring from an envelope that had lain on the table by a bundle of Barclay's possessions. "While Major Raymond and Mr. Dillingham are making up their minds about their problem, and before we question Barclay's men, it might be wise to look over what we brought from the cottage. Major, you managed to open the suitcase. Will you see if one of these keys fits that green box?"

They all leaned forward with fascinated curiosity to watch the Major as one by one he tried the keys in the lock of the green lacquered box he had taken from Barclay's suitcase. It was a box about twenty by thirty inches in size, and four or five inches high, secured with a sturdy lock. Daisy watched the firelight glance on its bright surface as the Major moved it, carefully holding it by the corners lest he blur a revealing fingerprint. At last he raised the lid. Daisy stood up to be sure that her eyes had really seen what she thought they did—six green cylinders, and two stacks of thousand-dollar bills.

There was a general murmur of astonishment, then Brett spoke with composure that sounded strangely without astonishment.

"Will you count those, Major?"

The Major's fingers rapidly ran over the edges of the stacks, turning back the corner of each bill while his lips moved in an inaudible count. Ignoring the whispers of amazement that buzzed around her, Daisy glanced at Brett Allison. He was watching the pile of bills bending in the Major's hands; once or twice his eyes moved and rested for the tiniest fraction of a second on Eva Shale, but it was a glance gone so quickly that one doubted if he had looked at her at all. Eva was watching the Major with a bewildered look, her hands locked under her chin; half turned away from Andrew, she seemed to be deliberately avoiding any recognition of what he was so evidently trying to hold out to her. Daisy thought with a sickening sense of hopelessness that she had never seen anyone so determined to relinquish sympathy and fight her way alone.

"Seventy-five thousand in one pack," announced the Major, "and sixty thousand in the second. A hundred and thirty-five thousand dollars."

There was a long unanimous flutter. Brett sent Andrew a look that seemed to suggest that there was another shock waiting for him, and a faint quiver ran along his delicate hands as he took from the green lacquered box one of the stubby tubes. Foster smiled as if it were a play at which he was the audience and the others the actors.

"I shall take the liberty of opening one of these," Brett said clearly. "The others can wait for the police." He held up the cylinder for them all to see. They were watching tensely, their eyes wide as though in an effort to see faster than his hands could work. Judith's ebony cigarette-holder dropped on the floor with a click; nobody seemed to notice.

"As you see," Brett was telling them, "this cylinder, like the others in the box, is made of bamboo. I should judge its length is about eight inches. This little cork at one end closes the opening and is made air-tight with a substance that looks like shellac. One moment." He took out his pocket-knife and worked carefully around the cork. "Here we are. Now we can see what it was that Barclay took such pains to safeguard, along with his hundred and thirty-five thousand dollars."

He tapped the closed end of the tube. Twenty tiny packages rolled on the table. Major Raymond sprang up with a smothered exclamation; Andrew gripped Eva's shoulder as he bent over for a closer view; Judith drew back, her whole body stiffening as she stared at the tiny white objects lying on the table in front of Brett Allison. Even Daisy was speechless.

"O-ooooh!" breathed Imogen. "Look, Tracy! What *do* you suppose they are?"

Brett had unwrapped one of the little packets. He held out his hand toward Andrew, and then toward the Major, and they saw lying on his palm a tight compact little square of white crystals.

"Cocaine," said the Major hoarsely.

CHAPTER SIXTEEN

"Exactly," said Brett. "I suppose we may assume that these other bamboo tubes have the same contents as this. It's a valuable cargo to be carried in a Gladstone bag, but getting it into Pass Christian tomorrow morning would have been easy, for as it is already on Paradise Island it has been technically brought into the State of Mississippi."

"I'm just too excited!" Imogen clasped her hands. "Think of it! Please let me see it up close? Could I just taste a teeny-weeny bit of it?"

"Don't be a fool, Imogen!" admonished her husband. "Put it up quick, Allison! Good Lord, I knew we were silly to stay on this island tonight."

"Well, I'm sure it wasn't my fault that Mr. Barclay got himself stabbed," Imogen began sulkily, but the others were not interested in the connubial disagreements of the Cuppings, and Major Raymond broke in with a curt

"Are you going through the rest of this stuff, Allison?"

"Certainly."

"Then suppose you open this." The Major took a little chamois bag from the suitcase and passed it to him. Brett loosened the drawstring and turned the bag upside down.

A handful of unset diamonds danced on the table-top.

There was a frightened cry from Judith and a gasp from Eva; Andrew pushed back his chair and stood up, as though too amazed to keep still; Imogen's mouth popped open and her eyes dilated excitedly.

"But how perfectly *gorgeous*! What *do* you suppose he was going to do with them? Aren't they—"

"A very suggestive concentration of wealth," Brett observed dryly. "What else is there in the suitcase, Major?"

The Major lifted out ten flat tin boxes and a memorandum book. In response to a nod from Brett, he opened the notebook and looked hurriedly through its entries.

"Very cryptic notes," he said after a moment. "All dated, and all including references to the latitude and longitude of various places in the Gulf. As for these—" the Major took the top off one of the flat tins and said something under his breath.

"Opium?" Brett suggested.

The Major nodded. His face was set in lines of uncomprehending anger.

"And now," said Brett firmly, "I believe that we all have a right to hear the subject of the conference that you, Major, had with Barclay and Andrew Dillingham just before Barclay was murdered." His voice, though low as ever, had a compelling penetration.

Andrew's eyes met Major Raymond's.

"If you hadn't been so secretive in the first place," spluttered Cupping, "we might all have been spared a great deal, sir!"

"I think, Major," said Andrew, "that we should tell."

The Major nodded slowly. "I am afraid you're right, Andrew. That conference, Mr. Allison—"

The outer door burst open and Warren exploded into the room. Behind him were two stubborn-jawed men, their visored caps pulled down over their foreheads, who halted just inside the doorway and surveyed the scene in front of them with appraising beady eyes. Warren had come up to the table.

"These men insist on seeing you now, Mr. Allison," he said.

"Now is right," interrupted the taller of the two men at the door. "If somebody bumps off our boss we want to be in on the know, see?"

They came further into the room. Daisy looked them up and down and whispered to Eva.

"Thugs. Eighteen-carat."

Eva nodded. "But I think he can manage them."

As the two men neared the table Warren stepped quickly behind them and stood there as if on guard. Brett was standing. Foster had pushed his chair back from the table, as if ready to spring up at any minute.

"If you can find out what has been going on," Brett said quietly, addressing the man who had spoken, "we shall be very grateful. What's your name?"

"Smith."

"Smith?"

"Yeah. John Smith."

"Very well, John Smith. What's your job?"

"Run the engine on Mr. Barclay's boat."

"How did you know that Mr. Barclay had been murdered?" Brett asked.

"This fellow," answered John Smith, pointing to Warren, "just told us. That's how we know."

"Yeah," agreed the smaller man. "He wised us up. Now we want the lowdown."

"What's your name?"

"Pedro Artinza."

"Your job?"

"I'm Barclay's captain."

"Very interesting," said Brett. "Mr. Barclay was killed about 6:30 this evening. Where were you then?"

John Smith blinked. "Say, you, don't try to pin nothing on us. We been right on the boat since three o'clock. Ain't we, Pedro?"

Pedro looked at John Smith and then at Brett. "Sure."

"What were you doing?"

"Say, I don't know nothing about who give Mr. Barclay the works. I been tending to my own business. Ain't I, Pedro?"

Pedro, half a head shorter than John Smith, raised his eyelids.

"Sure. You and me both."

Brett's cool, faintly sardonic politeness did not waver.

"I see. How did you spend the evening?"

"Fixing a clogged gasoline line," said John Smith.

"How long did that take you?"

"Don't know."

"Did you start fixing it before dark?"

John Smith scowled at the irresistible corroding of Brett's questions.

"Yeah. Still good light when I went below. Wasn't it, Pedro?"

Pedro, whose fixed glumness seemed hardly to need justification of words, nodded.

"Sure. Plenty light."

"And when did you finish?"

"'Bout ten minutes before that guy there—" he nodded toward Warren—"come to tell us we're wanted up here."

"I see. And you, Pedro?"

Pedro, his head still half lowered, let his black beady eyes slide up toward Brett's.

"On deck, cleaning up."

"But after the storm broke?"

"In Barclay's cabin. Around inside. Cleaning up."

He shut his mouth fiercely. His eyes moved over Brett's slight figure with sneaky contempt. Brett's manner did not change. He regarded the two men for a moment without speaking.

There was a crack of thunder. The storm, which they had half forgotten in their tense concentration, flung itself against Paradise Island with wild fury, as though the elements were enraged that such a tiny fragment of earth should stand in their way. There was another swoop of lightning that ended in a crash. The rain lashed against the windows and the flames in the fireplace writhed and twisted. Imogen squeaked with fright and clung nervously to her husband, whose jaw was set defiantly as though in angry protest against the intrusion of elemental noise. Pedro and John Smith blinked uneasily at the pounding wrath outside; John Smith shifted from one foot to the other and cleared his throat, and Pedro batted his shifty eyes in disgust.

"Well, I suppose that's the wind-up, ain't it?" Pedro asked with an air of finality. "We don't know nothing and we didn't see nothing. It's too bad about the boss, but that's the breaks."

He looked at Brett. "There's nothing we can do here. You're no flatfoot and me and my pardner, we ain't talking." He made a gesture toward the door. "Let's scram."

Brett smiled at Pedro as though he found that small, swarthy gentleman more amusing than exasperating. "I represent the police, Pedro. When did you leave the mainland?"

"'S morning. Whenja think?" Pedro's mouth curled in sneering rebellion.

Brett laughed. "Very well. Neither of you understands this situation, I am afraid, but if you don't want to talk freely to me you may wait and talk to the officers in the morning."

"Maybe," said Pedro ominously. "And maybe not." For several seconds Brett silently studied the two boatmen in front of him. Several feet behind them stood Warren, nonchalantly looking at Barclay's men, at Brett, at the group around the table, as if he had been placed to guard the door and thought the whole business rather boresome. Daisy, whose initial apprehension at the threatening appearance of the two men had subsided, glanced at the others. Eva sat looking at Brett's profile as if with growing confidence in his ability to direct events. Now and then she turned to look at Andrew, who was listening eagerly to Barclay's henchmen. Major Raymond was watching Brett with a sort of astringent admiration. Judith was watching him too. There was something indefinable in her expression that suggested neither triumph nor dismay, but an emotion halfway between; she was like a cat watching a strange bird that may escape or may be caught or may, with sudden unsuspected agility, turn and peck out the eyes of its pursuer. Daisy frowned as she looked at Judith, wondering what might be buried in the crevices of Judith's sinuous mind, but before she could no more than wonder her attention was caught by Brett's next question.

"Did you know what your boat was carrying when you landed on this island?"

Pedro shook his head in sullen negation.

"Don't know nothing," said John Smith.

"Well, all right," said Brett, with the air of a man brushing aside a couple of malodorous insects. "We'll let it go at that. You don't know anything about it, you don't want to talk about it, you would like to go back to your boat. Very well. Warren, go out with these men and get one of the chauffeurs to drive them back to their ship."

"Righto," said Warren with alacrity. "Come along, men. This way."

He held the door open with a lordly gesture. Pedro and John Smith obediently ambled out, and when the door had closed on them Brett turned inquiringly to Major Raymond.

"What do you think of them, Major?"

"Dangerous," returned the Major laconically.

"I'm sorry," said Andrew, "that they came in just after you had spread out their cargo on the table. That little fellow got his eyes glued to that collection and couldn't get them off."

"I certainly expected trouble," Eva whispered to Daisy.

Daisy grinned. "It seemed harder on them than it did on us. I think they were glad to keep out of trouble."

Eva's hand tightened on Daisy's wrist. "Daisy—do you think it's possible—" she stopped and glanced at Brett, who was talking across the table to Major Raymond—"that one of them might have done it?"

"Quite possible, my dear." Daisy patted her hand.

"Oh, I don't know—I don't know!" came back Eva's whisper. "A woman killed him. At least—"

Andrew turned with triumphant severity. "But you've been cleared. We'll make the police see that. Eva—please don't get desperate now! There are so many ways it might have happened."

"Yes, but to everybody but you and Daisy I'm still one of those ways." She smiled valiantly. "I'm trying very hard, Andrew."

"I know you are. And keep trying." He smiled. "If you go to pieces I'm afraid I'll lose my head, too." She was about to answer when Cupping's voice rumbled above their whispers.

"As for me, sir, I think you were very foolish not to have that pair of desperadoes locked up! Extremely shortsighted it was, Mr. Allison! The epitome of carelessness, sir! What assurance have you that they will not take a chance in spite of the storm and make their getaway while we all sit here dozing? Do you realize that a man has been murdered, sir? And that one of those footpads probably did it? And you treat them like guests at a dinner-party and let them get away, sir!"

He thumped the table. Imogen tittered. Brett answered with a long-suffering sigh.

"I hardly think your fears will be justified, Mr. Cupping. They know their boat would be swamped in this storm. We may take them in custody later on, if the storm lets up."

"There now, Tracy. So it's perfectly all right!" Imogen chirped, patting his knee.

"*Quite* all right," said Judith with venomous softness, to which Brett paid no attention. Warren had come in, and Brett was speaking to him.

"Go right down to the cottage and put two more men there. Give them shotguns. Then on your way back, go to the radio room and tell Beans to wire the police that Barclay's men are on the island. Give their names. Hurry."

Warren nodded and went off. Brett turned back to the job ahead of him.

"Mr. Dillingham, we want to learn what it was you and Major Raymond discussed with Barclay this afternoon."

Andrew looked gravely at the Major. "He's right, Major. After seeing this—" he indicated the bamboo tubes and the tins of opium—"we've got plenty of questions to ask."

"And," put in Foster, "a few to answer."

Cupping nodded a vigorous agreement. Andrew's eyes narrowed at Foster.

"Just what," he asked, "do you mean by that remark?"

"I mean," said Foster, "that some time ago you said the Major and Barclay were associated in business. Is this the business?"

"You fool!" Andrew was leaning over the table as if he would have liked to grab Foster by the throat. Daisy put her hand on his arm. Nobody else moved.

The Major spoke. "Don't get excited, either of you," he warned, and turned to Foster. "We will be very glad to answer your questions later on, Mr. Foster." His words came slowly; he looked like a man who has been whipped. "But I'll ask your permission, Mr. Allison, to postpone explaining my association with Barclay until I have had a chance to see if anyone else knows about Barclay's having this stuff in his possession. Mrs. Penn made a very puzzling statement before she broke down, about her having been in Barclay's cottage on an as yet unrevealed errand just before he was killed. Could we ask her to explain herself now?"

"It might be very intriguing," Judith murmured languidly.

"It might be, Mrs. Garon," said Brett coolly. "I'll speak to Mrs. Penn. Pardon me a moment." He bowed and walked over to the office.

There was a bubble of talk. Without the focus of Brett Allison's presence the groups seemed to disintegrate into eight scared people more eager for self-defense than for justice. Imogen was chattering, her golden head bobbing first at Cupping and then at Judith, neither of whom seemed interested, for Cupping was delivering oratorical opinions to Foster, and Judith, leaning back with lazy nonchalance, was giving Imogen only a faint and sarcastic attention. Such detachment as Judith's seemed to Daisy to be too careful to be real: her right hand, again dangling her cigarette-holder, was too relaxed; her left, caressing the scarlet flower at her girdle, had now and then a suggestion of a tremor. Daisy laced her fingers across her knee and looked at Judith, drooping and dramatic, and Daisy guessed that Judith dreaded something that had not yet been told. Linton Barclay was dead in his ship-cottage, and Judith was afraid.

Daisy looked at the glitter of Barclay's diamonds on the table and those little tubes and tins, shrieking without voices that Linton Barclay, chairman of the citizens' commission to halt the drug traffic, had been smiling over secrets of his own. And only this morning Eva Shale had received a strange letter.

She looked at Eva, who was quietly smoking a cigarette. Andrew and the Major had stepped away from the table and beckoned to Daisy to join them. Daisy went over. The Major was speaking with bitter grimness.

"Do you think this means what it seems to mean—that Barclay was the man we were looking for?"

"Very likely," she retorted. "He fits my specifications."

"If he was, I'm glad he met the kind of death he did."

Daisy looked at the Major. His face was white and hard. She guessed that he was remembering his son. Suddenly Daisy wondered if the Major could have stumbled upon this knowledge when he went to Barclay's cottage; if he had, she knew he would have killed Barclay as he would have a mad dog. The Major was speaking to Andrew.

"It all fits in. He let us arrest a minor agent now and then, who could tell us nothing. Whenever we seemed about to make an important discovery, we always just missed it. Barclay got all the Federal reports. He always gave warning just in time. But he was clever. We went as far as he dared to let us go, and I never once suspected him."

"Nor I," said Andrew. He thrust his hands viciously into his pockets. "And Barclay—*Barclay* nearly had us arresting Eva Shale!"

Daisy put a hand on the Major's arm and another on Andrew's. "Barclay's dead," she reminded them. "He got what he deserved."

"You're mighty right he did," said Andrew, but the Major seemed hardly to have heard her.

"I'd like to think," he said.

Daisy went back to the table and sat down, trying to reason her way through black confusion.

Eva had told them of an anonymous letter about dope-smuggling. Linton Barclay's bag had held a locked box of opium and cocaine. Eva had been found alone in the house with Barclay's body. Eva's origin and the source of Eva's income were riddles that Eva had said she could not answer.

Daisy roused herself and looked at Eva—her clear, challenging eyes, her firm young profile, her quiet sincerity. Fiercely' Daisy recognized again her own certainty that Eva was innocent of this or any other crime. She looked at Andrew's determined mouth as he talked to the Major. Her eyes met Eva's and they both smiled.

The office door opened and Brett came in with Mrs. Penn.

Mrs. Penn was completely at ease now. The cold force of Brett's personality seemed somehow to have dispelled her hysteria. Foster said something under his breath to Cupping and Cupping shook his head. Judith was reaching for another cigarette. Eva studied Mrs. Penn with puzzled attention. Andrew took his chair and the Major came over from the fireplace. They all waited for Brett to speak.

"Mrs. Penn," he said to them, "is going to tell us why she went to Linton Barclay's cottage tonight. Before she begins, I want to assure the rest of you that Mrs. Penn is fundamentally an honest woman. I have known her for many years, and while none of us is beyond temptation, what Mrs. Penn has to tell us will show—"

There was a scream from behind the desk. They exclaimed and started up. Felicia Meade was standing, her hands fluttering. Brett and Foster started toward her.

"What happened?" Andrew exclaimed.

Brett caught the girl's disjointed phrases and answered over his shoulder.

"Warren just called from the radio room. He says the radio set has been wrecked, and Beans is either dead or unconscious."

CHAPTER SEVENTEEN

DAISY breathed a deep sigh of relief as Beans opened his eyes and felt for the lump on his head. "Phew!" he said. "Who threw that brick?"

"You may have a heart of gold, young man," said Daisy, "but you've got a head of iron. No, lie still." She pushed him down and turned to McPherson. "He's all right now. Tell the others to come in."

Brett entered first, opening the gate in the office rail with his accustomed inscrutable courtesy. "Thank you, Mrs. Dillingham. The rest of you may come in if you like."

"Oh, the poor little boy!" cooed Imogen behind him. She clung to Cupping as to a rock in a weary land. Over her head he was glaring vengefully at everybody in sight, particularly Judith, who stood leaning against the door-post, serenely lovely as ever in her black satin sheath, smiling at Foster. Eva and Andrew came close to Beans' improvised cot, and Beans grinned up at her.

"Gee, Miss Shale, ain't I a bust? What happened, Mr. Allison?"

"That's what we wanted to ask you. Somebody wrecked your radio room, and tried to wreck you too. Do you remember anything about it?"

Beans wiggled one foot and then the other, and apparently satisfied that they were both in working order, he answered,

"Well, I'm just sitting out there, see? Just gotta message from The New Orleans Creole asking me if somebody had really bumped off Mr. Barclay, on account they wanted to put a piece in the paper, and I'm thinking I'll come down here and ask if it's all right to tell 'em yes, when I hears a noise behind me and before I can turn around out goes the lights, and that's all I know till I wakes up and Mrs. Dillingham says I gotta gold heart."

McPherson was holding a flask. "Here, laddie, drink this."

"Sure." Beans gave a mighty gulp and winked at Daisy. "Any time anybody hits me on the head McPherson can stand by with the cognac. Best I had since I made that trip to Havana."

"Put the flask in your pocket," said Brett smiling. "You might need it. Whoever knocked you out did a pretty good job of wrecking the plant—the aerial is down and all the tubes broken."

"They did a pretty swell job with me too." Beans' fingers warily felt around the bandages that swathed his head.

"You'd better get some rest in here, then. We'll talk about this later."

Beans grinned and held up his flask. "Okay, Mr. Allison. Here's bumps." He motioned to Warren. "Where do you keep your rod?"

"Rod?" Warren repeated.

"Your gun. Where is it? I don't feel so safe."

"In the drawer." Warren indicated the front desk. "But it's loaded. Be careful."

Beans winked. "Sure. Just wanted to know in case—"

Warren smiled as Beans paused expressively. He went back to the table, where the others were gathered. Imogen was babbling with scared shrillness.

"That poor boy! Somebody wants to kill all of us—I don't think we'll ever get off this island alive, do you, Tracy? It's a miracle he wasn't killed right away."

"Not that young man," said Daisy dryly. "He has a head like a gossip's heart. Flint."

"Suppose we go on," Foster was urging. "Beans isn't badly hurt, and we've still several points to clear up."

"Several points," Andrew agreed curtly. "And one of them is the coincidence in your sending that message and telling Beans to wait for an answer and having him get a rap on the head instead."

Foster smiled politely. "Yes, that is a coincidence. But only a coincidence, Mr. Dillingham."

"We'll see. It's early yet."

Foster looked at his watch and sighed. "So it is. Only a little after eleven."

Daisy caught sight of Mrs. Penn, who stood by Brett Allison's chair, a quiet and curiously dignified figure, and Daisy felt a sudden urge of sympathy. She resolved that Mrs. Penn should be kept waiting no longer.

"Let's go back to where we were," she suggested. "Mrs. Penn had something to tell us."

"You are ready to talk to us, Mrs. Penn?" Brett asked kindly.

"Yes, Mr. Allison, I'm ready." Mrs. Penn's manner had lost the jerkiness that had accompanied her breakdown, and she stood facing the guests of Paradise Island with square-jawed resolve. They met her gaze with characteristic varieties of attention—Cupping with bellicose defiance, Imogen fluttering as though she had forgotten what was trumps and had not the courage to ask; Major Raymond stern and attentive; Judith looked on with a sardonic tilt of the eyebrows that did not hide from Daisy the fact that she was apprehensive of what might be coming. Foster's suave assurance seemed unshaken. Eva and Andrew were frankly impatient; Andrew looked from Eva to Mrs. Penn as though defying the housekeeper to pile on another accusation.

Mrs. Penn did not sit down. She looked like a woman ready to make a speech, Daisy thought.

But she waited quietly for Brett's questions, which came only after a slow scrutiny not only of his club executive but of the martial array of his guests. As his eyes rested on each of them in turn their interest seemed abruptly to switch from Mrs. Penn and to gather upon him as the nucleus of all their questionings; Daisy thought she had never been confronted by such an imperative personality.

"Then it was you, Mrs. Penn," he said at length, "who returned to the clubhouse just ahead of Mr. Cupping?"

"Yes, it was."

Mrs. Penn spoke firmly, as though a sane decision had gripped her and was upholding her resolve to speak without regard for the consequences.

"Where had you been?" he asked.

"At Mr. Barclay's cottage."

"Why did you go there?"

"To get paid for being a thief."

An electric quiver ran around the circle. "A thief?" repeated Brett.

"Yes, a thief."

"Mrs. Penn," he said to her, "it will be necessary for you to tell us everything that happened between you and Mr. Barclay this evening."

"I know it," she said. "That's exactly what I am going to tell you." She looked steadily at him. He stood facing her, and their eyes were nearly on a level. "This afternoon I inspected the rooms as I always do. When I knocked on Mrs. Garon's door she said she was dressing, so I called through the door and asked if there was anything she wanted. She told me to come in."

"What time was this?"

"It must have been just after two o'clock, because that's the usual hour for the inspection."

They had all looked at Judith. Her lips were parted with a half-sneering, half-angry expression of denial. "If this detail is of any interest, Mr. Allison, I did call Mrs. Penn inside. Something had lodged at the back of one of the dresser drawers, and I asked her to help me open it."

"I'm sorry, Mrs. Garon," said Mrs. Penn inexorably, "but we're going to have the truth."

Brett's eyes turned full upon Judith with a reproof that chilled even her sardonic remonstrance. "Mrs. Garon, please let Mrs. Penn give us her version of what happened today. When she is finished, we shall be glad to hear you."

"Right!" thundered Cupping. "We've been polite to too many liars already."

"Mr. Cupping, will you be good enough not to interrupt? Very well, Mrs. Penn."

"Mrs. Garon," said the housekeeper with poisoned emphasis, "asked me if I wanted to make a thousand dollars. I told her I certainly did, because I need the money. I have a daughter who is sick in the East. She needs lots of attention, and I've already spent all the money I could get."

"Go on."

"Mrs. Garon told me to go into Miss Eva Shale's room and look in her suitcase and handbag and in the bureau drawers and get any letters I found and bring them to her. She told me if I did this without telling anybody she would give me a thousand dollars. I'm speaking the truth, and may God forgive me, Mr. Allison, but I said I would."

"You damned liar," said Judith with low fury.

Daisy clucked.

Eva had drawn back with a look of unbelieving horror. "Please go on!" she cried. "Did you go into my room?"

"Yes, Miss Shale, I did, and I've been well punished for it tonight."

Brett spoke evenly. "Did you find any letters, Mrs. Penn?"

"Yes, sir, I found three. I gave them to Mrs. Garon. She read them all and kept one and told me I could put the other two back."

"So that's where it went!" exclaimed Andrew. "Miss Shale said she had lost an important letter." Mrs. Penn nodded.

"Did you read the letters?" asked Daisy.

"No, I didn't. There was one in a blue envelope, and one gray and one white, with Miss Shale's name typewritten. That was the one Mrs. Garon kept."

"That's the letter," exclaimed Eva. "What do you know about it, Judith?"

Judith shrugged. "I've told you I don't know what she's talking about. I haven't the faintest interest in your correspondence, my dear."

('She holds herself well,' Daisy reflected. 'Brass backbone.')

Mrs. Penn's whole figure seemed to dilate. "Mr. Allison, I'm speaking the truth. Mrs. Garon kept that letter."

"And gave you," said Brett, "a thousand dollars?"

"No, she gave me a note to Mr. Barclay, telling me he would give me the money. She told me not to tell him what it was for. Just to give him the note." (Pieces of the puzzle tumbled together in Daisy's mind. But they didn't fit. 'Not to tell him what it was for. *Not* to tell him.' Strange, thought Daisy.)

"Is that why you went to Mr. Barclay's?" asked Brett.

"That's the reason. When I got there I was frightened. I knew I was doing wrong. I walked around to the back door. I was very nervous, and I saw someone in the shrubbery by the inlet. So I walked off a little way and then came back."

"This person you saw—who was it?"

"I don't know. I thought it was a woman. It was quite dark then, you see, and the shrubs are very thick between the back of the cottage and the road that leads down to the beach. I couldn't see very well. At any rate, I walked off a little way, and when I came back I didn't see anyone, and I went in by the back door and went through the little door from the passage that opens into Mr. Barclay's room. The door to his room was ajar, and I saw that he was mixing a drink. I called, very softly, for I didn't know whether or not this other person I had seen was in the cottage, and he came to the door and whispered to me to come in. I showed him Mrs. Garon's note. He read it and said, 'All right, tell her I hope she's lucky.' He gave me the money and held the door open. He whispered, 'Good night,' and I went out. He had taken the money out of a wallet that was lying on his dresser."

Mrs. Penn's lips closed in a thin line on the last word. She gave Judith a malevolent look, opened her clenched hand.

"There's the proof," she added, and threw a crumpled thousand-dollar bill on the table.

Brett picked up the bill and handed it to the Major, who took it gravely and unlocked the case, laying Mrs. Penn's bill alongside of the others.

"Thank you, Mrs. Penn," said Brett, and his voice was strangely gentle, without a suggestion of reproach. "Is that all?"

"Oh, I don't know—I'm so horribly ashamed and sorry." She turned from Brett and faced the others. "You don't know me," she went on more calmly, "except as an employee here. You can't understand what I've done by robbing a guest of this hotel, because you don't know how good Mr. Allison has been to me. He's the finest, kindest man I've ever known. He has lent me hundreds of dollars since my daughter was taken ill, and has let me spend weeks with her. He has been—"

"We needn't go into that, Mrs. Penn," said Brett, and Daisy had a feeling that he had withdrawn himself far away from them. "A single offense in a lifetime is very little. Most of us have sinned oftener and far more grievously than you." He smiled. "Don't you think it would be easier for you simply to tell us what happened tonight?"

"Very well, Mr. Allison." Mrs. Penn drew a long breath. "I took the long way back to the clubhouse. For awhile I simply walked around in the rain, thinking. I made up my mind to tell Miss Shale what I had done and return the money to Mrs. Garon."

"You say you came back 'the long way'?" asked Brett. "Tell us just what way you came."

"As I said, I simply walked around for some minutes—across the end of the golf course. I was wet to the skin before I had finally made up my mind to tell Miss Shale everything. Then I walked across the golf course and took the road leading to the clubhouse, and suddenly I saw a man behind me. I thought he was following me. I was frightened. I came on as fast as I could. I suppose he was Mr. Cupping. I went on to my room intending to go straight to Mrs. Garon and give back the money, and insist that she give me Miss Shale's letter. I was changing my clothes when the phone rang and Mr. McPherson told me Mr. Barclay had been murdered. I was horrified. Mrs. Garon had me in a trap. I remembered everything I had ever heard about circumstantial evidence. I knew I was in for trouble."

"Surely not when you can make up such fascinating stories," Judith murmured.

Brett pointed to the green lacquered box. "Did you see this?"

"No, I did not."

"Did you see this bag?" he indicated the Gladstone.

"It was on his luggage-rack, closed."

"Mrs. Penn," said Brett, "you have told a very clear story. But did you do anything in Mr. Barclay's room but hand him Mrs. Garon's note and take the money from him? Think very carefully, because the police will look for fingerprints in that room—or did you wear gloves?"

Mrs. Penn shook her head. "No, I didn't wear gloves."

"Did you do anything besides what you have told us?"

"Let me see." Mrs. Penn bent her head in thought. "I'm really so upset it's hard to remember everything, Mr. Allison." She looked at Major Raymond, who was rummaging in the bundle in which they had wrapped Barclay's miscellaneous possessions.

"O, yes—I did touch something else. He asked me to bring him his cane, that one on the table. It was lying on the bed."

Brett took up the cane, holding it carefully by its bottom end. "This cane?" he asked. He turned it and examined it thoughtfully. "What did he do with it?"

"Nothing, sir. He just said 'Thank you,' and put it on the little table where he had the fruit juice and the whisky. I told you that he was mixing a drink."

"He simply took the cane from you and laid it on the table? He still whispered?"

"Yes, Mr. Allison. And he told me to be quiet. He never raised his voice."

"I see. It seemed a simple thing to ask you to do. But the reason I am interested in this cane is that it was lying on the floor by Mr. Barclay's body. Do you remember seeing it, Mrs. Dillingham?"

"Yes. It was lying there—let me see." Daisy frowned and tried to remember. "The handle was away from the body, and the bottom end, the end you are holding, was pointing toward the body. Is that right?"

"Just a minute, Mrs. Penn. Foster, do you remember seeing this cane in Mr. Barclay's room?"

Foster nodded. "Yes, I remember. On the floor."

"Do you recall it, Major? And how it was lying?"

"Yes—handle away from the body."

Brett laid the cane on the table and turned again to Mrs. Penn, who had sunk into her chair as though her confession had exhausted her. "Thank you very much, Mrs. Penn. What is it, Mrs. Garon?"

When Judith spoke her luscious voice was rasped with anger. "Don't you think it's about time you gave me a chance to say that this woman is lying, that I have never spoken to her in my life except to ask her to send me a maid or something equally innocuous, and that while she may have searched Eva Shale's room, for all I know, she did not do it at my suggestion?" Judith snapped a flame from her onyx lighter, touched it to her cigarette and blew out a thin sarcastic line of smoke. "That's all."

"You say, Mrs. Garon," said Brett imperturbably, "you did not send Mrs. Penn to Miss Shale's room to look for a letter?"

"Certainly not."

"But she did get a thousand dollars from somewhere."

"And you did send her for it, Mrs. Garon," said Major Raymond with crisp distinctness. He held out a card. "I looked for this among the things we brought back from Barclay's. It was in the pocket of his jacket."

Judith glanced at it carelessly as the Major handed the card to Brett.

"This is your calling card, Mrs. Garon," Brett told her. "And on the back—" he turned it over—"is written 'Give this woman a thousand dollars cash. Will tell you about it later. Judith.'"

Judith sighed patiently. "I did write that. The storm was about to break, there was a long vacant evening ahead, and I happen to be fond of playing roulette. I had very little cash with me and I sent this woman to Mr. Barclay with this note, which is nothing more incriminating than a request for him to lend me some money. But for his death the thousand dollars would probably have been lost by now at your own roulette tables. He knew why I wanted it. Mrs. Penn told you he wished me good luck. In the shock I received when I heard of his murder I forgot all about it, and I suppose Mrs. Penn intended to keep the money, and but for Mr. Cupping's having seen her on her way from the cottage she would probably have said nothing."

"She's not telling the truth, Mr. Allison," said Mrs. Penn with fierce calmness.

Judith carefully flicked an ash-speck from her black satin lap. "I should like to remind you, Mr. Allison, that Mrs. Penn was in Mr. Barclay's cottage about the time he was murdered. Mr. Barclay was an old and dear friend of mine, and I should like very much to see whoever killed him tried and sentenced, but I will not be implicated in this affair because Mrs. Penn chooses to drag my name into her explanation of why she happens to be carrying around a thousand dollars."

"One moment, Mrs. Garon." Brett laid her card on the table by Barclay's cane. "For the time being it is sufficient to note that you deny everything that Mrs. Penn has said except that you did send her to Barclay's to get the thousand dollars."

"And also," said Eva rebelliously, "I'd like to know what she wanted with my letter."

"I'm sorry, Miss Shale. But Mrs. Garon says she hasn't got your letter, and I have no right to search her room."

"Just a minute," Judith exclaimed. "I'd like to ask Mrs. Penn one question more. Mrs. Penn, you didn't wear a raincoat—a red raincoat—to the cottage?"

Mrs. Penn bit her lip as if to bite back an angry retort. "I did not," she returned steadily. "If I had, Mr. Cupping would have told you."

"She didn't have on anything red when I saw her," Cupping inserted. "At least, I don't think so. It was dark."

Judith smiled. "But it's possible, isn't it, that Mrs. Penn might have taken a raincoat from the cloakroom—might have noticed a button missing—and might have thought it wiser to throw away the coat and walk back in the rain than to answer for the missing button?"

Mrs. Penn's eyes fairly blazed. "I might have," she answered with quivering fury, "but I didn't."

"So you say." Judith examined a speck on her pink fingertip.

Daisy wanted to slap her. She glanced at Brett, wondering how long he would let Judith go on. But Brett, without losing a whit of his easy authority, had taken up the malacca cane.

"Mrs. Garon, will you be good enough to let me question Mrs. Penn? This cane, Mrs. Penn—are you sure it was this cane Barclay asked you for?"

Mrs. Penn turned away from Judith with evident relief. "I'm sure it was, Mr. Allison."

"And you are sure he laid it on the table alongside of the whisky?"

"Yes, I'm sure."

(The cane, the cane! Daisy wondered what he was trying to prove.)

"Mr. Allison!" came Warren's voice from where he stood by a window. "The men from Mr. Barclay's boat are coming back."

Brett smiled. "I thought they might. Tell them to wait outside."

There was a pounding on the door. Warren turned from the window and crossed over to slip the latch. As the bolt slid from under his hand the door burst violently open and Pedro, shoving him aside, whipped out two murderous-looking automatics.

"Stick 'em up—everybody!"

PART FIVE

CHAPTER EIGHTEEN

THERE was a shriek from Imogen and the noise of a chair toppling over as Andrew leaped to his feet; Eva had sprung behind her chair as though with a wild idea that placing it between herself and Pedro might give her some protection; Foster gave an exclamation of fury and Cupping, his hands high, spluttered an incoherent threat as Judith in a shrill, horrified voice cried out, "You can't do this!"

"The hell we can't," retorted John Smith, who had edged into the room behind Pedro, slamming the door with his foot while his hands were occupied in leveling his pistols. "Get over to the wall and stay there. Step quick, now, like you meant it! You ain't gonna hang any murder on us, smart guys. Get over there." So this, thought Daisy, moving obediently backward, was what a stickup was like. Something to tell her grandchildren.

She glanced at Brett. He was quietly backing toward the sofa where he had flung his raincoat, his eyes measuring the distance between himself and the gun that was in the raincoat pocket. He still held the green cane. Andrew had one arm around Eva, angrily obeying Major Raymond's low command not to leap at Pedro. Mrs. Penn, stiff with fright, stood against the wall. Imogen was whimpering.

"Stay away from this table," ordered John Smith. "Anybody makes a move gets killed, hear me? Go on, Pedro."

Pedro was staring at Brett, his eyes almost glassy. "Drop that stick!" he commanded. "Drop it, y'hear?"

Brett glanced at the cane and laid it on a chair. Daisy could see drops of sweat on Pedro's forehead. He muttered a low imprecation.

His eyes still on Brett, Pedro warily tucked his guns under his arms and began sweeping the contents of Barclay's suitcase into an oilskin bag. For an instant there was a hysterical silence, broken only by the scrape of the green box along the table-top. John Smith's gun swept slow half-circles across the group. He spoke without turning.

"Ready, Pedro?"

"Yeah."

"Where's that rope? All right, you. We're gonna tie you up in here. Somebody'll come along in the morning. And we want you to know that if there's a dizzy move, somebody takes on weight—dead weight. Step up here." He held out the rope.

"Not me!" screamed Imogen. "Don't you dare touch me! I can't be tied up! Mr. Allison, tell them I can't be tied! I knew I was going to get murdered tonight! I knew—Ohhhhhhhhh—" her words were lost in a sobbing shriek.

"Quit yapping, you." John Smith pointed to Eva. "Grab that other dame too, Pedro."

"Don't touch that lady," Brett ordered. Except for his violent start when Pedro burst into the room he had kept himself under rigid control; still moving backward, he had nearly reached the sofa where his raincoat with its hidden pistol was lying.

Pedro leaped toward him. "We ain't gonna hurt her. Now all step up and be quick about it or we'll get nasty."

"Grab air, you monkeys!"

John Smith's arms went up. Pedro snarled and turned toward the voice. There was a shot, and Imogen shrieked again as Pedro tumbled head foremost and lay in a heap on the rug. With a yell John Smith leaped toward him and at the same instant another shot came from the corner.

"Drop those guns, you! Snap into it! That last one was a warning. The next one slaps home and you sprout wings."

John Smith had lowered his guns when Pedro crumpled up, but he had recovered his first fright and seemed about to fire, but a muzzle pressed against his ribs and a cool stern voice spoke at his elbow. "Drop them, John Smith," it said. The guns clattered to the floor.

"Thanks, Beans," Brett added.

They started and glanced toward the desk, where Beans was climbing over the office-rail with monkeyish agility—Beans, with his bloody bandage around his head and Warren's gun in his hand, and all the glory of a conquering hero in his voice as he yelled,

"Somebody grab that mug! Lord, did I get even for that rap on the dome? Get him, Mister Dillingham! These are the boys gave me my lumps. Say, ain't this swell?"

He was at the table now, marching grandly if unsteadily over to where Andrew and the Major, protected by Brett's gun, were forcing John Smith against the wall. Beans pranced on tiptoe across Pedro's crumpled person. His face was white and his lips pale, but he reeked with joyous bravado.

"Maybe that big ape can talk now. If he can't, I'll send him after his little playmate," he announced. Then he reached out for a chair and missed.

Beans had fainted.

CHAPTER NINETEEN

BEANS shook his head and slowly the lids fluttered back from his impudent brown eyes. He cocked his bandaged head on one side.

"You here again?" he asked, looking up at Daisy. "You too, Miss Shale? I know where I am, all right, but what happened after the lights went out?"

"You didn't miss much," Eva assured him. "John Smith's locked up in the garage."

"Good. Say, I didn't faint, did I, Miss Shale?" Beans asked unbelievingly. "Somebody musta blasted me." He felt around for bullet holes.

Eva smiled. "No, you fainted. But you did a good job first."

"And now," Daisy suggested, "if you feel all right, you'd better go outside."

They were in Warren's bedroom, just off the lounge. Daisy could see McPherson's broad back as he bent over the recumbent figure of Pedro, who lay on a cot near the window. Beans struggled to his feet and Eva half supported him to the door. As they went out, Daisy saw him look back toward Pedro and heard him whisper to Eva, "Ain't that guy dead yet?"

Daisy crossed to the bed and watched the blunt, deft fingers of the golf pro as he dressed the wound in Pedro's side. Pedro cursed weakly in Mexican Spanish, groaned and then was still.

"I'm not much of a doctor, ma'am," McPherson apologized, "and we've got no anesthetic. I can't find the bullet."

"Serves him right. He ought to suffer some," said Daisy, less gentle than the golf pro, for she was preoccupied. She had followed Warren and McPherson when they carried Pedro into the room, not because she had any hope of aiding Pedro by her ministrations but because she had a nebulous idea that possibly, if Pedro could be induced to talk, he might offer her some hint by which she could clarify the confusion that faced her. For Daisy knew that behind her, in the lounge room, there waited a tragedy more poignant than Pedro's.

McPherson reached out to take the bandage she was holding for him. "Well, there's naught we can do for him now but see what the morning will bring. Thanks for your help, ma'am."

Daisy almost chuckled. For McPherson was impressed by the manner in which she had volunteered to help him with the wounded man. She knew they were friends now.

"Do you think he can talk?" she asked.

Pedro's eyes moved slowly around to her. "Hell, I can talk, grandma. Who are you?"

She answered soothingly. "Is there something I can get you?"

Pedro gave her a grin that but for its weakness would have been impudent. "Sure. A drink. You don't carry a flask, do you, grandma?"

"No, I don't. But we can get you a drink, eh, Mr. McPherson?"

"Right away, Mrs. Dillingham." McPherson got up from his knees and went out, leaving her alone with Pedro. Pedro was pale under his swarthiness, and bloody; probably, Daisy thought with an effort at self-reproach, he was in great pain, but Pedro as an individual did not matter greatly just now, while Pedro as a possible source of aid in what confronted her seemed desperately vital. He must be made not only comfortable but talkative.

She watched in silence while Pedro lay with his eyes shut, waiting for McPherson to bring the whiskey. He was breathing heavily. She wondered if it was possible that he knew what she had seen out there. But no—he was not the sort to notice details like that. He had come for Barclay's dope and cash and diamonds, not to look for a subtle answer to a crude problem.

McPherson returned with a flask of whiskey and raised Pedro's head to give him a drink. Pedro gulped and sank back; McPherson turned to Daisy.

"Don't you want to go out with the others, Mrs. Dillingham? There's little you can do."

She drew him aside, toward the door. "Would you mind leaving him with me for a few minutes? I want to talk to him."

McPherson glanced uneasily toward the cot.

"Well, ma'am—I suppose we may say he's harmless—"

"I'm perfectly harmless myself, Mr. McPherson, and he knows it. White-haired old ladies don't offer much temptation even to gangsters. I want to talk to him, and I want to do it alone."

"Very well, ma'am. I suppose you know what's right. And I'll be just beyond the door, in the office. You'll call if you need me?"

His sudden tractability was a marvel. Daisy smiled.

"Yes, I'll call. Thanks. You've been a great help." He gave another shake of his head toward Pedro and reluctantly left her. Daisy approached the cot and sat down, the flask of whiskey in her hand.

"Do you want another drink, Pedro?"

His eyes opened. "Sure, grandma."

"Here, then. Don't try to sit up. I'll raise you." He gulped again and fell back heavily. Daisy set the flask on the floor and bent over him. "You've been very badly hurt," she said.

"Yeah." His voice was weak but vehement. "That kid sure gave me the works. But I'm tough. I'm not going out."

"I hope not. But I'm afraid you'll be a long time getting well."

"Yeah. Ain't it hell, granny?" He made an angry movement, and groaned. "My God—he did give it to me bad, at that."

With an effort, Daisy forbade herself to be mawkish.

Pedro was hurt; perhaps Pedro was going to die; but she had no time to spare him. There were stronger forces claiming her than pity for a wounded gangster. She spoke firmly.

"Pedro, I want you to talk to me."

"I—ain't talking. If I do—they'll say I did it."

"Did what?"

"Bumped off the boss."

"And you didn't?"

"No—I—didn't." Pedro stopped for breath and went on. "I didn't—kill him. And they can't—frame me."

"Well, they're going to try." Daisy spoke quickly. This was hard. But it had to be done. "The police will get here as soon as the storm goes down, and they're going to insist on talking to you whether you're able to talk or not. Did you ever try to reason with a policeman?"

"The cops? Yeah. The rotten buzzards. Ain't got no insides—" his words straggled off.

Daisy's hands were clenched on her knees. This was a role new to her. Resolutely she remembered that she was fighting for something more important than Pedro's feelings.

"Yes, I know they haven't much pity. They'll insist on your talking, because you're in a bad fix, and they won't stop to notice whether you're hurt or not. Don't you think—"

He interrupted slowly:

"Think what, granny? Hand me a drink."

She obeyed. When he had lain down again she went on, hurriedly.

"Don't you think it would be better if you talked to me, now, and signed a statement that I could give them in the morning? Then we could see that you got to a hospital and they'd let you alone till you were well."

"Hm. Maybe." Pedro's voice was stronger. "But they ain't gonna believe you."

"Yes, they will. You don't know who I am, Pedro, but the police will believe what I say."

"Yeah?" His eyes rolled up to her curiously. "Who are you, granny?"

"My father was a governor, Pedro, and my husband was a judge of the State Supreme Court. My oldest son is a judge. Judge Dillingham."

He gave a feeble grin. "Judge Dillingham? Yeah, I know. He's as lousy as the rest of 'em." He seemed to be considering. "You're a big shot, ain't you? What you want me to do?"

"Don't you see? If I tell the police you gave me a statement and signed it, and if I insist that they don't try to question you till you're stronger, they'll believe me."

"Yeah—I guess."

"All right, Pedro. I brought a fountain pen and some paper in from the office. I want you to tell me what you did tonight, and then I want you to sign it. Now first, when is the last time you saw Barclay?"

"Huh. You're quick, ain't you?" Pedro was breathing hard. "That bum that fixed me up ain't no doctor. It hurts bad where that punk got me. What'd you say?"

"When is the last time you saw Barclay?"

"Didn't see him to speak to since he left the boat. Saw him just before it started to rain, going into his house with a dame."

Daisy wrote rapidly. "Then you didn't stay on the boat all the time—cleaning up?"

"No. But I had a right to leave. He was gonna kill me. Or somebody. I thought it was me. He had that cane. Always kills somebody when he gets that cane. I can't talk. It hurts."

"You'd rather wait—for the police?"

"Oh—"

"Take another drink."

He drank. Again Daisy set down the flask and took up her pen. "How did you know he was going to kill somebody?"

"Well, it's this way. Ohhh—I feel like I'm going to die. I'm going to die, damn it. I know it."

Daisy wiped little beads of perspiration off her forehead with her handkerchief. But she had no time to be sorry for Pedro. She looked at the little handkerchief as she laid it in her lap—fine linen lawn, edged with lace. Queer that it should be wiping off perspiration forced out by the strain of questioning a dying gunman.

"Barclay sent for the cane," she prompted.

"Yeah. I ain't lying. Whenever he gets that cane, it's curtains for somebody. There's a devil in that cane." Conviction strengthened Pedro's voice. "I've watched it for years. Somebody always dies when he uses it. I've seen it happen. Voodoo, maybe. But it happens."

Voodoo. Daisy frowned as she wrote the word. The nearer one goes to the tropics, she knew, the easier it is to find voodoo substituted for reason.

"He sent for the cane this afternoon, yes. I remember. He told a boy from the clubhouse to get it."

"Yeah. The boy came to the boat. And I got the cane out of the safe. I had to. Gus, he's just a handy man. He don't know the combination."

"Gus?"

"Gus Michaels. The guy said his name was John Smith. So I had to send the cane to the boss. And the minute I done it I knew somebody was going to catch it. And I thought it was me."

"But how does he kill with the cane?"

Pedro drew a long sigh of weariness. "Grandma, if I knew it wouldn't be so bad. I'd get hold of that cane sometime and pitch it in the ocean. But suppose it's voodoo? Then I'd die anyhow. The man we had before Gus—he found out too much. Barclay gets the cane out of the safe. He goes up to see this guy. Then he sends him out. That was just off Tampico. Sends the guy to row to Tampico. We got men in Tampico, see, and all he had to do was take 'em a message. He didn't get there with the message and he never comes back, and we find the rowboat upside down. And Barclay still on our boat when we find the guy. He ain't been off the boat. I know Barclay didn't kill him. It was the cane. Time and time I seen it happen." Pedro's ardor was too much for him; his words trailed off. Daisy reached for the whiskey.

"Have another drink. There—do you think you can go on?"

Either the whiskey or his subject, so long guarded with fear and tremors, roused him to continue. "It's a devil stick. I tell you the truth; a devil stick." For an instant Daisy feared he was delirious, but after a moment's mumbling he went on more reasonably. "Remember when he had that aviator on the dope committee?"

Daisy nodded. "Sanders?"

"Sanders. That's the fellow. Well, Barclay killed him." Pedro wrenched himself over and rested on his elbow. "He killed him, I tell you. Killed him with that filthy green devil stick." He stopped and panted, then went on. "Remember when he busted up his plane? Barclay just put voodoo on him. Sanders was going out in that plane, and I guess he knew too much. Barclay says, 'Pedro, get me my cane. I must speak to Sanders.' I can see his dirty smile. He thought I wasn't wise, but I knew. Off he goes, and Sanders goes up, and Barclay ain't even been near the plane—he just talked to Sanders a minute. They had a drink in his cabin and he was carrying that cane, and the cane puts on the voodoo, and Sanders takes a wide dive to hell. I seen it over and over. And tonight I think it was going to be me."

He stopped again. Daisy waited till his breath came more easily, then she asked, "Why did you think he wanted to kill you?"

"I talked too much."

"About Barclay?"

"Yeah. About the dope. Barclay's playing smart, all these years. Slow and careful. Then he gets on the Federal committee. That blows the lid off. We bring it in by the bale. We all get in the big money. It was soft, until that woman put a crimp in it. Him and that woman."

"What woman?"

"That uppity one. You know." Pedro made a vague gesture with his uninjured arm. "She thinks she's a wise broad. But she ain't. She put me in the grease,"—his eyes blazed and his clenched fist beat the air—"but I'll put the finger on her before I go out, don't worry. Why, neither one of 'em could keep clear a week if it wasn't for me. I tell her that a few nights ago. I had a coupla drinks, see, and she was sore at the boss. She said she wasn't getting enough of a cut—enough money. She wanted to know what my end—my share—was. I'm special. I'm the boss' right hand man. I got him out of jail once. In Canada. That's where he and me gets together. I tell her that. And she has fits. She don't know he's ever been a con—a jailbird. I told her how we crashed out. Escaped, lady. Gee, you're dumb. But I'm dumb too. I tells this broad his name ain't Barclay, either. I'm fat-mouth, see? I spill the works. I get drunk and tell her all about the boss. She's plenty cagey, too. Just leads me on. Yeah, makes me feel like a big guy with them promising eyes of hers. But I think she tells Barclay, because this afternoon he sends for the cane. And this is the first time he's seen her since I blabbed. I know I been a chump, see? And I'm afraid to say I won't send him the cane. It might tip him that I'm wise, so when Gus goes below I think I'll wander up to his cottage and maybe knock him off before he can put the voodoo on me so I can get the cane and shake it over that damn woman—"

He stopped again, panting. Daisy mechanically held the whiskey to his lips. She was nervously aware that Pedro was getting weaker, and his story so far had told her nothing except that there was a great deal that she still did not know. At length he began again.

"So I go up to the house, see, and I hide in the bushes,, and before long he comes in, but he ain't by himself. There's a woman with him. And he's got the cane. And I don't know whether the voodoo is for her or for me. And I think, 'If it's for you, Pedro, the farther off you get the better, and if it's for her, and she dies somewhere around here, they might say you killed her, because he's too smart to let her die in the house with him.' So I gets off. And when I get back to the boat I tell Gus I been doing deck work. He's below fixing a gas line. But I got a charm. Old voodoo woman give it to me in Port au Prince. And I ain't never killed nobody with it, but I think maybe I can put it on Barclay. So I spit on it and throw it three times over my left shoulder and get some salt and make a cross on my bunk and put the charm by it. And pretty soon comes that fellow Warren. Then he says Barclay's dead. And I think I'm all right. But I ain't, the cane's working now. That's why I'm telling you things. I'm gonna check out, see, and I ain't killed Barclay, and I want that dame put in the grease, bad." He had been speaking faster, but his voice suddenly dropped. "They—can't—hang—a dead man—for—working—voodoo—backwards."

"No," said Daisy, "they can't."

"Sure—you're—Judge Dillingham's—mother you know that."

"Have a drink," said Daisy relentlessly.

After that, she asked, "Who was the woman you saw going into Barclay's cottage with him?"

"I—don't know. It was dark."

"How was she dressed?"

"Red." Pedro panted after the monosyllable.

Daisy waited a minute. "But you didn't tell me about the—the other one. The one you want to be revenged on—who is she?"

"Oh—she's the whole works. She's a big shot. Barclay's right-hand man."

"Was she in this dope business?"

"Sure—in big. She was sort of—middle man. She handled distribution—on the telephone—gave the mob the weekly layout—she'd put them wise to—where they could get it."

"But who is she?"

"Oh—you—know her." Pedro's eyes were growing hazy. His voice dropped. She had to bend closer to catch his words. "Can't think—name—"

"Try to remember." Daisy managed to speak with calm authority, but her heart was thumping in her throat. "Is she dark or light?"

"Good-looking—let me alone."

"Pedro, you've got to tell me her name!"

"Wait—I know. Judas. Funny. Judas—" He laughed a cracking laugh. "Judas. Garon. Damn her soul." He fell back.

Daisy took her little handkerchief and wiped her eyes.

"Thank you, Pedro. Now do you think you can sign this?"

"I—don't know."

"Here's the pen. I'll hold you up. There."

Pedro was very heavy. Daisy felt her arms quiver as she lifted him and put the pen in his hand. Yes, she was getting old. She smiled grimly as she watched Pedro fumble with the pen. She was past the age when most women could do anything but spin reminiscences and serve tea. But she was saving Eva Shale for Andrew.

Pedro squinted his bleary eyes over Daisy's fine script. "Tell them—to lock her up—she always—got in the way—I wouldn't trust her." He made a quavering scrawl that would legally pass for a signature. "That's me—Pedro Artinza. Killed by a punk—and a devil's cane."

CHAPTER TWENTY

IT WAS a relief to send McPherson in to Pedro and to go back to the familiar lounge-room. Daisy dropped into the first chair she saw, staring at the papers in her hand. She sighed and then chuckled, and looked down at the fine spiderweb lace that fell over her wrists, half hiding her delicate, blue-veined hands—strange hands to be holding a thug's confession. She looked around. Andrew and the Major were in a corner talking in low tones to Brett Allison. Mrs. Penn sat by the hearth, gazing into the fire. Farther off Eva stood facing the sofa where Judith had stretched herself in a long black satin undulation, one arm tossed above her head and the other gesturing airily. Eva seemed very tall in her white flannels, and her scornful voice came to Daisy clearly.

"Stop lying to me, Judith. *Where is that letter?*"

"Oh, please don't be melodramatic!" Judith was ironically petulant. "I don't know what happened to your precious letter. I've never seen it."

Judith looked full at Eva, and little lines shot out sidewise from her eyes—little lines that might have meant merely eyestrain, but which to Daisy, keyed to a new pitch of protective observation, suggested enmity and malignance. Eva retorted hotly.

"Yes, you have. And I want to know how you knew about it and why you wanted it."

Daisy stood up. "Eva, will you come here a minute?"

Eva started and turned on the heel of her flat oxford. She came to Daisy.

"Don't bother with Judith." Daisy slipped an arm around Eva and spoke in a low voice. "I'll attend to her."

"I almost believe you can!" Eva, half a head taller than Daisy, looked down at her with frank admiration. "What have you got?"

"Yes, what have you got?" said Andrew behind her.

Daisy looked up at them both and laughed. "I've been talking to Pedro."

"To Pedro?" repeated Brett, who had come up with Andrew and the Major. "It must have been an interesting tête-à-tête. Why didn't you call one of us?"

Daisy smiled serenely. "Because, Mr. Allison, the closer I get to this murder the more I'm convinced that its solution is a woman's job. Where are the others?"

Andrew grinned. "Cupping and Imogen and Beans went out to the veranda to catch a cigarette. Beans is having the time of his life. You'd think he'd just knocked down a duck in a shooting gallery."

Brett spoke with a sort of mild amusement. "Mr. Dillingham and the Major have been telling me why they came to Paradise Island. It seems that Barclay was hoping to have me play red herring to cover his misdoings."

"Yes, he was." Daisy had rolled the papers in her hand into a tight little cylinder. "Pedro gave me a good many details. Where's John Smith?"

The Major, who had been smiling in amiable satisfaction, patted her shoulder. "He's safe. We locked him up. I arrested him—Federal authority. He confessed to the attack on Beans and wrecking the radio room. Also to running in the dope today. They came from down the Gulf, not the mainland."

"Good." She glanced toward Brett. "Do you mind if I take charge for a few minutes?"

"Not at all. Might I ask why?"

"I've told you," she rejoined smilingly, "that this is a woman's job."

"Another Judge Dillingham," said Andrew, but Daisy hardly heard him. His banter was too superficial to be real, and she had noted how he and Eva were avoiding each other's eyes. She took Eva's hand in hers.

"Come over here, child. I want to see you." She led Eva to their old place by the table. "Do you feel very dreadful, Eva?"

Eva rested her chin between her fists and smiled ruefully. "Pretty rotten."

"Yes. I thought you would. But I think it's nearly over."

Eva's face twisted wryly. "You sound like a dentist saying 'Just one more pull and I'll have the tooth.' And then you know the last pull is going to be the worst of all."

"I'm afraid it is, Eva."

"What do you mean?"

Daisy looked at Eva's face, resolute in spite of its youth and tiredness, at her strong, sunburnt hands; and in place of the defiance of a few hours ago Daisy sensed a quality of almost tragic strength. She knew she must move carefully.

"Eva," she said, "can you stand a great deal?"

"I suppose so." Eva laughed. "I've been in heavy training since sundown. Why?"

"Because I want you to do something very hard." Eva sat up. A quiver seemed to run down her back. She sat straight and stiff, and looked at Daisy out of blue eyes suddenly grown frightened. "What?"

"Eva, why were you in such a panic to read that second anonymous letter tonight?"

Eva slowly twisted her hands together in her lap. Daisy's eyes still held hers as though by a mesmeric influence. At last she answered.

"I don't want to tell you, Daisy. Unless you say it's necessary." Her eyes carried a clear challenge. "I trust you, Daisy."

"It's necessary, Eva." The words were like a sentence.

Eva shook her head. Then she relaxed limply as though her strained muscles could hold their tension no longer. She hid her face in her outcrossed arms. "Daisy—you've been so good. Don't make it so hard for me now!" Her voice was low with rebellious pain.

Daisy put her arm around the girl's quivering shoulders. She had nearly everything in her hands now, but to make her work complete she must keep back Eva's old mutiny against them all. She would do all she could, but she knew that Eva must give her the last weapon she needed.

"Eva, I'm trying to save you from something more dreadful than you know. I'm afraid you'll have to tell me."

Eva sat up abruptly. "All right. But not all those others."

"Just me, and Brett Allison."

"I don't mind him. But nobody else. You can tell Andrew. Then maybe he'll understand why I can't marry him."

"My dear girl," said Daisy gently, "I want you to marry Andrew. Whatever it is you are going to tell us, it can't keep you from Andrew. Andrew loves you."

Eva bit back a sob; tears came very rarely to her, and she was ashamed of them.

"I know. I talked to Andrew while you were in there with Pedro. I can't help loving Andrew, Daisy. But I can't marry him. Won't you—"

"Sure, and I says to him, 'Whaddya think this is, a shootin' party?' And the old walrus thinks I'm low-down on account I didn't bump off both them mugs—believe me, Major, the Cupping family is a big pain in the neck!"

It was Beans, brightly making his way toward the table where he pulled out a chair and sat down like a man who has done a good day's work and is feeling particularly cheerful about it. Daisy watched the others as they came in—Major Raymond, listening and saying little, as always; Tracy Cupping, growlingly disgruntled that somebody shouldn't have disposed of all this unpleasantness before now; Imogen, fluttering at his coat-tails like a restless butterfly trying to light on an unsteady object; Judith suave and disdainful, only faintly suggesting by her nervous glance at Daisy that she had reason to fear what Pedro might have told; Foster looking tired, but only a trifle concerned; Brett inscrutably authoritative, directing them like the last of the line of a hundred kings; Mrs. Penn tear-streaked, but carrying herself with a certain indefinable dignity; Andrew trying very hard to be jocular but unable to keep from giving Daisy a look that pled desperately for her to do something about it all. Brett came over and spoke to Daisy.

"Do you want to talk to the others, Mrs. Dillingham?"

Daisy glanced at Eva, but Eva's face revealed nothing except a grim resolution to keep her self-control.

"I've asked Eva to tell us something, Mr. Allison. It's of a personal nature, and she quite reasonably doesn't want to make it public. Could we go into your office?"

"Certainly."

Eva stood up. Brett crossed to the door of his private office and held it open for them; Eva went in and stood by the desk, moodily watching the rain splash with dwindling force against the windows.

It was a large, many-windowed office, furnished with an austere lavishness that was like an exposition of its owner's purposeful and restrained personality. The vast glass-topped desk, the square book-cases, the filing-cabinets, the massive chairs, were the epitome of expensive and unostentatious competence. Brett opened a metal box of cigarettes that stood on the desk.

"Will you smoke, Miss Shale? Take this chair. Sit down, Mrs. Dillingham." He struck a match for Eva. "Does either of you object to my pipe? Thank you."

He did not speak again till he had filled his pipe and lit it. Eva was inhaling deeply, looking at an etching that hung behind Brett's chair.

"You had something else you wanted to tell us, Miss Shale?" asked Brett.

"Yes. I don't think it matters much to anybody but me, but I didn't want to offer it for Imogen's bridge-table gossip." Eva smiled faintly.

"We understand," said Daisy. "I don't think she need ever hear it." Daisy folded the sheets of paper that held Pedro's confession. She was glad Eva was going to talk; while she believed that the knowledge she already had would clear Eva of murder, there was something else she must find out, and she waited with mingled hope and apprehension to hear the detail that Pedro did not know.

Eva spoke with crisp determination. "Daisy asked me why it was so important that I read that second letter tonight. I'll tell you." She rapidly outlined to Brett the contents of the first letter and what the second letter was to reveal. "Now this man is head of a ring that's bringing dope into New Orleans," she finished. "The second letter was to give me his name. I felt I simply had to read that second letter tonight, because I was afraid—and I'm still afraid—that this man is my father."

"You poor child!" Daisy exclaimed, and through the tumult of her thoughts she heard Brett's voice urging, "Miss Shale, there is no need of your telling us this."

"I understand why I've got to tell it," Eva insisted. "I was in Linton Barclay's cottage when he was murdered. Just a girlish whim to take out a speedboat isn't sufficient excuse for my being there. But I *had* to go. Don't you understand?" She was speaking rapidly, as though afraid they might interrupt her again.

"I don't know who I am. I don't know my father's name or my mother's. The only tiny little bit of memory I've got of what happened before I was four years old is a sort of vague horror that my father was a convict.

"I was brought up in St. Helen's Convent. I've never had a chance to find out who my people were. But I suppose you know how young children remember things—vaguely, but very intensely sometimes—I mean, something may make an impression of an idea rather than of the specific event that caused it? Anyway, it's something like that that makes me think my father was a convict. Because the only thing I'm sure I remember about what happened before I was at St. Helen's was that somebody went to prison.

"I remember lots of snow—snow over everything. The first time I saw snow after I went to the convent was when I went home for Christmas with one of the girls who lived in Wisconsin, when I was fourteen years old, but I knew I had seen snow before that. I remembered snow. And I know that the snow happened in the same place where I remember about the prison. It's all confused and hard to tell about, but I know I got the feeling that it was something horrible, so horrible that nothing would ever be the same again in the world. I used to dream about it when I was a little girl—big dark prisons covered with snow, and I would wake up and wonder if it was my father who had gone to prison, and if that was why they had put me away off here where there was never any snow. As I grew up prisons had a queer fascination for me. I wondered what it was my father had done, and what made men commit terrible crimes, and I suppose that was the beginning of what Andrew calls my morbid interest in penology, because I was afraid and I wanted to help people in prison. I've tried and tried to find out things, but I never could.

"That's all—but when I got an anonymous letter saying that somebody thought I ought to know about the career of a man who had served a term in a Canadian prison about twenty years ago—don't you see that I thought that somebody was at last about to tell me who I was? I still haven't seen that letter—and I still don't know."

She stopped. For a moment there was silence. Eva sat very still, her eyes covered with her hand, as though the effort of telling the story she had guarded all her life had left her tired and spiritless.

For the first time that night Daisy wanted to cry. She glanced at Brett, who sat with his forehead resting on his hand, looking down; and she glanced back at Eva. Daisy understood a great deal now.

"Thank you, my dear," she said. "It was good of you to tell us."

Eva lifted her head. "I should have told you before, Daisy. Don't you understand now why I can't marry Andrew?"

Daisy smiled. "Don't be absurd, my dear. Of course, there's no reason why you can't marry Andrew."

"O, yes, there is." Eva stood up. "And when they want to make him the next Judge Dillingham he'll understand it, too. A Dillingham—it's like being a link in a chain. Suppose I was Andrew's wife—suppose we had children—and then the whole mess cracked down and it should be in the papers that the sixth Mrs. Andrew Dillingham was a convict's daughter? I can't do it, Daisy."

Daisy went to her, and took Eva in her arms. "You poor dear child—have you told Andrew this?"

"No. I couldn't."

"Tell him. Or I'll tell him if you'd rather. It won't matter to Andrew."

"But it matters to me." Eva stepped back. Suddenly she saw Brett, and a slow flush crept over her sunburnt cheeks. "I'm sorry, Mr. Allison. I—I forgot you were here."

Brett stood up and took Eva's hand with a gentleness strangely at variance with his usual impersonal irony.

"We'll both forget that I heard what was not meant for my ears, Miss Shale. But meanwhile, might I take the liberty of suggesting that my own observation of Andrew Dillingham makes it seem very unlikely that he would even consider such a remote possibility of disaster?" He smiled. "You have been very brave this evening, Miss Shale. I should like the opportunity to wish you happiness."

Eva smiled courageously back at him. "Thank you, Mr. Allison. You've been very good to me."

Brett stepped to the door. "Shall I leave you? Or would you prefer to come back to the others?"

"I'll go out," said Eva, and shrugged. "If we stay too long Imogen will pester us to death, trying to hear what we've been talking about."

As they entered the lounge Foster came over to meet them. He held his watch in his hand, and he was beaming affably at everybody.

"Just a word, Mr. Allison," he said. Brett stopped. Foster's smile broadened. "It's five minutes before midnight, and as there has been no notification of another formal bid's having been entered for Paradise Island, I take this opportunity to hand you—" he took a long pink slip from his pocket—"this check for the first payment of our purchase price." He glanced at Daisy and Eva as though awaiting an accolade. "That check," he added, "represents—"

"Balm in Gilead," said Daisy. She put out her hand. "Congratulations, Mr. Foster."

He bowed and smiled, looking from her to Brett. "It may be that Mr. Allison is to be congratulated. He sold the island and the mystery. We only bought it."

Brett Allison laughed as he slipped the check into his wallet. "Now if you've a fountain pen, Foster—"

"All ready." Foster took out a pen and a folded paper. "I've already signed it."

Brett smilingly wrote his name. "The other details can wait till tomorrow, I suppose?"

Foster nodded and was about to answer when Andrew, who had come up behind him to meet Eva, spoke to him.

"You'll let me apologize, won't you?" Andrew said. "For what?"

"For wiring to Washington to ask if you were straight." Andrew grinned. "I forgot about it in the excitement that Pedro and his friend gave us, but a minute ago Beans brought me the answer. It came just before he was knocked out, and he had been carrying it in his pocket."

Foster glanced at the message Andrew held out, and laughed. But it was Daisy who spoke.

"Apropos Andrew's apology, Mr. Foster, will you tell us one thing I've been wanting to know all evening?"

"Gladly."

"Then," said Daisy, squinting her black eyes and fixing Foster with deliberate mischief, "why did you try so hard to keep stirring up the pot and to keep everyone mixed up after the murder was reported?"

Foster laughed again. His successful purchase of Paradise Island had put him into high good humor. "You're a sharp one, Mrs. Dillingham, and you should be able to guess the answer. If Cupping hadn't been so confounded by the circumstances around him, he might have entered a last-minute bid for the island. That would have meant an auction, and might have wound up in a lot of financial complication. We wanted Paradise Island, you see, murder or no murder, and I knew it. So I thought it best to keep Cupping's mind off his work—to keep him busy elsewhere."

Daisy pounded her stick. "And a precious fine job you made of it," she commented. "That's all."

Foster bowed. "And now," he said, "I'll go tell Cupping our deal is closed." He walked over to where the Cuppings were sitting.

Daisy led Eva to a sofa and sat by her, thinking. Brett had crossed to a window and stood watching the faltering rain. The others were grouped here and there, talking. Daisy looked across at Judith. Judith lay back in a big chair at one side of the fireplace, blowing rapid swirls of smoke into the air; she showed no other sign of nervousness.

Frantically Daisy tried to put together the fragments in her possession. Linton Barclay had been in a Canadian prison twenty years ago. Pedro had told Judith. Judith, fiercely resentful of Barclay's attentions to Eva, must have sent that letter. Then Judith had tried a trick to get it back. Was it simply a jealous revenge on Barclay, or did Judith know something else? The other possibility horrified her so that Daisy would not let her mind dwell on it.

But there was something else that Daisy knew. It had nudged her subconscious observation, and then slipped into her consciousness, and now it rose like water behind a dam, stark and bitter truth beating at a barrier of ordinary experience. She had watched, wondered, disbelieved; but while she looked on tiny flakes of evidence had dropped before her, and she saw what a mountain the total had made. Daisy stood up and walked to the fireplace and back again—appalled and yet thankful, frightened and at the same time triumphant. For Daisy knew that she was standing in the presence of a tragedy, but a tragedy that was in some fantastic way so splendid that she felt a sense of awe.

The office door opened and McPherson came in.

"Mr. Allison?"

"Yes?" Brett turned and went toward him.

"I think he's going."

"You mean Pedro?" exclaimed Daisy. She hurried to where Brett and McPherson were standing. "Let me talk to him again. You say he's dying?"

"Gee, that's bad," piped Beans dolefully from a corner. "I just meant to nick him. Honest."

"I've got to speak to him again," Daisy insisted. "Yes, alone, Mr. Allison." She crossed hurriedly to Major Raymond. "Jack, take charge while I'm gone. Send Eva upstairs—she needs a rest. And in the meantime arrest Judith Garon. Yes, you!" she hurried on. "Don't stop me now—keep that woman in charge till I come back. She sent that anonymous letter to Eva and she has been hand in glove with Barclay—Pedro told me—be quiet,

Judith! I can't wait. I've got to speak to Pedro one more time before he dies. That's all."

She did not hear the jambalaya of voices behind her—Eva's cry of astonishment or Judith's raging protests, or Imogen's squawks. Clutching her papers tight in her hand she hurried toward the office door.

"Wait here, Mr. McPherson. I'll call if I need you."

She banged the door. Daisy always banged at least one door in a crisis.

PART SIX

CHAPTER TWENTY-ONE

THE storm was spending its last strength in a furious crescendo when Daisy came back into the lounge room. She had been gone nearly an hour.

She closed the door silently. She was very tired; and the hand that held the little wad of paper was shaking. Andrew, who had been waiting just beyond the threshold, hurried over to meet her.

"Please rest a minute. Has it been pretty bad?"

She nodded. "He's dead."

"Dead? And you were all alone with him?"

"No. I called McPherson at the last."

"Why didn't you let me come in? I wanted to go, but Brett said you wanted to be alone with him. Did he—did he talk?"

"Yes." She took the chair he had brought for her. "He talked, Andrew."

He sat down near her. "And you know now who did it?" he asked eagerly.

For a moment she did not answer. When she did speak, it was only to ask "Where is everybody?"

"Judith is locked in her room. Beans went out on the veranda with the Cuppings, to tell them more tales of his exploits, I guess. I think the Major and Foster went out there too. Brett's on the little side porch having a long cigarette."

She gave him a long look. "And Eva?"

He turned away from her. "Daisy, I don't want to talk about Eva. She's upstairs."

"She wouldn't talk to you?"

He shook his head.

Daisy stood up. "I'm afraid it's your job, Andrew—not only to make her talk, but to make her stop, look and listen while you talk."

He sprang up with a sudden grin. "Damn it all, it *is* my job!"

"Where are you going?" she asked, for he had already started away from her.

"Upstairs to Eva's room. I'm going to break down the door if she won't let me in. And don't you stop me. I don't give a whoop in hell who killed Linton Barclay. I'm not even interested."

He waved over his shoulder. Daisy smiled. For a moment she looked after Andrew, dashing up the stairs, then she walked slowly over to where the only other occupant of the lounge room, Mrs. Penn, sat in a corner wiping away quiet tears. Daisy laid a hand on her shoulder.

"Please don't cry, Mrs. Penn. I know you didn't kill him."

Mrs. Penn sprang to her feet, startled. "No, Mrs. Dillingham, I didn't. I thought you would know that." She indicated a serving-table at her side, on which was a coffee-dripper and a plate of sandwiches. "Won't you let me pour you a cup of coffee? Mr. Allison had these refreshments brought down."

Daisy took the coffee, but shook her head at the sandwiches. "Nothing to eat, thank you. Mr. Allison is very thoughtful."

"He always is." Mrs. Penn glanced down at the damp handkerchief in her hand. "He just gave me a check and told me to put my daughter in a sanitorium till she is well. That's why I was crying, Mrs. Dillingham—it's so much more than I deserve from him. Won't you have another cup of coffee? It will be good for you—you've been doing a lot tonight."

Daisy shook her head. "No, thank you. I've finished nearly all there is to be done. But I'd like to speak to Mr. Allison—will you step out on the side porch and ask him to come in?"

"Certainly." Mrs. Penn stood up again.

"Tell him," Daisy went on, "that there are one or two points I'd like to talk over with him—things I think he can help me clear up before we see the others."

"All right."

"I'll be waiting in his private office."

Mrs. Penn left her. Daisy went into Brett's sanctum and sat down by a desk. She had the voodoo cane in her hands.

It was only a moment before Brett came in. He closed the door quietly behind him and stood with his faint, formal smile, waiting for her to begin.

Daisy looked up. "Thank you for bearing with me, Mr. Allison. But there are several items I got from Pedro before he died that I think you should know. Then you and I together can decide what the rest of them are to be told."

Brett was still standing. "You have been very courageous, Mrs. Dillingham. Pedro is dead, then?"

"Yes. But before he died he told me a great deal about Barclay and his ring. The rest of the gang can be arrested in Tampico. I have the details—written rather illegibly, I'm afraid, but I can make a readable copy for you."

"It's all rather appalling, isn't it?" said Brett quietly. "What did he tell you about Mrs. Garon?"

"Judith has been associated with Barclay ever since soon after her husband died—about ten years ago. She handled the financial arrangements. When Pedro brought in a shipment of drugs Judith paid for them, for I understood from Pedro that neither she nor Barclay ever saw anybody from the mother ship. That was Pedro's job. The mother ship was a tramp steamer that runs from Calcutta to Tampico and from Tampico to New

Orleans and then on to New York. It isn't hard to see Judith's part in the plan. Usually the steamer transferred the drugs to Barclay's boat out in the Gulf, and Pedro would run it in to New Orleans. The head agent in New Orleans would receive it and give Pedro a voucher, to be redeemed in cash by Judith. Then the tramp would come in to New Orleans, deliver its legitimate cargo, and Pedro would get the cash from Judith and pay off the captain of the mother ship. Barclay's boat left the mainland early this morning and met the mother ship out in the Gulf. That's why he had that dope. He probably intended to plant a little of it on the island so it would be discovered tonight."

Daisy laid down her sheaf of papers on the desk and looked back at him with a smile.

"But that part of Pedro's story," she added, "is really for Andrew and the Major."

Brett nodded. "Yes. I confess I am more interested in the personalities of the case. Do you know why Mrs. Garon wrote that anonymous letter to Miss Shale?"

"I think so. Judith wanted to marry Barclay, or at least to monopolize his interest, and she did that very successfully till Eva appeared. Then Barclay paid Eva such marked attention that Judith became jealous. He excused himself by saying that he wanted to involve Eva in the suspicions of the dope commission, but Judith was clever enough to see that that was only an excuse. Personally, I suspect that he wanted to win Eva's confidence so thoroughly that when she discovered her plight she would appeal to him for aid. Then, as chairman of the investigation, he would clear her, of course winning her unbounded gratitude—" she shrugged. "It's really very simple."

"Devilish," said Brett under his breath.

Daisy went on. "So Judith, learning from Pedro that Barclay was an escaped convict, sent Eva that anonymous letter. Eva did just what Judith knew she would do—she told Andrew about it, and Andrew felt it his duty to tell Barclay and the Major. Barclay's state of mind can easily be imagined. Someone knew his past. He was afraid. It put Eva in another light. If she read that second letter she could expose him, and while he liked Eva, he liked Barclay better. He knew if Eva got to the mainland he faced disaster. For Barclay, there was just one way out. He had to kill Eva and make it look like an accident. Then he had to get possession of the promised letter. I don't believe Judith ever wrote a second letter or intended to write it, but at any rate Barclay thought there was a second letter, and he was desperate. Eva must be killed rather than get information that he knew she would at once give Andrew.

"So Judith got Mrs. Penn to take the first letter from Eva's room, so there would be no tangible clue, no matter what happened. All Judith wanted to do was get Eva out of the way, and if this took murder—well, Barclay had killed other people before, to protect his trade, and this doesn't seem to have worried Judith very much."

Daisy paused. Brett stood listening admiringly.

"You're an excellent detective, Mrs. Dillingham. So whoever killed Barclay did it just in time to save Eva Shale's life?"

"Exactly."

Daisy took up the voodoo cane, and told the story of Pedro's fear of it, of Pedro's horror when the cane was sent for, and of his certainty that Barclay used the mysterious power in the cane to cast a spell of murder. She turned it slowly in her hands and studied the jade handle.

"Somebody besides Pedro knew that this cane meant murder," she added, "but it's still a puzzle to me." She handed the cane to Brett. "What do you think?"

Brett looked at the cane a moment before he answered. "So Pedro thought it was a voodoo stick?" he asked. "He had no idea how Barclay used it?"

"So he said."

Brett was thoughtfully examining the cane. As he looked at it, between his eyes there appeared two opposing little wrinkles, curved outward like parentheses. He had heavy eyebrows like little black plumes, but when he frowned they curled upward at the outer ends and lay like two horizontal question marks above his eyes.

The silence crept over Daisy's consciousness. The storm had quieted, and over the island there had come a sudden lull of peace.

She spoke again.

"Won't you tell me about the cane?" she asked.

And then as Brett looked up, she smiled gently. "Won't you, please?"

Then, as if she and Brett Allison were in her own old-fashioned sitting-room, she went on,

"Please tell me. And please sit down—" her heart was thumping like a drum—

"—Mrs. Shale."

CHAPTER TWENTY-TWO

THE woman who had called herself Brett Allison slowly drew up a chair on the other side of the desk and sat down.

For a moment there was silence. Daisy looked at her, and she thought of Brett Allison's slight figure, his low, careful voice, his movements that were like well-rehearsed bits of a play. She looked at the bitterly controlled face across from her, and down at the long, delicate, fastidious hands clasped on the desk, and wondered that she had ever been deceived.

"It has been so many years," said the other woman. "Nobody has ever guessed it before."

"Do you want to talk now?" Daisy asked. "Or had you rather wait?"

The woman on the other side of the desk gave her a faint smile—a smile that was like and yet strangely different from the cool, impassive smile of Brett Allison.

"There's very little to tell," she answered. "I killed him. He was about to kill my daughter. There was just one thing to do—and I did it." With a hand that looked suddenly very strange beneath a man's cuff she wearily pushed back a lock of her dark hair that had fallen over her forehead. "All my life I seemed to have been confronted by that—a series of situations where there was just one thing to do. I seem always to have done it."

Daisy watched her with queer fascination as she took up the green-handled cane and twisted at a little gold band an inch from the bottom end. The end of the cane came off, and from the inch below the gold band she shook out a dozen tiny white tablets.

"There's what poor Pedro thought was the voodoo spell," she said. "They aren't poisonous. But any one of them makes a powerful sleeping draught. If he had given Eva one of these in a toddy and then let her go out alone in her boat, even in a comparatively calm sea, don't you see what would have happened?"

Daisy smothered a gasp of unbelieving horror.

"But of course—she would have fallen asleep—"

"And they would have found her body in the morning. Drowned. That's what happened to Tommy Sanders when his plane crashed. That's what has happened to anybody Linton Barclay wanted to get out of the way. It was so simple. Give him a sleeping draught just before he goes out alone, in a boat or an aeroplane or an automobile. There's a wreck. So simple—so diabolically simple."

Daisy only half heard her. For the first time she was understanding what twenty years of terrific self-control can do. Eva Shale's mother was speaking calmly, almost listlessly. There was not a quiver in the long fingers that were working carefully at the handle of the cane.

"And this," she was saying, "is how I killed him." The handle of the cane came off, and a thin, narrow blade about eight inches long sprang out of the cane. There were stains of dried blood on the steel.

"That's all," she said quietly. "I'll go with you to the police, or give myself up when they get here. Whatever you say."

Daisy shoved the cane aside and rested her elbows on the table.

"My dear child," she exclaimed, "you have just about the intelligence of a rabbit. Maybe the police would be satisfied with the scraps you've told me. But I'm not. Do you realize I don't even know your name—nor why you've kept up this ridiculous masquerade?"

The other woman met Daisy's eyes with a flash of understanding.

"'Dear child'—you're rather nice," she said.

"That's the first lady-like remark I've heard you make. Now, after all, trotting about in pants isn't going to change your nature. You'd probably love to sit back and have a nice long woman-to-woman talk, now wouldn't you?"

"It might be a relief. But I'm afraid I don't know how." She smiled. "I haven't talked like a woman in so many years."

"No—more's the pity. You should have. After all, you've got a grown daughter. You'll probably be a grandmother before long, if Andrew has the sense God gave him and knocks her down and makes her marry him, in spite of all her self-conscious notions that she's not fit to marry a Dillingham—"

"Stop, for God's sake! I can't bear that!"

And Daisy knew she had won. For the voice that had cried out to her was not Brett Allison's voice. It was the voice of Eva Shale's mother, and Eva's mother had covered her face with her hands, sobbing.

"There now. That's better. Take my handkerchief. I suppose you carry one of those baby tablecloths men use—they're no good for women's tears." She waited till the sobs had worn themselves out, marveling to discover what she had never in all her busy life seen before, the imperative dignity that sometimes belongs to surrender. "Now I suppose you feel better," Daisy said at last. "That's probably the first good cry you've had in years."

"Yes—it is." She looked down at the wet ball of Daisy's hand-kerchief. "When you start in a role like mine, Mrs. Dillingham, you carry it through. You don't dare relax it, ever."

"You did it very well, though I can't say I approve of it. But I suppose you had reasons of your own."

"Yes." Eva Shale's mother picked up the wet little handker-chief and began smoothing it out. Daisy wondered at the subtle change in her manner and all her movements: it was as though a tiny element had been suddenly removed from a chemical compound—so tiny that its loss could not be measured, but so potent that its presence had altered the nature of the whole, so that only after it was withdrawn could the essential quality of the whole be perceived.

"I am not asking you for sympathy, Mrs. Dillingham," the other woman continued with a bitter calmness. "I don't deserve it. But be good to my child. I've robbed her of so much—though believe me, I didn't know what I had done to her until tonight. I thought she would believe what I had told them—that her parents were dead and that she was living on the income of their estate. I didn't think she would have anything to remem-ber. Maybe you can understand that in all these years I've never known what depths of pain were possible till I sat in this room and heard her tell what I had done to her. And I had made myself helpless, for what good would it do to offer her a mother who had just broken the last of the ten commandments?"

Daisy patted her hand. "No doubt you've committed a great many sins, my dear. Our job is to see if we can't save Eva from the consequences of them. We've got a great deal to talk about, you and I, for all I know is that you are Eva's mother, and that for years you've been going around dressed like a man."

Eva's mother gave her a look of whimsical courage. "And I thought I had done it so well. How did you know?"

"It was all very plain, really. I simply put two and two together and made twenty-two. You see, it seemed obvious that a woman had killed Barclay, and I knew perfectly well it wasn't Eva.

Though I never saw Eva till this afternoon, it isn't hard to see that she's too honest even to be tactful. She's a very splendid girl, your daughter."

"I think she is. Go on."

"Well, I wouldn't put murder or much else beyond Judith Garon, but Judith is not the sort to act without visualizing the consequences. She might have killed Barclay, but she would not have risked herself by leaving in his room evidence that he was the head of the dope ring. Imogen Cupping hasn't got the nerve to prick a pimple, much less put a knife into a man, and Mrs. Penn is an honest sort of person—anybody with your arrowy way of asking questions would have struck the facts if she'd known them. I suspected that there was another woman somewhere. Unless some man had dressed up in a woman's clothes. But the fact remained that Imogen had heard Barclay call this strange woman Eva—I suppose your name is Eva?"

"Yes. She did hear him call me Eva."

"At first I thought there might be a woman hiding somewhere on the island. But you gave yourself away. When poor Pedro and his friend came at us with guns—"

"I was horribly frightened for a moment."

"You were. You had been under a terrific strain all evening, and it isn't surprising that you forgot your role. At the instant that they broke in and shouted 'Stick 'em up!' you started back with a woman's primitive gesture of self-protection—you caught your arms in a cross over your breast. That's a woman's gesture, my dear child, and no man has ever done it—it's her instinctive movement of defense."

Daisy's listener gave a short little laugh of astonishment. "Did I do that? I don't remember."

"Yes, you did. In another second you were Brett Allison again, very quietly backing toward the sofa where you had left your raincoat with a pistol in the pocket. For a moment I was so startled myself that what I had seen hardly registered, but when things were quieter I looked at you, and I wondered that

I could ever have thought you were a man. Your sex seemed so obvious. You have a woman's hands and a woman's face, and a woman's way of thinking—a woman's terrifying persistence, and her attention to minute details. I knew you were a woman, and I knew you could have killed Barclay. You said you were at home, but you could have slipped out of the house and back again in time to get Miss Meade's call."

Daisy's listener nodded as if accepting a not very surprising fact. "I ran my electric launch across the inlet. The water was fairly quiet there and it took less than five minutes each way."

"I thought you might have done something of the sort. I believed you had killed Barclay, and that you were not going to confess unless you had to, but from the beginning it was evident that you were not going to let Eva suffer for it. If you had wanted, you could have virtually convicted her of murder; you could have hounded her and tortured her till her denials sounded like the hysteria of guilt; but you had not done this. You had insisted that all the rest of us give any facts we knew about the events connected with Barclay's death, and your questions were all pointed to one conclusion—that every fact brought out made it plainer that Eva could have had nothing to do with it.

"Over and over I had been asking myself why you had taken her part, and I had concluded, even before I knew you were the woman who had killed Barclay, that you had some strong connection with that mysterious past of Eva's that she told me about this afternoon. It was obvious that Eva herself did not know what this connection was, for she was as surprised and as grateful as Andrew for what you were doing. I watched you both. Your name was Eva, so was hers; you are dark and she is light, but you have blue eyes like hers, and you both have a crisp way of saying just what is necessary and no more, and in a queer fleeting way that I can't explain she does look like you."

Daisy paused. The other woman sat watching her with an intensity that was almost frightening.

"Eva had told me this afternoon that she had a vague memory of her early childhood. She didn't say what it was, but I gathered that it was a recollection that terrified her. I thought it must have something to do with her frantic anxiety about what could be in that promised letter. So I asked her."

The calm, impassive mask of a face across the desk was almost gaunt. But suddenly Daisy saw in it a glimpse of a tragic and fugitive beauty. She went on, with a gentleness that softened as much as she could the torture she was inflicting.

"You heard her tell me why she was afraid, and why she couldn't marry Andrew."

Eva's mother lowered her head, resting her forehead on her two tight fists. Her shoulders jerked with quick breaths that were more bitter than sobs.

"I wanted you to hear what she had to say then," Daisy went on, "because I wanted to see how much that story meant to you. I watched you while she talked, and after that it would have been hard for me to doubt, for not even your years of desperate self-control could keep your suffering out of your eyes. Then, when you came in here with me, you looked at Linton Barclay's cane with that same funny little frown that she has, and I was sure."

For a moment there was silence. At last the other woman looked up. She had regained her self-mastery, and when she spoke it was without a tremor.

"What do you want me to do, Mrs. Dillingham?"

"Why, first," said Daisy brightly, "I want you to tell me what it's all about. Why you separated Eva from you, and why you've been going around in these grotesque clothes. Where's that idiotic pipe of yours? Light it up—and let's get the story told."

Eva's mother smiled slightly. "The pipe's outside. But I would like a cigarette, if you're sure you don't mind."

"Why should I?" Daisy pushed the box of cigarettes nearer the woman opposite her. "After all, a pipe isn't a very nice accessory for a lady. I'll have a cigarette too and we'll both be comfortable. Oh, for heaven's sake!" Daisy laughed and shook her head at the fine hand of Brett Allison, which had struck a match for her. "Quit being a gentleman."

The other woman lit her own cigarette and looked up with a frank smile. "You're very nice to be so decent about it."

"It's curiosity, not decency, my dear. Now suppose we talk."

"About what?"

"Why, about you, male and female. You've got a great deal to tell me, you know. Remember, I'm old enough to be your mother and I assume I'm old enough to judge how much of a thing needs to be repeated. So we'll start. What have you been doing all your life?"

"Principally things I shouldn't have done, Mrs. Dillingham. It isn't a pretty story. I suppose it should begin when I was a girl."

Daisy regarded her judiciously. "You must have been a very beautiful girl. You've got lovely eyes, and your hair must have been wonderful before you cut it off."

"Thank you. I was always just too tall and slim to be the Gibson girl type that was so popular. You made a good guess about my hair, though." She smiled reminiscently. "Cutting it off was Brett Allison's first hard job."

"There must have been lots of difficulties before you really made a man of him."

Eva's mother laughed. "The really hard thing was to keep up the pretense of shaving every day. I used vanishing cream and an empty safety razor to go through the motions, and I must have wasted thousands of blades, just to keep my servants from being suspicious."

"There's a lot of details I'll want to know," Daisy said merrily, "but they'll wait. Let's get this mess straightened out first. You were going to start with your girlhood."

"Well—a number of men wanted to marry me."

"Yes," nodded Daisy. "They would."

"I began by being very foolish. I listened to an ambitious aunt and married a stern Puritan about fifteen years older than

I was. We lived in Maine, and he was settled and a success, a power in the community and all that sort of thing."

"And you found it, I suppose, deadly dull?"

"Exactly." She lit a fresh cigarette and crushed out the stub with a disgusted gesture. "I was too young and too spoiled to know how fortunate I was. He was very fond of me, and of my baby when she was born, but he didn't show it very much. I was full of life—wanted things—and there wasn't much to please me down in our part of Maine."

"You should have been spanked," said Daisy.

"Yes, of course, but I wasn't. I was an orphan, and my aunt who had brought me up had pampered me dreadfully. I suppose I expected too much—at any rate, when I met Linton Barclay I thought he could give it to me."

"Linton Barclay?" Daisy's voice must have expressed the relief that had been growing in her mind, for the answer she received was sharp as a whip-lash.

"Good heavens—did you think he was Eva's father?"

"I've been praying for an hour," said Daisy thankfully, "that no matter what else Eva had to face she'd be spared that."

The other woman looked aside toward the window, where the last rain was dribbling down the pane.

"Tell Eva, if you must, that her father was a fine and splendid man and that her mother was a feather-headed fool who didn't know what she was throwing away till it was too late." She stopped. Her long fingers began breaking a match into little pieces.

"You haven't finished," Daisy reminded her.

"It's a very old and ugly recital, Mrs. Dillingham. I thought Linton Barclay was a romantic hero. His name wasn't Barclay, by the way—it was Burfield, but I don't suppose that matters now. He was a Canadian; his mother's people were French. The French Canadians are dashing and delightful, like the Louisiana Creoles, and he was young and rich besides. I ran away with him."

"You took Eva with you?"

"Yes. She was a baby. We lived in Montreal. My family name was Lashe, and I turned the letters around and made it Shale, because I knew Eva's father would move heaven and earth to get her back, and I didn't want him to find us. His name was Curtis—that's Eva's name too; you can tell her if you think it's necessary."

She was still looking at the window; after a pause she turned to face Daisy.

"I don't suppose all this is much pleasanter to hear than it is to tell. Barclay was rich, as I said; at first I didn't know how he got his riches, and it was only gradually that I found out. He was part of a syndicate that smuggled drugs into Montreal. He always had this cane."

She took up the slim green-handled cane and let it fall with a clatter on the desk.

"Once," she said, "one of his sailors got angry and threatened to talk. He killed him by slipping a pellet like these into the sailor's bottle, and sending him out alone in a boat. The knife was hidden in the cane to be used for more direct crime if he ever found it needful."

She took up the cane again and looked at it, and put it down with a shiver.

"Before long it began to be pretty dreadful. He was tired of me, and I had to hold on, because I was completely dependent on him, and somehow I had to take care of Eva. Then the catastrophe came. He went to prison, and the whole silly structure of my own life came shattering around me—and around my baby."

CHAPTER TWENTY-THREE

SHE looked narrowly across the desk at Daisy. "I suppose you remember how they brought up girls of my generation, Mrs. Dillingham? To be charming and decorative and as helpless as kittens. When Linton Burfield went to prison I was alone with a child to take care of, and I could play pretty tunes on the piano, I could chatter in French without misconstruing more than half the verbs, I was a good dancer and I had a knack of wearing smart clothes."

She stopped, and Daisy laid her own hand on the suddenly tremulous fingers that had just dropped a half-smoked cigarette into the ash-tray.

"Go on, my dear child. I know this isn't easy, but I'm afraid you'll have to tell me all of it. What did you do then?"

"I took the last money I had and bought a railroad ticket to take me back to Eva's father. I knew he wouldn't let me come inside his house, but I thought he would take care of her. Even if I never saw her again, it seemed better than anything I could do for her alone. He was dead. I went to my aunt, and she gave me a check for a thousand dollars and told me never to come near her again. I took the thousand dollars and paid most of it to the Mother Superior at St. Helen's Convent, keeping out enough money for railroad fare back to Montreal."

She stopped again. Daisy waited silently, and after a moment the story went on.

"Let me skip the next couple of years. They were pretty terrible. But I managed to keep Eva at the convent. You'll understand why I couldn't keep her with me."

For a moment she looked down at her knees, as if the fabric of Brett Allison's trousers had become suddenly strange to her. Then she looked up again.

"There was a man I knew who gambled heavily in the stock-market. He told me about the ups and downs of money, and it fascinated me. I had saved a little, and I played a tip he gave me.

My money nearly doubled. I sent the quarterly payment to the convent and bought stocks with the rest. I was very lucky. I was completely intrigued, for I had discovered that I had what I'd never suspected—a talent for business and a gambler's instincts. I was suddenly sure that if I could go into business, I could make money. And I wanted to make money. My own experience had given me an obsession about money; I had learned that the only independence that matters is economic independence, and I had determined that whatever it cost me my daughter was going to have money. Not just enough—a great deal of money. That seemed to be all I could give her that was worth having.

"I studied stenography and tried to get a job in a stockbroker's office. But they didn't like to employ women in those days. It's different now, but then business was an affair for men, and I was a woman.

"But I had a flair for business. I was sure I could make Eva rich if I were a man.

"I had made enough money in stocks to take care of her for the next few years. But I didn't want to be able just to take care of her; I wanted to make her rich." She smiled. "It seemed another of those crises where there was just one thing to do. I cut off my hair and put on men's clothes and set out to make money.

"I went to New York alone, and practised walking and talking like a man; I watched men and copied masculine mannerisms. If I may say so—" she glanced up whimsically—"I think I did it rather well."

"Yes," said Daisy, "you did. You were fortunate?"

"Very. I've made a good business man, Mrs. Dillingham."

"And so," said Daisy, "you bought Paradise Island."

"Yes. I wanted to be close to her. I had brought her South because the Canadian winters had seemed hard for her, and when I was at last independent I wanted to come as far from Montreal as I could. I've never been back. My memories of Montreal are not very pleasant." She stopped again, and thought a moment before she went on.

"I came South to look around. I had to have a one-man project, where I wouldn't be brought into continual intimate contact with people who might be too observant. The Gulf Coast was beginning to boom as a playground. There were all these islands—many of them like this one, jungles of palms, ready for anyone with a few ideas and plenty of nerve. It seemed ideal. I bought this pile of sand and made Paradise Island.

"At first it nearly killed me. I worked sixteen, sometimes eighteen hours a day. It took more endurance than I ever thought I had, and more financing than I had any idea I could swing. But I swung it, and it was worth the trouble. Tonight I sold Paradise Island for four million dollars."

She hesitated. "Perhaps you can arrange to give the money to her, Mrs. Dillingham. I'm afraid it's asking too much to suggest that you let her know where it comes from. After all, it may be better that she shouldn't know."

She stopped again. Daisy spoke.

"Did you intend ever to tell her that she had a mother?"

"O yes—I meant to tell her. I didn't plan to keep up this masquerade of mine indefinitely. I thought that when I had enough to assure her safety, I'd tell her who I was. Then, if she detested me for all I had robbed her of, at any rate I'd know I had done what I could to make up for it. But it took such a long time to make Paradise Island pay, and at first the profits came slowly. I used to drive by the convent, and watch her playing with the other little girls, and she seemed healthier and happier than she could have been anywhere else. As Brett Allison, I could hardly take her to live with me; and Brett Allison could hardly turn into a woman and stay on Paradise Island. I meant to wait till I had made enough money to take her and go away. I thought then that this would be very soon, but it took years.

"Then, recently, since I have been able to give her all I wanted to, it seemed cruel to interrupt the jolly sort of life she had, with a tragic knowledge such as I would have to bring her. She seemed so happy and so vital, and her life seemed so complete as it was—what good would it be to introduce her to a mother who was strange to her, and who could give her nothing she did not seem to have already? She came over here often, and it was evident that she and your grandson loved each other. I thought she was satisfied that her guardians were simply paying her the income of her parents' estate, and that she had no idea she might have a tragic background."

"Did you know," Daisy asked thoughtfully, "that she was a friend of Linton Barclay's?"

"No. Not until a week or two ago. I knew they were acquainted. He had been coming here very often of late—I'm afraid I'll have to confess that it gave me a sort of sardonic amusement to over-charge him. I nearly fainted the first time I saw him here. It was several years ago, after Paradise Island had become a fashion-able resort, and at first I thought I had been misled by a chance resemblance. It was some time before I was sure."

"You didn't know he had gone back to his old trade?"

"No. I never inquired. You see—" she began to trace angles on a blotter with the end of a match—"you see, whatever I had felt about him had been dulled by the passage of time. If I had seen him sixteen or eighteen years ago, I don't know what I might have done. But now—I thought I was secure. I thought there was nothing else he could do to me."

"And he never recognized you?"

The other woman raised her eyes from the blotter and smiled—Brett Allison's ironic, enigmatical smile.

"He was a very vain man, Mrs. Dillingham. He seldom wore glasses. Even you never guessed that he was so near-sighted he couldn't recognize his best friend twenty feet away. I was careful never to come near him."

The match punched a hole through the blotter. The smile of Brett Allison faded, and the next words came in the gallant, tired voice of Eva Shale's mother.

"Suddenly I became aware that he was a friend of Eva's. I saw that his admiration for her was so great that it had made

Judith Garon fiercely jealous. I'm afraid I've been simply sorry for Judith, Mrs. Dillingham. Because except for that disaster in Canada, I might so easily have been Judith. But when I realized he was getting tired of Judith, and had begun to admire Eva—I was nearly frantic. I've spent a good many hours walking up and down in my room, wondering what was the wisest thing to do to separate Eva from that man. Perhaps I relied too heavily on the fact that Andrew loved her. I didn't dream that her own lack of knowledge about her people would make her turn deliberately away from him in an attempt to find companionship somewhere else.

"But this afternoon, when she came in from her ride with Barclay, I was standing in the lounge by the office door, speaking to Warren. She said she was going to take her boat back to the mainland. Barclay offered to mix her a drink if she would come by his cottage.

"This, of course, might mean anything or nothing. But as she talked to him, she looked up at him with a queer mixture of confidence and comradeship that made me know that there was danger if she continued it. I wasn't sure just what was her relationship with Andrew, but I knew that between Linton Barclay and myself there was going to be a crisis. I was going to him and order him to let my daughter alone. I wasn't sure he was smuggling drugs now, but I knew that I could expose his real name and his past record, and I intended to threaten to do so if he ever spoke to Eva again.

"Then one of the clubhouse boys came in and gave Barclay his green-handled malacca cane."

She shuddered.

"That green-handled cane—I hadn't thought of it for twenty years. But like Pedro, I knew it carried death.

"I was aware of no reason why he should want to kill Eva. The death in the cane might be for anybody. But he had offered to mix Eva a drink before she went out, and there was just a chance that because of something I did not know, the pellets in the cane might be meant for her.

"I didn't think very clearly. All I was sure of was that I had to see that man, to forbid him ever to see my daughter again and to stop a murder."

She took out another cigarette; her hands shook, and the match scraped futilely across the edge of the box away from the sandpaper. Compassionately Daisy took it from her.

"Here's a light, child. Wait a minute before you go on."

Eva Lashe slipped wearily back into her chair. Slowly she mastered her quivering nerves.

"I can finish," she said steadily. "I'm nearly done." She laid the cigarette across the edge of the ash-tray.

"I went by the servants' cloakroom and took a white uniform and a red raincoat—the regulation attire for maids who have to go out in bad weather. I left the lounge room before Eva and Barclay did, and I wasn't sure she had gone to the cottage with him. I slipped out of my house and took my launch, and crossed the inlet. I anchored at the wharf nearest Barclay's cottage and walked through the shrubbery. Then I saw Mrs. Penn about to go in, and waited. She caught a glimpse of me, you remember.

"I had carried keys, but the back door wasn't locked. I went in, and found Barclay in his bedroom.

"He didn't know me. I had on a hat, and he didn't see my short hair. I had simply opened the bedroom door, and he came out into the passage between the bedroom and the living-room when he saw me—that was when Imogen Cupping caught sight of us in the passage. I simply told him I had something to say to him that must be said at once, and he opened the bedroom door again and we went in. That was because Eva was in the living-room, but I didn't know it.

"It was not until we were in the bedroom that he suddenly saw who I was. He was astounded beyond words, but I hardly noticed. I had seen the whiskey and fruit-juice on the table, and lying near them the green-handled cane. I picked it up and told him what I had come to say—that he was not to see or speak to my daughter again, and that I was going to throw that cane into the Gulf.

"He didn't try to get it back then—I suppose because he didn't want any noise of a struggle to rouse Eva and bring her in to ask what was going on. He tried to laugh at me. I told him I had heard him offer Eva a drink, and asked if she was in the cottage. I said if she was there I was going to see her at once, and tell her who I was and who he was, and that for some reason I did not know he was planning to kill her.

"I opened the door into the foyer. Imogen didn't hear all he said. What he said when I opened the door was, 'She's not here. Don't be a fool, Eva. You can't bluff me.' He slammed the door and backed into the bedroom. He was in a fury. My mind was racing in circles. I knew that he was making a drink for somebody, and that he had told Eva that he would give her a drink if she came by his cottage. I knew that if he had made up his mind to kill her, he could knock me senseless and do what he had planned. I thought Eva might come into the cottage at any minute. Whatever I did had to be done then."

She spread out her hands in a comprehensive gesture.

"Again—there was just one thing to do. I killed him."

CHAPTER TWENTY-FOUR

FOR several minutes there was silence. At last, with the relieved brusqueness of one who is nearly through with a bitter undertaking, Eva Lashe spoke again.

"I ran my boat back to the wharf next to my house and hurried upstairs. I got out of the dress, and while I was putting on my own clothes the telephone in my room rang and Miss Meade told me Barclay's body had been found. I said that I would be over there at once."

"What did you do with the red raincoat?"

"I knew the button was missing, so I tied the coat and uniform around an old anchor and threw them into the bay."

For a moment Daisy sat looking at her, this woman who was so plainly a woman, in her impeccable clothes that were suddenly not elegant, but absurd. The office was very quiet, now that the storm was over, and the low beat of the surf and the wind were less like sounds than like a soft background for silence. After a moment Daisy roused herself with brisk energy.

"If that's all, my dear Eva—I suppose I may call you Eva?— you and I have only a very little more ahead of us. What do you propose to do?"

"It seems very simple." Opening a drawer at her side, Eva Lashe took out a sheaf of Brett Allison's letterheads and a fountain pen. "I'll write to my attorneys, giving them the details of the sale of Paradise Island. My will is already in their hands— signed Brett Allison, and leaving everything I own to Eva Shale. When I've finished the letter to my lawyers, I'll write a confession. It won't be long—simply a statement that I killed Linton Barclay, and signed Brett Allison. I'll leave these in your hands, and then I'll go for a walk."

"And then step quietly into the Gulf?" Daisy asked quickly. "Yes."

"Nonsense," said Daisy. She gave an impatient shrug. "Listen to me, Eva Lashe. You've been wearing Brett Allison's personality so long that you can't think independently of him. Brett Allison was a charming and gallant soul, and no doubt that's what he would do. But you are Eva Shale's mother, my dear. What would she do?"

"Eva Shale's mother," said the other woman simply, "would do whatever seems most likely to save Eva's happiness."

"Of course she would. Now, my dear, use your brains. What will Eva think when she receives a four million dollar legacy from this man Brett Allison, whom she hardly knows, and then learns that Brett Allison's body has been washed up by the tide and that it has been discovered that he was a masquerading woman? That's poetic gallantry, my dear girl, but it isn't common sense."

The other woman sighed wearily. "But is there another way?"

"Certainly," said Daisy. "Listen to me. We've got to do three things—tell Eva that she isn't a convict's daughter, arrange for her to have your property, and satisfy the police about who killed Linton Barclay so they won't be asking a lot of questions about what's none of their business. You can't be considered just now. You've committed a great many sins, my child, and I've got too much old-fashioned moral sense not to believe that where there has been sin there should be retribution. Are you listening?"

After a pause of a moment Eva Lashe nodded silently.

"Good. Now about our three problems. Why doesn't Brett Allison tell Eva that he has been thinking things over, and remembers that he used to be an acquaintance of her father's?"

"Of course—how beautifully simple?" Eva Lashe caught Daisy's hands in hers with spontaneous gratitude. "Thank you."

"Absurdly simple, my dear. Brett would have thought of it himself if he hadn't had so much else on his mind. Why doesn't Brett have his attorneys advise Eva that she is now at the age at which according to her mother's will she was to come into her full estate? That can be done shortly after Brett Allison leaves Paradise Island—just as soon, say, as he can conveniently arrange it. She's quite capable of taking care of her property, if I'm any judge."

"Splendid. I'll arrange that."

"Brett had better keep back enough to provide Eva Lashe .with a modest competence."

"Then," said Eva Lashe with Brett's slow, whimsical smile, "she isn't going to pay any penalty for her misdeeds?"

"Don't be foolish. To be sure she is. Her daughter won't know her. Yes, my dear, I'm sure that's wisest. There's nothing you can give her now. As for the rest—" Daisy shook her head. "You have done a great many things that you shouldn't have done, my child, the latest of which is murder. Now murder is a great crime, and the law insists on the right to punish a murderer according to its own idea of justice, but the justice of the law is always the result of a formula in which two and two make four.

"The world will be better off without Linton Barclay in it. If the law had done its work perfectly, he would not have been on Paradise Island tonight to threaten your daughter's life. Murder is reprehensible, but after all, Linton Barclay was killed with the instrument in which he carried death meant for your daughter. Now you and I, Eva Lashe, are going to be conspirators in one more crime."

"I'm afraid that I don't understand, Mrs. Dillingham."

"Pedro Artinza is dead," said Daisy, slowly and very distinctly, "and it was Pedro, when all is said, who was directly responsible for Linton Barclay's death."

Eva Lashe had gone white.

"Then you mean—"

"I mean," said Daisy firmly, "that I have Pedro's signature on a paper covered with my own handwriting, on which I purposely left a space to be used only in the event that Pedro died. He is beyond any injury or help from us. And he started the chain of events that forced you to kill Barclay when he told Judith Garon that Barclay had served a term in a Canadian prison."

Daisy rose and went around to the other side of the desk. For an instant she stood looking down into the tired, incredulous face of Eva Lashe. Then, with swift impulsive sympathy, she bent and kissed her.

"My dear girl, I have had a very happy life. I never even had any temptations to speak of. I think it's about time I did something sinful." She gently smoothed back the thick dark hair under her hand. "Please don't cry. My husband used to tell me that only arch-criminals tried to block the law, but I think if he knew what I was doing now he'd forgive me. That little handkerchief of mine is no good any more, child. You'll have to use your own."

She drew up a chair. "Now then, that's much better. What absurd handkerchiefs men carry. You'd think they all had chronic bad colds. You're all right now, aren't you?"

Eva Lashe crumpled up Brett Allison's handkerchief and then carelessly put it back into her pocket.

"I'm all right."

"Then for the rest. It all fits in. Pedro went to the cottage, intending to kill Barclay. Pedro was Barclay's aid. Imogen will believe that Pedro stole a red raincoat and that she mistook 'You can't bluff me, Pedro' for 'You can't bluff me, Eva'—if it's properly suggested to her."

Daisy patted the hand that lay in hers. "That's nearly all. Just one more detail. There's a pretty little cottage with a garden on Prytania Street, in the Garden District. It's very near my own house. When Brett Allison has arranged his affairs, I think he might leave for parts unknown. Then I think that some time later Eva Lashe might like to buy this cottage. It has beautiful roses on the lawn. She had better not come to live there until she has let her hair grow and has practised wearing skirts and walking in high heels, for we dowagers who live in the Garden District don't approve of masculine women. She won't be entirely happy there, for she won't be able to tell her daughter who she is. Not for a long time, anyway. We'll see how things go. But if she is a very nice lady, as we expect ladies of the Garden District to be, I would ask her in for tea now and then. Perhaps sometimes I might arrange for the sixth Mrs. Andrew Dillingham to drop in for tea with us. And there might be some little Dilly-Dally Dillinghams to be made to mind. It's not a bad thing to look forward to, for a couple of hardened criminals, is it?"

Eva Lashe drew a deep breath. "It sounds," she said, "like heaven."

Daisy chuckled. "Here's the rub. There's just one thing that won't fit in the picture. That damn pipe you've been smoking all night. It just won't do."

THE END

Printed in Great Britain
by Amazon

36541441R00118